I0770668

Hollywood Glitz and Glamour

Ariella Talix

Copyright © 2026 Ariella Talix, all rights reserved.

The main characters and their experiences portrayed in this book are fictitious. With the exception of references to known historical individuals and events, any similarity to real persons, living or dead, is coincidental and not intended by the author.

No part of this book may be reproduced or stored in a retrieval system or transmitted in any form or by any means, electronic, mechanical, photocopying, recording, or otherwise, without express written permission of the publisher.

Cover Design by Dar Albert, Wicked Smart Designs

E-Book ISBN: 979-8-9936972-0-8

Paperback ISBN: 979-8-9895156-9-1

Hardcover ISBN: 979-8-9936972-1-5

To love and be loved is to feel the sun from both sides.
David Viscott

Dear Reader,

The language in this book has been carefully researched line-by-line to give you an authentic sense of life in California in 1939 and what people sounded like. It was not as common then for people to swear as much as we hear now. However, throughout the story, emotions run high, so there is a certain (and I hope appropriate) amount of cursing. Common names for things and idioms are as accurate as I could find.

I have also attempted to tell the story within the legal, social, and moral framework that existed then. It is not necessarily how we see things in 2025.

I hope you enjoy reading my story as much as I did telling it.

Happy reading!

Ariella Talix

Chapter One

Rosalie

"Rosalie, would you please pass the gravy?" Daisy asks, barely taking a pause in her story about the gossip she heard this week at MGM. I'm surprised she can keep eating at the rate she's carrying on. In spite of myself, I can't stop listening. She swears it's all gospel truth.

"So then I heard that not only did they make Judy Garland wear these weird things called nose discs inside her nostrils to make her nose look prettier on film, and fake caps on her teeth, they wrapped her chest so tight, she could barely breathe because they didn't want her bosoms bouncing around. I guess there were some rather nasty remarks made during the early filming before they settled on that solution." She shovels some potatoes and gravy into her mouth and continues after barely swallowing. "And I also heard she was given lots of pills. Some to keep her awake, and some to get her to go to sleep at night. Can you imagine? It's like that poor girl has no say in her own life. *And* they made her take pills to keep her weight down too. She's just a little bitty thing! But it was important to them that she look like a young girl about ten years old, even though she's sixteen. I bet she's glad she's done with the shooting of that movie."

My heart drops, and I put down my fork. I'm not fat at all, but I do have a healthy appetite. Maybe that's why I haven't been able to get any movie parts yet. I look at the mashed potatoes on my plate, and suddenly the mound looks like it's laughing at me and challenging me. I've always been happy with the meals we have here at the boarding-house, but now I wonder if I'm *too* happy about food.

I work different waitressing shifts at the Beverly Hills Hotel. Sometimes I'm on for breakfast and lunch, but I prefer the lunch and dinner shift because I get better tips. I'll switch to that tomorrow. I can't complain. Waitressing jobs are hard to come by in Los Angeles because there are so many ambitious young women flooding into town all the time. It always sounds to me like the 1849 Gold Rush when hopeful miners flooded into California with hopes of striking it rich. Now it's hopes of another kind of golden success, but the level of determination and naïveté are certainly the same. Experienced waitresses are a dime a dozen, so you just know that a few minor slips in your performance means they'll give your job to the next girl before you can blink. I'm the envy of most of my friends because I often get to serve studio executives or actors and actresses. Some of them are pretty nice, but not all of them. I guess that's people.

Daisy is the only girl in the boardinghouse who actually works in one of the studios. She works in costumes at Metro-Goldwyn-Mayer (she usually calls it MGM), so I'm sure there are lots and lots of stories floating around about the making of *The Wizard of Oz* there. I'm just surprised anyone talks about any of it. From the stories she's sharing, I would think the studios would have everyone sworn to secrecy.

"Do you think they treat all their actors and actresses that way, Daisy?" I ask. "Or is this just because she's so young?"

Daisy shakes her head sadly. "I don't think she's a special case, but the other stories I've heard are probably more about carelessness than actual abuse. You know, Buddy Ebsen was the original actor hired to be the tin woodsman, and he was hospitalized because of the makeup they put on him to make him look like he was covered with tin. He got so sick from it his lungs almost shut down, so they had to hire Jack Haley to take his place. Haley's been sick too from the new makeup they came up with, but it was just an eye infection they could cure, so they're making him continue with the role. And poor Margaret Hamilton—you know, the Wicked Witch of the West? She got second and third degree burns when she left Munchkinland because their safety precautions didn't work. Also, they used a stunt double for her when she was supposed to ride her broomstick that was shooting out fire, but the broomstick was made out of a pipe that exploded! The stuntwoman was hurt so badly, she had internal injuries and had to have a hysterectomy, and her leg was all gouged up pretty badly too. Isn't that just awful? I don't think I'd ever want to be an actress after hearing this!

"They try to keep it all quiet on the set, but you know how people love to talk. The studio doesn't care much about anything but the money they're going to make from their movie, and they would come down like gangbusters on anyone who went to the press with these stories. I do love making costumes, though." She looks down at her plate, having run out of scary stories for now. But then she looks up and laughs. "I'm probably pretty safe from harm unless my sewing machine falls on me or I get stuck with a pin. But anyways, don't tell anyone I told you all of this because I could end up in a real jam if my name got back to the studio bigwigs."

"Who would I tell?" I laugh. "I don't know anyone." Just as I thought, she's not supposed to be blabbing about this stuff.

"You never know who you might meet at work, Rosalie. You rub shoulders with famous people all the time."

"I see them and hand them their food, but I'm virtually invisible to them, and we certainly never get into any long conversations," I protest. "You probably have more contact with actors and actresses than I do when you do fittings and such."

"Yeah, maybe. They really don't pay us much attention though, do they?"

I can't help but hope that one of these days that might change. In the meantime, I go to work and go to acting classes. Once in a while, I try to get a part as an extra, but so far that hasn't panned out. I'm hopeless when it comes to singing, so voice lessons would be a waste of time, but I'm also considering some dance classes. We'll see.

I sure don't plan to sling hash forever, even in a ritzy place like the Beverly Hills Hotel. I have ambition!

Chapter Two

"Ollie, come out to dinner with me," I plead for the fiftieth time. "I'm sick of these boring Hollywood nincompoops who either want to be seen with me or tell me how to run my life. I want to enjoy a nice meal and have a real conversation for once."

"You know the rules," he answers me, giving me that stern look he's perfected so well. It just makes me want to throw him down on the bed and kiss that frowny face away, and then I'll do all kinds of other...he breaks my reverie by continuing, "Everyone thinks I'm your majordomo, and that's *it* as far as the public is concerned, and no one goes out to dinner in this town with their household steward. Besides, you're supposed to be meeting with Moe tonight. I'd only be in the way."

Moe is Morris Frankle, my humorless agent who's about as much fun as the chickenpox. I can't help rolling my eyes. "Can't we forget the rules just this once? We'll tell Moe that the cook has a migraine and refused to fix any dinner for you. A man has to eat—especially one as big and strong as you!" I run my finger up his chest, and what a fine chest it is.

I hope if I flirt enough and play up to his ego, he'll relent. But Oliver Shackleton has an iron will. He glares at me a moment, then says in a sad voice, "Don't tempt fate, Troy. All it would take is one long look or an inadvertent touch to get tongues wagging. You've come too far with your career to see it all fall down around your ankles now."

I snort. "You mean the way you love to see my pants?"

"Exactly. I could ruin you, sweetheart." He reaches out and strokes my cheek the way I love. "I'm not a talented actor like you. I'd give us away with one stupid glance. You'd smile at me, and I'd get hard, then you'd get hard, and we'd be drummed out of town...or arrested for illegal, immoral behavior." He takes my hand. "Go meet Moe and then come home to me. I'll always be here waiting. You know that."

"I hate that you're always relegated to the shadows. It's not fair!" I sound like a petulant eight-year-old, even to my ears.

"Who says life is ever fair? But let's be clear. I get to live in this gorgeous mansion we bought with our sizeable earnings from our brilliant careers." He grins at me. "I have my needs taken care of, and I get to live with the man of my dreams. I don't mind being out of the limelight at all; I prefer the quiet life. I read all I want and have plenty of time to work on my novels. The anonymity of the pen name Robert

Oliver keeps me hidden from prying eyes. So don't feel sorry for me. I chose this life, and I chose you. Now go get dressed for dinner."

He kisses me and turns to leave the room. I sigh, looking at his long legs and broad shoulders as he strides away. Ollie keeps fit by swimming in our pool for an hour each morning. But this time of day, he'll probably sit down at his typewriter and get lost in his manuscript before I'm even changed for dinner. Then Zelda, our talented cook, will have to pry him loose to eat while her food is still hot. She hates it when we're not prompt to meals. Zelda is a gem. She does all of our cooking and manages the household staff indoors and out with an iron fist. She's the true majordomo around here. And...she protects our secret while we keep hers. It's the perfect setup for all of us.

Damn. I guess I have to go. I've been cooking up too many excuses to avoid Moe lately, and I finally need to face whatever folderol it is he wants to discuss with me. It's interesting he didn't want to meet at his office. Maybe he thinks I won't argue with him in public.

We'll see.

SOMETHING IS DEFINITELY up with Moe, and I don't like it. His eyes are shifty, and he has that smile like he knows a secret. But he keeps talking about *As Always*, the movie we're in the middle of making, like he's obsessed with it. It's not anywhere near ready for release because we have the majority still left to shoot, but the studio, Premier Works, is ramping up the promotion for it like crazy. I guess it's going to turn out fine. It seems like we're doing a decent enough job with the acting—well, *I* am at least. The story could be a lot more original in my opinion, and even the title seems insincere, but nobody asks the actors what they think. We're told where to stand, what to do, exactly what to say, and how to look while we're saying it. We're primped and prodded, dressed and coached, and some days I feel more like a talking piece of clay than a real person. But...when I'm in the middle of a challenging scene, and it's all coming together right, it's a rush. It's like the best feeling in the world—so much so that I've become addicted to it. I love being an actor, and I've worked on being one my whole life. Unfortunately, this current production has more than its share of difficulties for me, so I can't be sure the scenes will all come together as smoothly and convincingly as I'd hoped. I wish I had a more cooperative co-star. One with some talent too, if I'm honest. There. I said it. My co-star is awful, and I'm not going to save this movie all on my own.

I let Moe carry on, barely listening to him, until he realizes my attention is elsewhere. I just got a load of the waitress working at the next table. My God, she's perfection. Yes, I'm madly in love with Oliver, but I also have an eye for women, and this one is something, alright. Even in the gawdawful waitress uniform she's wearing, I can't take my eyes off her. Her curves make my fingers tingle. Her honey-blonde hair shines like the sun, even with a stupid hairnet on, and her shapely legs...well...she's just about the prettiest thing I've ever seen, and in this town, that's saying a lot. I wonder what she's doing waitressing. She should be in the movies or on the stage—or at least a model. I try to catch her voice over the general chatter in the room as she asks the dinner patrons what they'd like to order, but she's soft-spoken. I like that about her too.

"Troy!" a frustrated voice breaks through my reverie with a hiss. "Pay attention."

Sighing, I turn back to him. I was being rude by staring at Dollface anyway. "Yes, sir, your Magnificent Highness? You were saying?"

"Cut the crap, pretty boy. I was just getting to the good part."

"Pray tell, what is that, Professor Brilliance?"

He rolls his eyes at me and says, "The studio says it's time for you to get married." I immediately wrinkle my nose at that notion, but he carries on like I'm in complete agreement. "You're twenty-nine now, and if you wait much longer, people will start to wonder about you. You know—what kind of a man doesn't want to marry by the time he's thirty? That kind of thing. So they gave me a list of possible candidates, and one of them was...uh...your co-star in the current film."

"No."

"No what? No to your co-star or no to marriage?"

"Gloria Dumont is an insufferable narcissist who never shuts up, and she refuses to brush her teeth even before a kissing scene—after eating raw onions. She drinks far too much and says terrible things about people all the time. And I bet she eats boiled kittens for breakfast. So you can forget that."

"Oh, stop exaggerating and acting spoiled. Gloria needs

a little boost to her image because word is leaking out that she's kind of a...uh...well...a bitch. Pay the woman some attention, and I bet she'll shape up. We need *As Always* to be a success, and when people really believe you're in love with each other, they adore that kind of crap. They'll chalk up the bad stuff to jealous gossip or falsehoods or something. They'll convince themselves that you have great chemistry in the movie. The studio wants you to start courting her publicly and then make a big splashy proposal."

I'm vibrating with anger. "Well, sic her on some other unsuspecting patsy if her image needs some help. I *won't* do it. Who else ya got on that dumb list? Lizzie Borden? Bloody Mary?"

"Troy, be reasonable. It wouldn't have to be a real marriage..." He regards my face and probably notices the steam pouring out my ears. "Fine, you got me, there was no list. They want you to...uh...marry Gloria. And it wouldn't hurt your image either, you know. No one ever sees you out on the town. You need to project what a romantic guy you are if you want to continue getting these kinds of parts."

I've completely lost my appetite. I feel like jumping up and running out of here, but I politely place my napkin on the table and ask, "What will the studio do if I refuse?"

He looks me in the eye and answers, "They won't hire you for any more leading roles after this movie unless you can convince them you're committed to their values. They said you seem apathetic about Gloria, and that's the kiss of death, sonny boy. If you won't marry her, we're going to have to find her someone else *and* a woman for you too. This idea of the two of you getting hitched is just killing two birds with one stone. I think it's the best scenario."

Well, that doesn't sound too good, but I halfway don't believe it. I'm a real star in this town. So I try a little bravado to see what will happen. I skewer Moe with a look that says I mean business and tell him, "If I'm supposed to middle aisle it with some dame, I'll do it. But only if you can convince *her*." I point to the knock-out blonde who is now delivering a shrimp cocktail at the next table to a florid-faced, corpulent studio exec. She's smiling at him like he's Tyrone Power himself, and he's eating it up.

Moe looks and then turns to face me. "The waitress? Why?"

I shrug. "I like the looks of her. See what you can do. Remember...you work for me. Not the other way around."

As I get up to leave, he hisses, "But I already told them you'd marry Gloria."

Glaring at him, I order a little too loudly, "Fix that."

I can't wait to tell Ollie about my evening so we can hopefully laugh about it. Fat chance anything will come of my demands, but I swear on my sainted mother's life, fake or real marriage, I'm *not* marrying or even dating Gloria. Just thinking about her gives me the heebie-jeebies.

The only reason I feel bad about leaving dinner early is that I didn't get to ogle that stunning blonde anymore.

I'm sure glad I have Ollie at home.

Chapter Three

OLLIE

I'M surprised to hear Troy slamming the door and trudging into the house. I thought he'd be out for a couple more hours at least, partly because our house is pretty far from the Beverly Hills Hotel where they were having dinner. I hope things didn't go horribly wrong with Moe. That man can be truly awful sometimes, but he's great at his job, and so far, he's done well with Troy.

When Troy showed up in Hollywood, Moe sent him to a dentist, a fancy barber, a stylist, and a voice coach, then he changed his name from Lester Beanblossom to Troy Kingsley. Huge improvement, if you ask me, but I was already in love with him despite his slightly gap-toothed smile and his ridiculous name. I never liked calling him Les because he's so much *more* than *less*. I saw tremendous promise in him and knew in my heart he had what it would take to be a star, so I joined him out here from Ohio. My writing career was already a success, so I knew we wouldn't starve.

The funny thing is, we both broke up with girlfriends to be together. I didn't know I had a queer thought in my mind until I set eyes on him, but it was love (and lust) at first sight. It just felt so natural and right to be together; it's hard to explain. We have to take great pains to keep our involvement a secret, and that's no fun, but he's worth it to me.

I'd been dating Louise for a couple of months back in Cleveland, Ohio, and I bought us tickets to a popular play so we could have a fun night on the town. Troy—who was still known as Lester back then, of course—was the male lead in the production. There was something so raw and honest about his acting, I couldn't take my eyes off him. He's stunningly handsome with jet black hair and light-green eyes. He's tall like me, but more muscular, and he fills out a suit looking like a dashing duke in a bespoke tuxedo. There's something truly majestic about the guy. When the play was over, I asked Louise if she wanted to try to meet him backstage, and I could see the stars in her eyes when I asked, so apparently he affected her the same way.

When we made our way backstage and I caught his eye, something strange happened to me; my reaction to being close to him was visceral. He and I had this instant connection like nothing I've ever experienced. I had to remember to introduce Louise, who blushed her head off when he politely shook her hand, but he only had eyes for me.

Long story short, after one heartfelt conversation to explain that I felt I was wrong for her, I never called Louise again, but I bought myself a ticket to every one of Troy's performances after that until the play's run ended.

Each night, I sat spellbound in the darkened theater while soaking up Troy's deliciousness like a gift of ice water in the desert. After joining a well-deserved standing ovation —I was often the first to jump to my feet—I would rush backstage to his dressing room, and we gradually got to know each other. If any of the cast asked who his new friend was, Troy told them I was a writer who was interviewing him to get ideas for a novel about stage actors. He told them it was research.

Our friendship started out with interesting, diverse chats, then we progressed to late-night, after-theater suppers at a nearby little hole-in-the-wall restaurant in Little Italy. We would sit in a dark corner and "acciden-tally" brush each other's hand from time to time or bump knees beneath the table where we would eventually splay our legs, letting them rest against one another. Finally, after quietly acknowledging the current that ran between us like lightning, I asked him if he'd like to come back to my place for a nightcap. That's when our love affair began in earnest.

He was as baffled about it as I was.

A few months later, he quietly moved into my house with me. I knew he had aspirations about acting in the movies, and I had no doubt he'd be a success. Women and men responded to his charisma and sex appeal, so we made plans to head west. Because I can write anywhere, it was nothing for me to leave Cleveland. I had to be with Troy.

I sold my house, earning a tidy profit, and we loaded our

trunks into a train bound for Los Angeles on which we had a deluxe drawing room. Nothing but the finest for my beloved.

And yes, I am besotted with him. But now and then in my most private thoughts that I wouldn't dream of speaking aloud to my delectable paramour…I miss the softness of a woman.

So when I hear Troy grumbling down the hall toward my office and stomping his feet like a Clydesdale, it not only sets my teeth on edge, it worries me. I can't imagine what would have gotten him so worked up. Was he fired? That can't be right. He's one of the most popular and successful actors in Hollywood, not to mention he has an ironclad contract with Premier Works. I'm sure he was hired to star in *As Always* because they knew the script was a dog, and they needed someone with appeal and talent to salvage it. Whoever green-lighted that script should be the one who's fired. They can't pin it on Troy if it bombs. Before I see his stormy face as he bursts into the room, I'm already thinking up ways to ease his mind and pouring him a whiskey.

I silently hand him his tumbler and lead him to the couch. He's furious, but there's something else besides anger going on. I can read the man better than anyone. "Tell me," I say and run my fingers through his hair, ruffling up his perfection just a bit.

"They're idiots," he squeezes out through clenched teeth.

"Who?"

"The studio execs. They want me to marry that…that *creature* Gloria Dumont. They say her image is poor and she needs a big boost, plus I'm getting to be too old to be single, so they want me to pretend to fall in love with her, drag her around town like a pet dog and then make a huge, public marriage proposal to her. I could gag."

"Hmm. Sounds dreadful." I try to sound calm, but I'm seething inside.

"She makes my skin crawl. I'd sooner marry one of those hideous flying monkeys! I told Moe no." He shudders. "My God, she was nothing but a bit player before this movie, so I wonder what she did exactly to get the lead in *As Always*." He downs half of his drink and looks me straight in the face. I'm starting to wonder if what else is on his mind will show itself.

"Even if I refuse to marry smelly Gloria..." he winces, and I guess it's because of his memory rather than because he feels bad calling her that. "They still want me to marry. So I told Moe to find out what he could about a waitress at the Beverly Hills Hotel."

My chin drops. "You would *leave me* for a waitress?"

"No, of course not. I lost my temper and I just...I just picked her out of the crowd. I know it won't go anywhere, but I have to admit, there was something about her. She's way prettier than anyone in the movies now. I gave Moe an ultimatum that it was her or no one for me. Nothing will come of it, so I'll just have to figure out how to deal with the studio. After he fails miserably with Dollface, that is."

"Dollface?"

"I don't know her name, so I have to call her something in my head. That's what came to mind as soon as I looked at her."

"Should I be jealous?"

"Not for one minute. It's only you for me, Ollie. You know I love you. Plus, like I said, Moe won't make it to first base."

As I contemplate that news and Troy finishes his whiskey, the phone rings. Of course it's Moe calling. Troy listens for a while and then says, "Huh...alright...sure... Thanks, Moe." He hangs up and looks at me like a deer startled by the headlights of car. "Moe says he did some fast digging. Her name is Rosalie Channing, she's twenty-four years old, single, lives in a boardinghouse with three other women, and she wants to be an actress. She's working the lunch and dinner shift for the next six days. I'm supposed to have lunch tomorrow with Moe and Grant from casting, and they're going to offer her a screen test. He says they don't want me marrying some nobody, but if she can act as good as she looks, then we might have a deal." He looks at me with haunted eyes. "Ollie, what have I done?" I don't know what to say to that, especially when his face grows even more anxious and he murmurs, "If someone at the studio tries anything with her, I might have to kill him."

Good God, this is quite the turn of events, and my heart is about to shatter into bits. That Troy would even consider marrying anyone after I helped him and moved out here with him, selling my house and leaving everything I was used to and happy with in Cleveland? Unthinkable. My parents are getting old, and I haven't been able to see much of them at all since moving out here. But mostly it's just heartbreaking how the studio wants to control Troy's life to the extent that it will ruin what we have. I don't even know what to say to Troy. All I can do is stare at him for a while, noting his miserable expression. Finally, I ask, "So you're attracted to this Rosalie? Do you know anything more about her?" I also note that he's quite protective of someone he doesn't even know.

"Ollie, don't look so glum. You know you're the love of my life. I'm not planning to marry anyone, but yes, she is something special. I only know what Moe told me about her, so you now know as much as I do. But that information was certainly not what a sane person would base a marriage on. I'll have to convince him that I don't need to be married. Anyway, I'll meet her tomorrow and learn more."

I feel about two percent better hearing Troy say he's set on not marrying anyone, but I also know how persuasive the studio heads can be. When they say, "Jump!" the actors are expected to ask, "How high?" We may be in for some nasty heartache in the near future.

"Troy?" I ask softly.

"Hmm?"

"Will you come to bed with me now? I have this terrible need for you all of a sudden." Maybe I can convince him to never leave in non-verbal ways.

Finally, I see a smile on his face as he looks at me hungrily. "You bet."

Chapter Four

Rosalie

I'm exhausted after a long day on my feet, and I'm just about to head for home via the hotel's service entrance when a strange man approaches me. He's vaguely familiar, but he's definitely not anyone I've met. He holds out a business card to me and smiles, showing lots of teeth as if he wants me to understand he's a good guy. "Evening, miss. My name is Morris Frankle, from Frankle and Associates. I'm a talent agent, and I work with Troy Kingsley, Guy Harrison, Selma White, and several other top names you've undoubtedly heard of."

Now I remember. He was sitting at a table earlier tonight with Troy Kingsley before Mr. Kingsley got up and left in a huff. I wondered what that was all about. He didn't even finish his meal, and it was a lovely Chateaubriand. Who leaves food like that? This guy must have said or done some-thing to really make him angry, so I'm suddenly leery of anything he has to say to me.

"Yes?" I say, straightening my posture. I don't have it in me to be rude, so I'm glad there are other people milling around. His card looks legitimate, and he was with Troy—I mean Mr. Kingsley—an actor who is about the most dashing man on earth. I had to force myself not to stare at him while I was serving the people at the table next to his. It was hard, believe me. I've never seen anyone who's better looking, with his piercing green eyes and those muscles. I get shivers just thinking about him, and he's a fabulous actor. He never overdoes a scene the way so many actors do. He doesn't oversell, so he's completely believable.

But this Morris character is still talking, so I look up at him and try to pay attention. "Troy Kingsley is going to be starting a new movie soon, and Premier Works is looking for a fresh face to act opposite him. Are you by any chance an actress? You have just the look they'd like."

I blink a few times wondering if this is a joke, and I have to keep myself from swiveling around looking for whoever is in on the prank. But I gather myself and answer, "Yes, I'm an actress. I've had a few roles." I don't tell him the bit parts I've had were in high school productions back in Idaho. I've been studying and working hard since leaving that little one-horse town, so I'm sure I'm better now. Besides, the mayor's daughter used to get all the good parts. I was a nobody, even back there.

"May I ask your name?"

"Oh, um, yes, I'm Rosalie Channing. Pleased to meet you,

Mr. Frankle." I finally have the sense to stick out my hand and shake his like a sane person.

"Nice. We wouldn't even have to change it. Your parents should be commended for giving you a marketable name."

"Thank you. Actually, I made it up myself. My real name is Rosemary Chester, but I got sick and tired of hearing, 'Hey, Chesty!' each time I walked into a room." To his immense credit, his eyes crinkle with laughter and do not drop to my bosom. I can't believe those words came flying out of my mouth to a perfect stranger. I'll chalk it up to nerves.

"Good choice," he says with a satisfied nod. "We also don't want people thinking of you as a spice cabinet."

I smile ruefully because that's not a new one either. "What would you like me to do? Perform a screen test for the role possibly?" I hope I sound like I understand how it's done in this town.

"Eventually, yes. I'll have to set something up. First, I'd like to introduce you to Troy, if that's suitable."

Now I'm getting a weird feeling that things might not be on the up-and-up, so I say, "I'll be serving lunch and dinner here tomorrow if you'd like to stop by, even though I'll be busy serving and won't have much opportunity to chat. You can ask to be seated in my section. But now I must be leaving or I'll miss my streetcar. It was a pleasure meeting you." I step away to leave, but he stops me with a hand on my arm. I do *not* like it, but he drops his hand as soon as he sees my cold expression.

"Can I have my driver take you somewhere?"

"No thank you, sir. I'll be fine on my own. I hope to see

you tomorrow though. Good night, Mr. Frankle. I have to hurry now." And I scoot away.

Wait until I tell Daisy about this! I wonder if any of what he said was real.

WHEN I GET BACK to the boardinghouse, I check to see that Daisy's light is on. I can see it shining from the crack beneath her door. I knock lightly, and she opens up right away. She looks tired, so I want to make this brief.

"Daisy, do you know anything about this man?" I thrust the card he gave me into her hand. "He approached me after the dinner service tonight and wants me to do a screen test."

Her jaw drops, and she loses her sleepy expression immediately. "Come in, Rosalie, and have a seat." Her room is tiny—even smaller than mine—but there is a chair beside the bed, so I take it while she climbs onto the bed and looks at me with shining eyes. "He's on the level, if it was really him. What did he look like?"

So I describe him: "Not too tall, a little paunchy, dark hair and eyes, bushy eyebrows, and a big, toothy smile."

"Sounds right. What did he say to you?"

I proceed to relay every word of the conversation. It's etched in my mind, and I went over every nuance of it while I rode the streetcar back to the boardinghouse.

"Wow, you lucky duck, that's aces! And you get to act with Troy Kingsley! Maybe you'll get to kiss him." She fans her face, and it makes me laugh. "I hope you get the part. Too bad it's with Premier Works and not MGM though. That way we'd get to see each other on the set."

"Yes, too bad." Honestly, I don't care one way or the other which studio wants to possibly hire me. "It sure would be something, though, wouldn't it? But now that I think about it, he just said he wanted me to meet Troy, not that I'd be doing the screen test with him. They probably wouldn't want to waste his valuable time on someone like me. Anyway, I don't mean to keep you up, but I had to talk it over with someone. Thanks, Daisy. See you in the morning. Get some rest."

As tired as I am, my head is spinning, and it takes me a while to drop off to sleep. Why did Troy look so angry? I can't help calling him that in my head, even though I've never met the man. I guess seeing him in movies over and over has made me feel as if I know him personally, even though that's a silly notion.

Chapter Five

Moe reserved a lunch table for us so we might be able to chat with Rosalie during her shift. I'm not so sure that's a good idea, but we'll see. I can't understand why I'm feeling butterflies in my belly as I head over to the hotel, though. Besides Moe and Grant, a couple of other bigwigs are suddenly joining us to get a look at this girl. I hope she doesn't feel like we're ganging up on her. But she's an aspiring actress, so maybe she'll look at this as the big break she's been hoping for. Knowing how hungry young actresses are in this town, it's far from impossible.

I try to tell myself that if Rosalie doesn't work out, someone else will. After all, if I truly have to marry someone, anyone would be better than Gloria. But my heart isn't in it.

I had a morning shoot that had plenty of retakes thanks

to you-know-who, so I'm running a bit late, and I'm the last to join everyone. I see them several tables away—all with cocktails, and they're talking and laughing as I make my way through the crowded dining room.

I spot Rosalie coming out of the kitchen just as I'm about to sit down. Our eyes lock, and…holy cow. She's even more gorgeous than I remember. She has one of those perfect china doll faces with enormous blue eyes and plump lips made for kissing. I'm instantly convinced she's both intelligent and sweet, just by looking at her, so I stick out my hand and introduce myself.

"Troy Kingsley, Miss Channing. I understand from my colleagues here that we're possibly going to do a screen test together." Her hand feels perfect in mine. It's soft, yet her handshake is firm and confident.

"Pleased to meet you, Mr. Kingsley. I wasn't sure, but that's what these gentlemen tell me. It's a wonderful opportunity, though I don't know whether I'm right for the part. If you'll have a seat, I'll bring you a menu right away."

Her voice is lovely—low and sexy, and she has roses in her cheeks. She has to pull her hand out of mine to make me let go.

"Call me Troy, please."

"Yes, right. I'll do that." She turns to go. Wow. She looks just as good walking away as she does coming toward me. I'm spellbound watching her hips sway.

As I sit down, the laughing and gabbing at the table stops, and they all stare at me. "What? Do I still have makeup on my face or something? I washed up before I left the studio." I put my hand up to my chin and wipe.

Moe breaks the silence. "You look just fine, pretty boy. And I must say, you have quite the eye for the ladies. Your new girl here is quite the looker. We all agree, don't we?"

Everyone grins and nods in agreement, and their attention immediately shifts to Rosalie again as she approaches with a menu for me. "Oh," I say. "If everyone else has already ordered, I'll just have the poached salmon with asparagus and new potatoes." Then I get embarrassed and add, "If it's not too much trouble." I don't like ordering this woman around. She's meant for so much more.

She rolls her eyes at me a tiny bit and says, "Don't worry. I don't have to catch it and clean it; I just have to bring it to you. It's my *job*." Then she smiles—although it looks pretty stiff—and asks, "Would you like something to drink in the meantime, sir?"

I feel myself blushing. "It's *Troy*," I say looking at her right in the eye. "Just an iced tea, please. With lemon." I don't seem to be making a very good impression on her, and that's making me a little sad—or maybe I'm just frustrated. I possibly have a lot riding on this woman.

"*That one has some sass in her,*" Moe whispers to me once she's out of earshot. "*I like that in a woman. Makes for more fun between the sheets, if you know what I mean.*"

"Shut up, Moe."

He shrugs at me. "Suit yourself." He turns to the other guys and asks, "How soon can we do this screen test anyway?"

"We can fit it in this afternoon," Grant tells him. "But since we don't have a script for this so-called movie we're supposedly trying her out for, we'll have to use something else."

"Can't we just use a scene from *As Always*?" I ask.

The general consensus is that as ideas go, it's good enough. So the next thing is to schedule the lovely Rosalie for later today.

When she returns to the table and starts to distribute each of our meals, it's once again Moe who speaks up. "Miss Channing, we'll provide a car to take you to the studio as soon as you get off work today. These guys want to see you test right away."

She plunks his plate down with a startled look and says, "I can't today."

One of the studio guys asks, "Don't you realize what you're saying? How many people are offered screen tests with a leading actor at one of the top studios, and you say you *can't* do it? What's wrong with you?" He's a little rude, but he does have a point.

"I have just enough time after lunch to get to my acting class and back for the dinner shift, and I need to be there, or I might lose my spot. There's a waiting list for the class."

"Who are you studying with?" I ask.

"Bruno Metzler. He's very strict, and my scene partner will be left in the lurch if I don't show up."

Grant speaks up. "Metzler's good, and I've heard about his reputation, but your screen test is way more important. He'll understand. I can even give him a call for you so he won't boot you out of his class. A car will pick you up here unless you want to drive back with us. We're leaving as soon as we finish lunch."

I hope to ease the tension and say, "I'll wait here and drive her so she can *finish her shift*, Grant." She's looking rattled, so I hope I can calm her down. These guys can sure come on strong and bossy. "I brought my car, and I have the rest of the afternoon off, so this works out great. We can get to know each other on the drive over." I look at Rosalie and ask, "Do you need to go home first and change?"

She smiles softly and says, "I brought a change of clothes. Thank you. I'll take you up on the drive, Mr....um...Troy." She looks at the table at large and asks, "Is there anything else I can get you gentlemen?"

This must be so awkward for her. She's trying to do her job, and clearly she doesn't want to lose it by being unprofessional, but she also needs to make a good impression on these studio vultures. I want her to be successful, but I don't exactly trust these guys around a beautiful woman. Well... just about any woman, actually. I'm relieved when she excuses herself to tend to her other customers. The studio will pick up the tab for lunch, and I sure as hell hope these characters tip her well.

The rest of lunch is awkward for me. The execs discuss more of the complaints they have about Gloria Dumont and look at me like I ought to be delighted to help out that woman's public image. They also make it clear to me that I'm expected to do what they say, no matter what they decide. My stomach is twisting at the very thought of spending more time with Gloria. I pray that the screen test with Rosalie goes well. Seeing as how she's a waitress rather than a seasoned actress, I don't have a lot of faith in her success. But even if it does go well, that might be great for

Rosalie, and I'll still be railroaded into stepping out with and ultimately fake-marrying Gloria. I make a couple of pronouncements to the effect that, "I am *not* marrying Gloria Dumont," but I just get glares instead of responses. Marrying her to salvage her reputation *was* their brilliant idea, after all.

Finally, the other guys all get up to go back to work, and I let Rosalie know I'll be waiting for her in the lobby whenever she's ready to go. I have Ollie's new book out in the car, so I go out and grab it before making myself comfortable in a quiet corner. The lobby is generally a bustling place because a lot of their guests like to see and be seen, but I know of a quiet alcove where I likely won't be bothered. I hope.

I get lost in Ollie's book, and I'm not even aware of how much time has passed when I hear Rosalie's voice telling me, "Sorry to keep you so long. I'm ready to go." She's wringing her hands and looking as nervous as a cat. But she also looks beautiful in a white skirt and a pale blue blouse that matches her eyes. She's positively exquisite without the hairnet and waitress uniform. No surprise there. Her hair is loose, falling in soft waves just past her shoulders, and she's added a lovely color of lipstick to her delectable mouth. This immediately makes me wonder how her kisses taste.

I realize I'm staring when she starts to fidget with her hair, so I hop up and offer her my arm. "You're gorgeous," just kind of spills out of my mouth, so I clear my throat and say, "I mean, let's go."

She sees Ollie's book in my hand and asks, "Oh, his new one is out? I haven't read that one yet. I'm a huge fan. How is it?"

She has great taste! I smile proudly. "Just as terrific as all the others. I'll get you a copy."

"You don't have to do that."

"It would be my pleasure. I can get it autographed for you too."

"Oh? You're friends with the author? I understand he's something of a recluse and no one ever sees him."

"We're acquainted. He's actually a great guy. My car is just over there." I need to shut up. The book isn't even out in stores yet and won't be for a couple more days. I don't want to explain how I got my hands on a copy so early. "So tell me about your acting classes," I say by way of changing the subject. Hopefully, she will be interested in talking about herself. If this were Gloria, she sure would be. *Ugh, don't think about Gloria Dumont.*

We have nearly half an hour to get to know one another, so we talk about our backgrounds—not that I have a lot to say about mine before coming to California. I tell her I grew up the youngest of four boys on a farm in North Olmstead, Ohio, and I acted in several stage productions in Cleveland before moving to Los Angeles, and that's about it.

I discover she's from a little town called Emmet, Idaho where her parents have a cherry orchard. It sounds like a nice place, but I understand her wanting to leave if she had ambitions to act in Hollywood. She has younger siblings—a sister and brother who are twins, but they aren't particularly close to her due to a six-year gap in their ages and because the twins are so close to one another.

Her parents were not thrilled with her when she left town because they felt she was deserting them and ought to want to eventually inherit the orchard. She was not the least bit interested in becoming an orchard owner, however.

My parents were alright with me leaving because my older brothers embraced farm life far better than I ever did. They all recognized I was born to be different.

I'm enjoying listening to her voice and discover she has a good sense of humor, but all too soon, we're at the studio and I have to park and take her in. I liked having her all to myself for a little bit.

Right away, Rosalie and I are handed a short script, and one of the studio flunkies whisks Rosalie off to makeup. "They said you're good enough the way you are, Mr. Kingsley, because they know what you look like," she says as she leads Rosalie away. "You can find Mr. Packard on the set where he wants a word with you."

The director of *As Always* is John Packard, and he's usually a reasonable guy, so he probably just wants to chat. I'm not prepared at all for what he has to say, however.

Smiling, he greets me, but he beckons me close and says in a low voice, "Troy, thanks for doing this, although I'm not exactly sure what's going on. Listen, between you and me, I can't *stand* working with Gloria, and I heard a rumor that she's bugging the shit outta you too. So I need you to try to butter her up a little and make the scenes go a lot smoother. Play up to her some between takes so she feels more of a connection to you. You know what I mean? I'd like to get the shooting finished on this crap and move onto something better. But you didn't hear this from me, got it?"

I let out a long sigh and answer, "I'm doing my absolute best, but...I'll try harder. Every minute I spend with that woman feels like torture. How'd she get the lead role anyway?"

Packard looks over his shoulder, mutters to me that "She gets around and isn't picky," and then makes a crude gesture with his hand and mouth. I nod. Just as I thought. I can't help wincing. Lucky me. I've had to kiss those lips.

Sitting down next to him, I take a look at the scene I'll be doing with Rosalie. It was originally one of my favorites, but that feeling was quickly squashed when Gloria got hold of it. It should be tender and moving, but she bulldozes her way through it like a buffalo dancing the rhumba. The woman has no finesse whatsoever. I'm not sure we'll ever get it right. I get the feeling this is going to be trial by fire for Rosalie, and I have this burning desire to seek her out and discuss it with her before the camera rolls. But all too soon, she's being escorted to the stage set again, and at the same time the producer, casting director, and Harry Walken, the president of Premier Works, arrive to watch the proceedings. I'm shooed out of my seat and told to go stand on my mark next to Rosalie.

I know the scene by heart, so I leave my script on the chair I vacate, and as I approach Rosalie I'm once again floored by her beauty. I take her hand and whisper, "Break a leg, beautiful."

With no rehearsal at all, the director calls, "Action!" and Rosalie looks deeply into my eyes, projecting the feeling that we've been in love for a long time. She cocks her head with a private smile that goes straight to my heart and delivers her lines like she's Olivia DeHavilland or Bette Davis...no, not like them—like herself.

She's Rosalie Channing, and she belongs here, doing just what she's doing, and she's incredible at it. My heart swells as I respond to her and take her gently into my arms. She lays her head on my chest as if it lives there, and my heart begins to race. Our conversation is gut-wrenching and powerful, and we end the scene with what was supposed to be a sweet kiss, but I am so wrapped up in her, I hold it too long. She tastes so sweet, I can't stop kissing her.

"Cut, Loverboy! You'll give the censors a heart attack if you keep that up," the director hollers, and there is stone silence on the set. I turn to the panel of men assessing our chemistry together, and I see slack jaws and bulging eyes from each of them. Suddenly, they all burst into applause.

"Where's Moe?" the director hollers. "This woman needs an agent *now*."

Grant, the casting director, hisses at Harry Walken, "How can we get Gloria out of her contract? Morals clause? Shift her to another movie? Trade her to Paramount for something? Give her a bunch of shitty parts in lousy movies? We *need* to have this actress instead. That was movie magic!"

"I'll figure something out," Walken states as he beckons us to approach him. "Miss Channing, we've never done anything like this before. We'd like to formally offer you the lead female role in *As Always*, but I think we're going to have to make some serious script alterations, and we'll change the name of the movie to...um...*Forever Yours*. I never did like that *As Always* crap; it sounds insincere. Nice job, Troy." Then he winks and says, "I think we have a winner here now. Miss Channing, you'll want to meet with Moe Frankle, unless you already have your own agent, and have him work out your contract details with our financial guys. Standard protocol is a seven-year deal. I look forward to seeing what else you can do." And he strides away, not even stopping to ask Rosalie if she wants a contract. He obviously assumes anyone in Hollywood would give their soul to get one.

I hadn't let go of her when the director hollered "cut," so I notice she's trembling all over. I take a good look at her and ask, "Are you alright, sweetheart? You're not going to faint or anything, are you?" I turn to the ever-present flunky and order, "Get Miss Channing a glass of water right away, please."

Rosalie looks up at me and says, "I can't believe that just happened. Are those men serious?"

"As serious as a heart attack. You were incredible, Rosalie. I'm over the moon at the thought of working with you. You'll sign the contract, won't you?" I add that last part so I don't sound as presumptuous as the studio execs.

"Of course I'll sign. This is my lifelong dream. Thank you so much for doing the scene with me."

"My pleasure, believe me. The funny thing is, they didn't even bother to go back and watch us on film to discuss it. They know you're a gem already." I give her a squeeze, "I'm so happy!" The assistant hands her a glass of water then, and it's apparent that Rosalie is still shaking. I frown a bit and ask, "Have you had anything to eat today?"

"Oh, um, no. I slept late and missed breakfast, then I had to rush to get to work. I am a little lightheaded, actually. How embarrassing."

"I'm going to show you to the studio commissary. It's not the Beverly Hills Hotel's caliber, but the food is decent, and you can iron out the details of your contract when you're feeling better. I know how much acting can take out of you emotionally too, so it's understandable that you're a little shaky. I'll give Moe's office a call and let him know where he can find us. That'll give him time to work things out and have stuff ready for you. Don't worry. He'll get you a decent deal, but you'll want to read over the contract carefully before you sign it anyway. Have a seat, and I'll be right back." I hope that wasn't too pushy.

I cannot wait to tell Ollie about this day. And get an autographed book for Rosalie.

Chapter Six

ROSALIE

PINCH ME! What just happened? This morning, I was a waitress at a hotel restaurant, and suddenly I'm the lead actress in a major motion picture with one of the best studios in the country. And with Troy Kingsley! I guess I better quit my job at the hotel so some other girl can take it. And I'll need to write home to my family. They'll be so shocked. I hope they're proud of me. I'd telephone them, but they were so angry when I left, I'm afraid they might just hang up the phone if they hear my voice.

We have a small café on the premises of our cherry orchard—well, I should say it's *my parents'* orchard. They made it pretty clear I gave up my rights to any of it by leaving, even though I send them what money I can spare now. I'd been working there since the age of fourteen, so I had lots and lots of waitressing experience by the time I showed up in California. That certainly helped me get settled here. I'd saved up every last penny I ever earned so I could pay my way out here and afford the boardinghouse. One could say I've been extremely lucky, but I've also worked incredibly hard to make it this far.

But today was a whole new level of...I can't believe it. I got to meet Troy Kingsley and act with him—even *kiss* him, and the studio loved what I did. Or at least what we did together. I can't take all the credit. He definitely brought the best out of me the way he looked into my eyes like I was the most beautiful woman he'd ever seen and he was deeply in love with me. I almost believed it myself. And they're offering me a part! I can't say that to myself enough times. I have a part in a Hollywood movie! A *big* part!

My mind keeps jumping back to that delicious kiss, and it makes me all squiggly in my belly. I remember all that Daisy has told me about actors. She says the kissing part is always fake, and the actors can't kiss for longer than about three seconds because of the Hays Code that upholds a moral standard. Well, that's not what I experienced. Our kiss felt as real as can be. So I suppose that Troy is a great romantic lead if he can sell it that way, but then I remember the director's reference to the censors, and I wonder if we both got carried away. We'll have to be careful, I guess. I hope there's lots of kissing, but I think the Hays Code limits the number of instances as well. Maybe we can practice a lot.

As I sit sipping my water and woolgathering about my fabulous fortune and great kissing, Troy comes striding back into view, beaming at me. "Ready to get something to eat?"

he asks. "Moe is on his way, and I also took the liberty of alerting Jack Cramer, my lawyer, so he's coming over as well. I don't mean to overstep, especially if you already have your own attorney…" He's blushing a little. That's a surprise.

Laughing, I assure him, "I've never had reason to hire a lawyer in my life, so I appreciate your thoughtfulness more than you'll ever know." Then I get a sick feeling in my stomach and say, "But I don't think I can afford one."

"Don't worry. You'll be making enough to afford him, and he's all about making sure you get the best deal. Between Moe and Jack, you'll be in good hands if you can get past Moe's personality. They were both salivating over the idea of making a new contract for a budding star with Premier Works. Let's go. We don't want you fainting away from hunger." He offers me his arm like a gentleman, and I delight in the contact with him again. I've always had a bit of a crush on him, but now it's more than just a Hollywood idol crush. This man is suddenly real to me, and jeepers, do I like what I see!

"I need to be back to the hotel in a couple of hours for the dinner shift, Troy. How long will this take?"

He bursts out laughing. "You won't be getting back there tonight, Dollface…Sorry, I mean Rosalie." Now he's blushing for real. "They'll spend lots of time going over the contract with you and making sure you understand their expectations. And when the execs are all done with you, unless it's so late that they've already gone home, you'll probably be sent to visit the ladies in the costume department to let them measure you and whatnot for your wardrobe. There won't be any time for waitressing ever again, believe me. Do you have anything you need to go back and pick up at the hotel? Because I can drive you.”

He sure is being helpful. “Thank you for offering a ride. I’ll accept. No, I don’t have anything at the hotel, but I do need to make a call and let them know that they’ll have to get someone to take my shift.” Now the nerves are suddenly overtaking me. “But what if this doesn’t work out? What if what we did today was a fluke, and I’m actually terrible on camera? Don’t I still need to keep my job?”

He throws back his head and laughs like it’s the funniest thing he’s ever heard. “Rosalie, you were magnificent. They all saw it right away. You’re not going to get fired from the studio, and in a couple of hours you’ll have a contract that protects you from getting canned anyway.”

“What happens now to the actress who had the part already? Won’t she be upset? I feel terrible taking someone else’s job out from under her.”

“Just between you and me…good riddance. They were foolish enough to cast the wrong actress for the worst of reasons in her case, but she’s still protected with her contract, even if it’s a more limited one. She’ll be given a different script, and they’ll make it sound to her like a promotion, no matter what it is. You’ll see. You didn’t hear it from me, but that woman can’t act her way out of a paper bag, but sometimes certain women manage to get parts anyway, if you catch my meaning. Anyway, I could see how delighted they were with you. Well, here we are.”

He opens a door for me, and even though I’m still reeling by the suggestion about some people and their behavior, I’m suddenly starstruck seeing a bunch of well-known actors and actresses, some in costume and others casually dressed, sitting around eating, drinking, smoking, and looking like normal people. *I'm going to be one of them now*, I tell myself—but only in the tiniest of internal whispers. I don't want to jinx myself.

But then Troy goes on to say something truly extraordinary as he stands still and looks me in the eye. "If you're still worried about whether or not you'll be a success, you could always marry me, and I'll take care of you." I assume he's joking, so I laugh, but something in his expression makes me stop and stare. I know he's an excellent actor, but there is sincerity in his gaze that I swear looks vulnerable. *Oh my.* Before I can venture any response, though, he breaks the mood by asking, "What do you feel like eating?"

Chapter Seven

I simply cannot believe I said that to Rosalie. Thank God she thought I was joking when those words about marrying me and taking care of her came out of my mouth. I *was* joking to some extent, but the excitement over getting rid of Gloria and being partnered with this delightful young woman suddenly got to me, and I blurted out what felt like my heart's desire. What am I thinking? She's taking care of herself just fine, and I probably sounded like an overbearing fool who thinks all women are weak or something.

And then there's Ollie. If he knew what I'd said to her, he'd be crushed. I love Ollie. Deeply. It's just that sometimes, in my heart of hearts, I would also love to be with a woman. Since I can't marry him, and I can't marry a woman and keep him, I don't know what to do. But if anyone could tempt me away from the man I adore, it would be Rosalie. We're hardly acquainted, and yet I feel as if we've known each other for ages. Another possibility starts to tickle the back of my brain. I'm glad I asked Jack Cramer to show up. I might have a word with him.

Rosalie settles on having a club sandwich and a piece of apple pie. Pie sounds good to me too, so I plan to join her for dessert. Unlike most of Hollywood, I do not elect to sit around smoking a cigarette while she eats her sandwich. I tried smoking one awful time when I was sixteen, and it caused a frightening asthma attack. It wasn't terribly severe, but it was the first I'd had since I was nine or ten years old. I was sure I'd outgrown it, much to my family's delight, but inhaling that smoke just scared me to death when I felt my lungs seize up. When Ollie found out about my episode, he immediately quit smoking. He's so good to me. Anyway, as long as I don't smoke, I don't have attacks, and I'd like to keep it that way. I've had to make the studio adjust a few scripts because of that. It's one of the things I had stipulated in my contract, in fact. I explain this to Rosalie about my asthma when I was a kid and then add, "If there is anything specific you need them to consider for your health, religious practices, or whatever, now is the time to let them know. They can't come back at you and tell you how you must do something their way if it's already in the contract."

She considers this for a while and then decides, "I can't really think of a thing." She's finished with her sandwich about the same time Moe shows up, but before they can get into anything, she asks, "Is there someplace I can go make a quick phone call? I'll be right back."

While she's gone, Jack also arrives and I tell him, "Don't leave before I have a chance to speak to you privately, please?"

Rosalie comes back to the table, so we all stand, and I pull out her chair again and introduce her to Jack. He seems thunderstruck by her appearance. I guess Moe is getting used to seeing her by now because he just looks like he sees dollar signs when he looks at her. Frankly, I can't blame either of them. She's something alright.

Rosalie has a long conversation with both men, and I'm impressed with how businesslike and savvy she seems for someone new to this town. It's as if she'd taken a primer course in contracts and negotiations already. Eventually, one of the studio flunkies seeks us out and tells Rosalie to follow him to one of the meeting rooms to meet with the execs.

"Thank you, but I'll be bringing my lawyer, my agent, and my...uh..."

"Fiancé?" I interject. I take her hand, and she laughs.

"Friend," she says, and I pretend to be broken-hearted, but Moe and Jack get a kick out of her.

"Friend and co-star," I say more definitively.

"Told you I liked her sass," Moe whispers to me as we head out. *"You lucky dog."*

"Shut up, Moe," I mutter. To Rosalie, I say, "I'll meet you all in a couple of minutes. I have to make a quick call." I head for the nearest phone to let Ollie know I might be a little late getting home, but I have a lot to tell him when I get there.

As I head to the meeting room, I'm a bit surprised to see Rosalie, Moe, and Jack still waiting in the hall, and they've been joined by a couple more guys from finance. Just the sight of her takes my breath away. As I approach them, I hear a familiar voice screeching inside the room at the studio execs. "You bastards! I don't believe for one minute that you've trashed *As Always* so I can have a bigger, juicier role in *A Soldier's Wife*—that maudlin crap. You just loaned me to Paramount so you can play your dirty games with some new little piece. Well, I'm done sucking your nasty dicks anyway! I should call each of your wives and clue them all in." The door flies open, and Gloria Dumont stomps out jerkily with tears streaming down her cheeks. She shoots daggers at me and then catches the sight of Rosalie. Gloria stops dead in her tracks, and an evil look comes over her splotchy face. "Watch out, bitch!" she hisses in Rosalie's face, then she continues staggering down the hallway like she might already be drunk in the middle of the afternoon. I'm not sure whether she was warning Rosalie to watch out for the people she's about to work for or for Gloria herself. In either case, I vow to myself to look after her closely.

Despite Rosalie's appalled expression after her face-to-face with Gloria, we all file into the conference room. Rosalie calms down and gets right to business, and the next couple of hours are spent going over a very basic contract. The only surprises come at the very end of the talk. Harry Walken speaks up, addressing both Rosalie and me. "I'm glad you decided to join us for this, Troy." He smiles blandly at me. "I know Moe has already broached this topic with you." My heart sinks just thinking about what he's going to say, but it's not as bad as I feared. "We did want you to help Miss Dumont's image, but frankly, she might be beyond repair at this time. Too bad. She had potential." He doesn't look too busted up about his opinion, and he sounds terribly insincere to my ears. "Up to now, we've been far too lenient with you, Troy, and I still think we need to have a romance between you and your leading lady so people will have something to talk about. So from here on out, you and Miss Channing will be seen around town at each of the restaurants and parties we send you to. You will behave as if you are falling in love, and since you are both consummate actors, I expect the public to eat it up. My secretary will alert the press as to when and where they can take publicity shots, and she'll send you a weekly list that you will both abide by unless someone is deathly ill, and in that case, I'll need proof. We shouldn't have too many impromptu events to add to the list, but if so, you will also be expected to attend when and where we send you."

He turns to Rosalie. "We'll provide you with stylists for your clothing and hair, and from time to time we will ask you to wear certain jewelry that will be sent to you on loan. Again, you are *in love* from today unless we decide for some reason to release you from this stipulation. Don't count on that, however.

"And, Troy, we want a dramatic, heartfelt proposal when we deem the time is right. One of our script writers can help you with that. Don't look so shocked, Miss Channing. We won't rush this too badly. You'll have a wonderful wedding that the studio will pay for, and then we'll send you both on a honeymoon to someplace nice where we will see to it you have a luxury suite. Upon your return, you will move into Troy's house. What you do or don't do when you have private time together is entirely up to you, but you will get married. Legally. This arrangement falls under the 'expected behavior' clause in your contracts.

"We plan to schedule your wedding shortly after the release of the movie, so you'll have plenty of time to get to know each other, and the public will be going crazy with excitement. With your looks, you two will be Hollywood's Golden Couple, and we expect your public behavior to reflect that favored status. If the kiss you two participated in during the screentest is any indication of your attraction to one another at this point, I doubt much of this will be a hardship. I can see why Troy suggested you. Now, it's past my dinnertime, so let's all get out of here and go home. Miss Channing, it was a pleasure meeting you. Be on time tomorrow and every day after that."

"Wait! What...?" Rosalie begins to ask, but the studio bigwigs get up and march out. She looks at me like I'm going to say something brilliant, and I wish I could. Nothing comes to mind, unfortunately. With wide eyes, she asks, "You knew about this and didn't warn me? And what did he mean you suggested me? I've never even met you before!"

"I...well...Moe actually told me they wanted me to marry Gloria, to be fair, so this is a much better option." I don't tell her I selected her as my preferred option after spotting her across the room of the hotel restaurant.

"Option? I'm an option? Are you out of your mind? We just met, and these men want us to *marry*? How did this happen? Why did you choose me without even speaking to me once? What am I supposed to tell my family?"

Moe, who is still sitting with us, pipes up and says, "You could do a lot worse, Miss Channing. Troy's a great guy." He gives her his best toothy grin, and I shudder inwardly as I think about the impending complications of my home life. Moe is unaware of my relationship with Ollie.

"That's not the point!" Rosalie huffs. "I can't agree to this. It's crazy." Looking fit to be tied, she stands up and grabs her purse like she's about to bolt out of the room.

"Look," Moe says like he's trying to soothe a spooked horse. "You can do as you like, but this opportunity won't come around again anytime soon. I wouldn't be too hasty if I were you."

Suddenly, my life is spinning out of control. I need to fix this. I need to speak to Ollie, and I need to speak to Jack privately. He's sitting silently next to Moe, taking everything in. Clearly, he knows I have something on my mind, but he's remaining quiet, thank God.

It's way too late to send Rosalie to see the wardrobe ladies, and I did offer her a ride home, but I need to speak to Jack. I also need to calm Rosalie down. She looks like she's about to cry. I make a split-second decision and ask, "Jack, can I call you later tonight? I told Rosalie I'd drive her home, and it's getting late." Jack gives me a shrewd nod, so I stand, take her arm gently, and smile at her as kindly as I can. "May I drive you home now? We can talk on the way if you like."

Chapter Eight

Rosalie

This has been the most exciting and confusing day of my life. First, I am offered a *lead* in a movie, then I'm given a seven-year contract with a major studio, and finally I'm ordered to marry a virtual stranger. What has happened? I'm nobody special. I'm a waitress from a cherry farm in Nowhere, Idaho, and now all of this? Maybe it's all a dream, and I'll wake up pretty soon. It sure feels real, though.

I'll say one thing for Troy: he has good manners. He offered me a ride home from the studio, and even though, for some reason, he seems a little nervous about something with his lawyer, he's following through. I told him I'd take the streetcar, but he wouldn't have it. "They're going to have to provide you with car service while we're making the movie," he told me. "I might not be able to chauffeur you around exactly when they need you. We might have different sched-ules on some days." I understand the practicality of this, but I wouldn't mind having him chauffeur me around. Frankly, I love his car's cushy leather seats, the purr of the engine — like a powerful cat—and the slight woodsy scent of Troy's cologne. It's faint, but it's masculine and makes me want to get wrapped back up into his arms again. Even if he was just acting, being close to this man is addicting.

On the ride back to the boardinghouse, I say, "Thank you again, Troy. I understand that without your interference I'd never have gotten this role—or probably even the screentest. But I really need to know—what is this business about you choosing me somehow? I'm terribly confused."

"Please don't be offended or upset; I mean this only in a complimentary way. I was having a conversation over dinner with Moe, and he told me I was going to be ordered to marry Gloria Dumont to save her lousy image. He also suggested that the consensus is that I am getting too old to be single, so they would be—as he said—killing two birds with one stone by having us marry. Since I absolutely cannot stand Gloria, I panicked. I saw you serving at the next table, and you were so lovely—possibly the most beautiful woman I've ever seen. And you seemed polite and, well, I never thought Moe could possibly follow through, but I made a grand sort of state-ment that I'd never marry Gloria, and the only woman I'd consider would be you. I didn't know your name or the first thing about you, and yes, I see how impetuous...well...*crazy* that was of me. I thought Moe would take it as a joke, but he took it as a challenge and found out about you—where you lived, the fact you were studying acting, and so forth. He worked incredibly quickly. And you know the rest. We'll have a few months before we need to tie the knot."

"So you think we really have to do this?"

Troy looks resigned. "If we don't, we'll never act again. They'll see to it. Working with the studios is a double-edged sword. You play by their rules, and you become a huge star. Step out of line, and you're nothing for the rest of your life. It's definitely a deal with the devil for a lot of folks. But, hey, I'm not a bad guy," he tells me as he pulls up and stops in front of the house while knocking me out me with his gorgeous smile. "You might even get to like me eventually." He gets out of the car, but I'm rooted to the spot after what he said.

Just as Troy is opening my door, Daisy walks by the car, heading to the front path. She stops and does a double take, so I take Troy's proffered hand and step out of the car. "Hi Daisy, I'd like to introduce you to my co-star, Troy Kingsley. Troy, this is my friend Daisy Dillinger who works for MGM." I wish she'd close her mouth or even blink; she looks like a fish.

Ever the polite one, Troy extends his hand. "Pleased to meet you, Miss Dillinger. I'm sure Rosalie has a lot to talk about with you this evening, so I'm glad she has a friend handy. I'll say goodbye now. And Rosalie, I'll stop by at eight in the morning to pick you up, and then we'll see if the studio can arrange car service for you. It was a pleasure spending today with you." He leans in and gives me a sweet peck on the cheek. "Good night, ladies."

He steps back into his lovely, sleek automobile, and he's gone.

Daisy still hasn't uttered a peep.

I do have a lot to tell her, and I can't wait to get inside.

For once, Daisy isn't the one monopolizing the conversation over dinner. I have everyone's spellbound attention as I relay what happened to me today. But I stop short of telling anyone about the studio ordering us to get married. I'd love to maintain the illusion that it's all real, so I'm keeping that to myself. Also, I don't want to get into trouble for letting word leak out that our engagement is less than authentic. Who knows? Maybe by the time we get married, we'll be hopelessly in love. Stranger things have happened. And I'm already attracted to the man. What could possibly go wrong?

Chapter Nine

ZELDA HAS LEARNED to be flexible with our mealtimes, but even so, it was nice of Troy to call ahead and say he'd be late getting home. I'm so busy writing my next best seller (positive thinking!), I don't even consider being hungry or upset with him. They often keep him late at the studio when they're shooting, so Zelda and I are used to it. When this filming is done, life will go back to normal for a while until they start shooting his next movie. I've just learned to have a late lunch—just in case. So I'm pleasantly surprised when he walks through the door only a tiny bit late. The inscrutable expression on his face is hard to read, however. I stand from my desk chair to give him a welcome-home kiss, but Troy wraps his arms around me and burrows his face into my neck. This is odd. He's often affectionate, but not usually clingy.

"I'm glad you're home, Troy, but what's going on?"

He sighs and pulls away. Noticing the whiskey bottle and empty glasses on the credenza, he steps back and pours us both a drink. He hands one to me and takes a swig, then leads me by the hand to the couch.

"I don't know where to begin," he mutters. A chill goes down my back, but he doesn't look particularly sad. More... confused maybe?

"Are you ill?"

"No. I'm fine."

"Is your job in jeopardy?"

"Not really. I suppose if I made some truly horrible decisions it could be, but that's not an immediate concern. Well... maybe, actually."

"Clear as mud, Troy. Don't you want to tell me?"

"I have to tell you, Ollie. You're everything to me, and I can't keep anything from you. You know that."

"As you are to me. I assume this has something to do with the studio then, right?"

He sighs again. "Yes."

"Take your time. I'm not going anywhere."

"I hope that's always going to be true."

I narrow my eyes at him. My suspicions are growing by the second. "Go on."

"Alright, I'll get right to the point. I have a new co-star as of today." He tries for a smile, but it's not his normal, joyous look. "Gloria Dumont was fired from *As Always*, and she has been sent over to Paramount to star in some second-rate movie that may never make it to theaters because she'll ruin it. She's furious, and I'm relieved to be rid of her."

"That doesn't sound too bad. Well—at least for you. She's probably fuming. At least you won't have to marry her now."

"Oh, Gloria's fuming alright, and she left making parting threats, but I'm not even sure what she was threatening. The important part is that my new co-star is the exquisite young woman named Rosalie Channing I told you about last night. It turns out she's a brilliant actress and so beautiful it's almost hard to look at her. She's a huge fan of your books, too, by the way." He takes a healthy swallow of his whiskey.

"Well, I'm half in love with her already. What's the hardship that has you so wrecked?" I'm not stupid, but I need for Troy to say it.

"She's perfect."

"And...?"

"We did a screentest, and I...kissed her."

"Oh. So? You've kissed lots of actresses."

"Not like this, Ollie. I got so carried away, the director said the censors would have a heart attack! He loved it though; I'm sure of it."

Now my hands are starting to shake, and I have to swallow some whiskey so I can speak. "So, you really like Rosalie?"

"I don't just like her, Ollie. She's amazing and nice, gorgeous, and...I can't wait for you to meet her. I told her she could have a signed copy of your book, even though I didn't tell her we live together or that I'm in love with you."

"Yeah, well, good thing. I'll be happy to sign a book for

her, but why do I have to meet her? I don't think that's the best way to keep my identity under wraps." Maybe somehow I can stall the inevitable.

Troy's eyes go a bit wild and he stands abruptly. He starts to pace around the room, running the hand that isn't gripping his whiskey through his hair. I wait. Finally, he stops, looks me in the eye, and says, "There's no easy way to say it, so I'll just…I'll say it. I've been ordered to marry her, and she'll be moving into this house with us!"

My hand shakes as I lift my glass and down the rest of its contents in one gulp. "Did you try telling them no?"

"It wouldn't do any good. They reminded us about the section in both of our contracts that says we need to act the way they deem the best at all times, and they say we're getting married. You know it's just a publicity stunt. They want to capitalize on our on-screen chemistry and turn us into Hollywood's Golden Couple. Packard's own words."

"How did Rosalie react?"

"She was shocked, and not particularly pleased, so I don't think she's starstruck or anything. She was also concerned about what her family would say. They live in Idaho, so at least they aren't around here." He takes a last swallow of his drink and flops back down onto the couch, too far away for me to reach without scooting toward him, and I instantly fear a fissure between us that may start to grow exponentially. Troy's career is everything to him, and I doubt he'd jeopardize it. Maybe I ought to offer to sell him my half of the house and move back to Cleveland. I might even get over him in a decade—or two—if I'm lucky.

Troy jumps up and announces, "I'll go let Zelda know we're ready for dinner, and while she's getting it on the table, I need to make a phone call to Jack Cramer." He's out of the room before I have a chance to question that.

He needs his lawyer?

Chapter Ten

Troy

If ever there was a time to make sure of a lawyer's discretion, this is it. I ring up Jack and don't waste a moment of time. "Jack, I need you to draw up a confidentiality contract for me to give to Rosalie Channing to sign. She needs to be alerted that there is a situation with my living arrangements that she can never discuss outside of this property."

Jack doesn't even hesitate. "Sure, Troy, I can put that together first thing in the morning. It's fairly common practice, actually." He chuckles. "There's a lot going on in this town that people would prefer nobody knows about. I'm a bit surprised this request is coming from you, however. Is there anything in particular I need to spell out in the contract?"

I take a deep breath and feel lightheaded suddenly. "Before we get into that, I can't risk anyone in your office reading it. If word got out, I could not only lose my job, I would most likely be arrested."

"I see. You understand that our secretaries are sworn to secrecy about our clients too. Not just the lawyers."

"But can you trust one hundred percent that if someone were in possession of some truly tempting Hollywood gossip that none of the secretaries might spill the beans? I mean, even just telling a friend, asking her to keep it to herself, could be enough. That friend could do the same to another friend, and before you know it, a whole boatload of people knew the gossip that was just too good to stay quiet about in the first place. I mean, my career means the world to me, but someone else would also be affected just as seriously if word got out. I can't risk that."

"Alright, Troy. I understand. I'll keep it brief and type it up myself. It'll take a little longer that way because I'm not one of those sixty-words-per-minute typists, but I'll do my best."

"Look, you can write it up in longhand if that makes it easier. In fact, that would be just fine." I take a deep breath and begin, "So here goes. I need you to include that Oliver Shackleton's employment status *and* identity are never to be mentioned to anyone."

"Just out of curiosity, why? Are you harboring a fugitive of the law or something?"

"No, nothing like that. Look, you don't have to add this part to the contract, but the reason for this is that he is the author who goes by the pen name Robert Oliver, and he is not my majordomo. He's my life partner, or boyfriend, if you will. He owns the house with me, although my name isn't even on the deed for privacy's sake. I'm certain this would become as clear as a bell to Rosalie once she moves in, but I'd like her to be aware of it before she and I are forced to marry. I don't want to compound a lie with more lies that would be impossible to avoid if we don't come clean right away. Right now, only two other people know about this. The first is our live-in cook and housekeeper Zelda—who is our real manager—and now you because I see you as not only my lawyer, but also my trusted friend, Jack. We've given up a lot to keep this secret, and we're never seen in public together. It's my fervent hope that Rosalie can be tolerant of us."

"I see. Mind if I give you some unsolicited, friendly advice?"

"You can try."

"That young woman has it bad for you. It's written all over her face. So if she finds out you prefer men to her, she's likely to be crushed. She might do anything when her ego is squashed."

"She's not like that."

"Troy, how can you say that? You've known her for a few hours. She's an actress, and you know quite well the kinds of egos that go along with the profession. I'm just saying to tread lightly and do what you can to make her feel loved and wanted. I also got the feeling from you that you are pretty taken with her, unless you really are the best actor in Hollywood. So I don't know what you have going on with Oliver, or how serious that is, but you might have to make a hard choice. You might want to break things off with Oliver. Many homosexual men marry women and deal with their lives… somehow.”

“I’m not homosexual.”

“Yeah, right. Look, no judgment from me, but then what are you doing being with a man?”

“I’m apparently sexually ambidextrous, and Ollie’s special. He’s been the only man for me ever. I’ve only dated women prior to meeting him. I do *not* plan to give him up, so I’m hoping we can work something out. Mostly, we don’t want the studio to find out, and we don’t want to end up getting arrested for so-called immoral behavior. It’s not immoral to love someone!”

“Whatever you say, Troy. Frankly, I don’t need the details. I’ll draw up the contract, and we’ll have Rosalie sign it. Can you bring her by my office when you get done tomorrow? I can keep the contract sealed up here in my safe. No one will ever see it that way, unless she wants another lawyer to take a look at it. That would be her right.”

“Well, let’s hope she doesn’t feel the need to do that. I’ll get her there tomorrow. Thank you, Jack. I’ll call and let you know when we can get away. Just please make it clear in the contract that she can never mention this to anyone at the studio or anywhere else, and that the contract extends for her entire lifetime, alright?”

“You got it. One more thing, though. What is the penalty if Rosalie were to tell someone and her indiscretion resulted in the end of your career? Can you put a dollar amount on that?”

"Twenty million dollars." I have no idea why that figure even entered my head. It's utterly ridiculous, but it ought to get Rosalie's attention.

"Got it. I'll see you tomorrow." Apparently, twenty mill wasn't unheard of because he took the amount in stride.

"Thanks, Jack."

I KNOW how uncomfortable Ollie is. Zelda keeps giving him quizzical looks, and he's avoiding looking at her. He's not doing a great job of looking at me either, if I'm honest. I make a promise to myself that I will let him know just how much I love him as soon as we're done with dinner. In the meantime, our supper is largely silent except for quiet thanks and compliments directed at Zelda for her delicious meal. Since we're not pretentious people, the three of us eat family style in the kitchen. I wonder if that will change once I have a wife. Maybe the dining room will finally see some use. I can't say the prospect does anything for me one way or the other. Thinking about Rosalie reminds me that I should tell Zelda about my plans.

"I have some business to do late tomorrow," I tell her, "and I'll no doubt go out to eat after that, so don't wait on dinner for me."

As soon as we're done with coffee and dessert, I rise and take Ollie's hand. I look at him with such longing, he has to understand the depth of my love for him. Zelda ignores us and goes about cleaning up after dinner, so I lead my beloved man down the hall and up the stairs to our suite. "You're done writing for the day. I need you too badly," I tell him and get an understanding nod as a reply.

As soon as the door is firmly closed, I begin to remove Ollie's shirt. His smile looks a little sad, so I kiss a trail across his body as I expose more and more of him. A sudden notion pops into my head that I might be doing this in the future with Rosalie and feel a strong stirring below the belt. I'm glad Ollie can't see my thoughts, but I know my face has gone red. I feel the heat. Let him think my arousal is all for him. *Oh my God. I can't do this*, I think to myself. *I cannot pretend with the man I love so dearly*. I can't be making love to him while fantasizing about someone else, so I try to banish the thought of Rosalie and her delightful kisses out of my mind and start on Ollie's pants. Once they're undone, I reach for him and find he's hard for me. I stroke him and then drop to my knees in front of him. One of his hands threads gently through my hair while the other grips my shoulder.

My Ollie. My beloved. My best friend in the world. How can I break his heart, even if it means my career? But...

I take Ollie into my mouth, and he gives a long moan of arousal. I've discovered he loves having his cock sucked more than almost anything, although he also loves it when I screw him. We've tried it in all sorts of ways. Me in him, him in me, facing each other, front to back...But oral pleasure definitely gets my man Ollie going. For myself, I love putting my dick in people. I love women, and I love Ollie's tight, muscular ass. It's all good. But if he needs to be sucked, sign me right up. I adore him, and I'd do anything for him.

"I love watching you on your knees for me, Troy. You're such a good boy, still all dressed, with my dick practically down your throat. Do you think we might be able to teach Rosalie how to do that for us?"

I'm so shocked, my jaw drops open, and I lose the suction hold I have on Ollie. "What?" I croak. I cannot say the thought hadn't crossed my mind, but it seemed so far-fetched, I barely acknowledged it to myself. Now that Ollie has brought it up, my erection is so hard it hurts, and I have to be rid of these clothes immediately. I stand and tear them off. My dick is red and angry-looking in its tumescence.

"Oh, my sweet boy Troy, I heard every word you said about Rosalie, and I know you're taken with her. And now I'm going to admit something I should have been honest about long ago." He takes my dick in his hands and strokes it just the way he knows I love. "I miss having a woman some-times. You know I love you with my whole heart, but once in a while, I think maybe it's not enough. I crave the feel of a woman. I love their softness and the way they smell. I love their soft breasts and the noises they make in bed, and I love the feel of my cock sliding in and out of a tight, wet pussy."

"I'm not enough for you?" My heart cracks a bit, even as I know that's unfair. After all, I'm already fantasizing about fucking Rosalie while I'm fellating him. I lean back in and start sucking even harder.

"Yes, Troy. You are enough because I love you, and I could be happy the rest of my life with you." He stops speaking a moment and moans. "Oh, yes—just like that. It feels so good." He takes a deep breath and continues, "But if you're going to marry Rosalie, I think we might have a few new options. First, you and I cease having sex." I pull off with a small pop and stare at him. "That's a terrible, ridiculous solution, so don't look so appalled. Second, I could find my own woman and move her in with us too, and we could convince both the women somehow that while we love making love to them, we also need each other. That one has a lot of limitations because I'd have to get busy and find a compatible woman in a hurry, and there's no telling how she'd react to my crazy plan. Third, we can *share* Rosalie and still have each other. I'm not talking about taking turns with Rosalie. You've heard of a ménage à trois, yes? That might be just the thing, if she's up for it. I know it's a big *if*, but I read a book once about a threesome, and…well…it was quite enlightening, I'll say that. All three participants were equal, and I found it quite arousing and beautiful at the same time. Reading that book helped me open up to you in a physical way because the sex between the men was so superbly written. I wasn't afraid to explore."

"I, um…wow. Do you think it might be possible? Number three, I mean. That would be my greatest fantasy in the world, Ollie." I get up off my knees and pull Ollie to the bed.

"I thought it might," he answers sweetly as we lie down face-to-face.

"You're not just saying this to placate me then, are you?"

"Not in the least. So…you think about it, and once Rosalie is comfortable with you, bring her home to meet me. In the meantime, I'll find that book so the two of you can read it. It's no doubt on a banned book list, but I'll see if I can locate it somehow. Now, let's get back to what we were doing. I was enjoying your mouth on me before you stopped. Shall we resume?"

We don't get much sleep. Both of us keep coming up with

wonderful possibilities, and we keep each other as hard as iron pokers that we have to relieve—over and over. I love the way Ollie's mind works.

And I can't help but wonder how convincing we might be with Rosalie. I bet she's never had anyone ask her to enter a ménage à trois.

Chapter Eleven

Rosalie

I'm so nervous, I could just die. It's my first day as an actress employed by a real major Hollywood studio. I hardly slept a wink last night, so I hope I don't have dark circles under my eyes. I don't know what to expect, so I'm glad Troy offered to drive me over. He might be able to answer some of my questions on the way. I get dressed and then nibble at some toast and sip some tea, but I'm in too much of a flutter to eat. I'm staring at the food when there is a polite knock at the front door. Daisy jumps up with a gleam in her eye and races to open it before I can get my napkin out of my lap.

"Troy! How lovely to see you again," she purrs at him like they've known each other forever. "Come in, come in."

"Good morning, Miss...uh..." he falters.

"Daisy. Daisy Dillinger."

"Right, sorry. Dillinger like the gangster. Any relation?"

With a decidedly frostier tone to her voice, she answers, "None at all." I have to stifle a snort by coughing into my hand. Apparently, Daisy doesn't appreciate having her name forgotten or linked to a bank robber. Poor Daisy. She's a good egg, though.

"Good morning, Troy. You're bright and early. I'll just run and grab my purse, and we can go." I scoot up the stairs trying to look graceful and not waste any of his time. I quickly brush my teeth, check my hair, and almost leave again without my purse. I swear—my head isn't on straight this morning. The sight of that exquisitely handsome man took my breath away. I still can't believe I'm starring in a movie with him and I'm supposed to marry the man. Hollywood is a crazy place.

When we get into the car, I notice that Troy keeps blushing about something. Unlike yesterday, he doesn't seem too anxious to talk. But I can't keep my mouth shut. I jabber about the beautiful weather and the lack of rain in Los Angeles. I comment on the palm trees and colorful bougainvillea I never saw in Idaho. Then I carry on for a while about the Hollywoodland sign up on the hill. He just nods or grunts. Finally, I try to be more focused on what he might like to talk about. "This is a lovely automobile, Troy. It looks new, and it's so shiny."

"Uh-huh."

"What is it? I've never seen one like this before. Such an interesting design."

"It's a Mercury. They're new."

"I see. It's lovely." I already said that, and now I probably sound like a dope. I could tell him about the tractor I drove around the orchard, but he also grew up on a farm, so he no doubt knows his way around a tractor and wouldn't be all that impressed. After a long, uncomfortable—to me anyway—silence, I ask, "What do you think they'll have us do today?"

"No doubt you'll be measured for your outfits, and we'll do some rehearsing while they're shooting scenes that don't involve you yet."

Now we're getting somewhere. Full sentences at last. "Did you do a lot of scenes with Gloria already that they'll have to cut?"

He shrugs. "A couple of them maybe. Mostly we just rehearsed because she wasn't taking any of the director's advice, and she wasted a lot of time acting like a spoiled brat. I think Packard was ready to wring her neck; he had a terrible time directing her." Troy seems to shake off the mood he was in and adds with a smile, "Having you on the set instead of Gloria is going to be like a breath of fresh air."

"Oh! Thank you. I hope I live up to that prediction."

"Just please don't smoke or eat raw onions, and we'll be fine."

I laugh easily. "No problem."

"Look, Rosalie," he starts in a far more serious tone that has my nerves returning. "I need for you to run an errand with me as soon as we're done for the day. I can't explain it right now, but I need for you to sign something, and we... well, we'll have to leave the studio to do that. Please don't say a word about this to anyone." As he says that, we approach the gate to the studio lot, and I don't have a chance to ask him about it anymore, but I sure wonder what the heck we have to leave the studio to do together.

The next few hours are a whirlwind of meeting people, including having my measurements taken by a friendly bunch of ladies in the wardrobe department. I tell them all about my friend who works at MGM, and they're such a bunch of chatterboxes, they tell me all about the differences between the studios. Sharon, one of the ladies, tells me, "You ought to have your friend look into getting hired here. I like it better than when I worked for MGM." I don't get to ask why, however, because just then an assistant says I'm wanted in rehearsal immediately. I hope I can get something to eat pretty soon. I haven't seen Troy in hours, and I'm getting terribly hungry and even more curious about the errand he wants us to do.

It turns out the rehearsal isn't even with Troy. It's with another actor and actress I've seen in movies, and I'm immediately starstruck. They're supposed to be my parents in this story. The man, however, looks me up and down in a terribly unfatherly way, and I'm instantaneously put off by him. On screen, he has always seemed like such a gentleman, but he's certainly far from that in real life. His comments get more and more lewd until his "wife" tells him, "Knock it off, Harold. This is the poor girl's first day on the set. We don't want her running for the hills because you're acting like a tomcat." Just when I'm thinking she has a soft spot for me, she adds, "And we sure as hell don't want this production dragging on any longer than necessary now that we've lost Gloria."

I'm starting to get a little shaky since I haven't eaten.

This is getting to be a thing for me, so I need to make myself eat a hearty breakfast before I get here, apparently. But for now, I ask, "Is there any way I could get something to eat? I'm not feeling quite right."

My "mother" actress looks around and snaps her fingers at someone. She barks, "Miss Channing is feeling faint from hunger. Take care of that right away."

"Oh, um, thank you. I didn't mean to put anyone out. I just need a quick sandwich and maybe a glass of water if I have time to go grab something..." No one is paying me any attention, and then the director, Mr. Packard, comes in and starts telling us how he visualizes this scene.

The assistant silently returns with a glass of water, plunks it down in front of me with a little pill, and then scurries away.

"What on earth is this?" I ask. I was expecting possibly a ham sandwich or at least a cookie.

"Just take it. You could stand to lose a few pounds, and this will take the edge off," my dear "mother" advises me.

I'm offended, but I drink the water, hoping that will help some. When I ignore the pill, she scoops it up, swallowing it dry.

Harold chuckles at her.

"What? It's a shame to waste a good bennie," she says with a shrug and a smirk.

The glamour of this job is wearing off quickly for me.

Finally, we get down to business, and the two of them suddenly transform themselves into loving, caring parents who want the best for me. Mr. Packard is happy with how the scene goes and dismisses them. In walks Troy, and he's a sight for sore eyes. Not only is he happy to see me, he's carrying a cheeseburger and a chocolate malt that he sets down in front of me.

"I was afraid you hadn't had a break for lunch yet, sweetheart," he says quietly. "I heard you were in here rehearsing, so I grabbed this for you. No onions." He winks. "Eat up. Then you and I have a bit of rehearsing to do."

"If you're trying to make me fall in love with you, you certainly have the right idea, Troy. Thank you so much." I take a monstrous bite of the burger and then wash it down with icy, chocolaty goodness. Apparently *he* doesn't think I need to lose a few pounds. I immediately feel better.

We spend the rest of the day going over scenes and taking suggestions from Packard. No one got angry or short with me, so in my estimation, it seems to be going well. Finally, Packard tells us we can take off. Troy grabs my hand and says, "Come on, beautiful. We need to hurry."

Our drive isn't far, but I'm surprised when we end up at Jack Cramer's office. I remember the lawyer from yesterday. Not wanting to waste any time, he sets a paper in front of me, saying, "Miss Channing, Troy has requested that you sign a confidentiality agreement that you will not discuss his living arrangements or any details of the individuals or staff living with him. You may not discuss this with anyone, and the contract is binding for the duration of your life. The penalty for breaching this contract is twenty million dollars." I take in a gasp of air and stare bug-eyed at Troy, who looks pretty calm considering this conversation.

"Really?" I ask.

"Yes," they say in unison.

"How on earth would I come up with that kind of money?"

Troy looks as serious as a heart attack when he says, "Then you better not discuss it with anyone."

"It is legally binding, Miss Channing," Cramer adds. He looks as solemn as Troy, and I feel like I've stepped into some strange new reality.

I look back and forth between the two of them, and ask, "Is anyone going to explain this to me? What terrible thing do you have going on at your house that I have to stay quiet about? Does someone from the Mafia live there? Are you a drug dealer?"

Troy softens a bit and takes my hand. "You have an interesting imagination, but you are way off base, I can assure you of that." He sighs and runs his hand through his hair before continuing, "Sweetheart, this town is full of gossips, and the press is constantly looking for the new scandal or the new victim to skewer. I'm just trying to protect myself. I am a very private person. Think of what you've read about me in the past; have you ever seen anything the least bit titillating? Or was it all just hype about my newest movie? I can answer that for you. I've *never* been caught in any situation that would appear the least bit controversial, and I aim to keep it that way. This contract is to protect me from any misunderstanding or gossip that starts small and blossoms into a story that becomes a runaway train. This will also protect you, you understand. The privacy works both ways."

"I see, and I appreciate that, but I can't help but think that where there's smoke, there's fire. Are you hiding something? If I am to marry you, don't you think I ought to be made aware?"

Cramer speaks up quickly saying, "The studio unfortunately can insist that the two of you marry. That is their right, even though it sounds heavy-handed. They have a history of arranging marriages to suit their needs, and it's basically become an accepted custom in Hollywood for actors and actresses. And, I might add that divorce also doesn't carry the same stigma here as it does elsewhere around the country. So even though you feel as if you need to know everything about Troy, you're going to marry him anyway. The only alternative to that would be if you flatly refused, and then your career would be finished before it even began. If your ambition is to become a successful actress with the full support of the studio behind you, my recommendation is to sign Troy's contract, abide by the studio's decree to get married, and act your heart out." He chuckles briefly and adds, "You both may deserve Academy Awards for the acting you'll be doing."

Troy flinches a little as his grip on my hand increases and he glares momentarily at Jack, and I wonder about that. His expression vanishes quickly, so maybe I misread him, and he's excited about the possibility of being nominated for an Oscar. I narrow my eyes a little and look at Cramer. "Troy says the privacy goes both ways, but I don't see anything in this contract that protects me—just him."

"You're right. That was an oversight. Let me add that right now," Cramer says.

I look at Troy, and he's smiling and nodding. "Good catch, Rosalie. I respect that, and I have no problem agreeing to it." Of course I have nothing to hide, so I can't imagine what he might gossip about me. Maybe that I used to bite my fingernails when I was little? Or that I have refused to eat okra ever since a boy in my first-grade class told me it was actually cow snot? Heady stuff!

Troy interrupts my reveries by saying, "Should we ever decide to separate in the future, you understand that this contract still holds. I hope, of course, that we will find married life suitable, however, and will stay married for a long, long time."

I can't help but notice Jack Cramer's eyes flit quickly to look at Troy's face. He has an indecipherable expression on his face, but I get the feeling he doesn't hold our marriage to a high standard for success, and that suddenly makes me a little sad.

I get an idea and tell them, "Just so you both understand a little more about me, I told Daisy and the other boarders where I live about my new part in the movie, and of course Daisy met you, Troy, but I didn't breathe a word about our upcoming marriage plans. I hoped it would all seem natural and like it was meant to be in their eyes if I didn't tell them we were marrying on orders from the studio."

"Excellent thinking," Troy says and gives my hand a little squeeze. He seems to be enjoying holding it.

I like it too.

Cramer is writing away on the contract and finally sets his pen aside. He looks at me seriously then and says, "I would be remiss if I didn't offer to let you hire another attorney to look over this agreement before you sign it."

I sneak a peek at Troy, and I see his jaw clench.

"Why do I need another lawyer?"

"Because right now, I represent both of you, and that might be construed as a conflict. I need to be looking out for both of your interests."

"Do you feel the contract is swayed in any way toward either of our favors?"

"No, definitely not, especially with this addendum."

I look at Troy, who is looking at Jack, and I decide there isn't really any point to adding someone else to the mix. It's only about not gossiping, for heaven's sake. "Give me a pen and the contract please, Jack."

He indicates where to sign in two places, and I scrawl my name. "Do I need to also use my legal name?"

"Actually, we can have your name changed legally if you'd like."

"Yes, please."

"Then your new name is fine."

I scoot the paper over to Troy who also signs with a small, relieved sigh. Silently, he pushes the contract back to Jack who makes a rather showy deal of sealing it into an envelope. "I'll put this in my safe before I leave for home. Thank you both for coming in, and best of luck with the movie and...everything else."

Chapter Twelve

TROY

I FEEL SO MUCH BETTER. It's like some dark cloud that was following me around has lifted and let the sun back in. This makes me think about sunsets, so I ask Rosalie, "How would you like to have some dinner? We could drive out to the beach. I know of a quiet little place where no one will bother us."

"I'm not really dressed for a night out..." she starts to protest.

"It's alright. This place is casual—right on the beach. And it's such wonderful weather, it'll be fun. It'll be sunset by the time we get there, so we can watch for the green flash."

"Okay. If that's what you want to do, let's do it. I've never seen a green flash. Are they actually real?"

"So I hear."

Not long after this, we're sitting at a picnic table outside of a beachside fish market. It's not the least bit fancy, but the fish is fresh and delicious. I love this setting and sometimes come here with Ollie because it's the one place I can breathe and not be photographed or stopped for an autograph. Rosalie and I sit side by side and watch intently as the sun sinks into the Pacific. As promised, the only other patrons are far more interested in themselves than us.

We don't see a flash, but that's alright. I wonder if they're a myth. I have yet to see one.

"I thought we could take advantage of our last bit of privacy before the studio starts sending us to their sanctioned events where the press is encouraged to follow us around," I tell her quietly. "At this point, no one knows you yet, but once they do, it's going to be a new ballgame."

"They certainly know you, though."

"I've learned to keep my head down and avoid eye contact with anyone. Sunglasses and a hat also help a little." I took mine off when we sat down to eat.

Rosalie smiles. "I feel like we're playing hooky in a way. This is fun. I'm so glad you suggested it, Troy." Then she gets a troubled look on her face and asks, "Is it normal at the studio to offer diet pills instead of food to actresses?"

I look at her sharply. "Who did that?" She explains what happened during her rehearsal, and I feel like punching someone. How can anyone look at her and think she is anything less than perfect to begin with, but also to offer her drugs? Inexcusable. I vow to have a serious chat with...well... someone. Unfortunately, I'm fully aware that this is standard procedure, and I now have a strong sense that I need to protect Rosalie from a lot of what goes on at the studio. Realistically, I know I can't be there with her all the time, but I wonder if by marrying her, I can exert some pressure that will keep her out of harm's way somewhat. The pressure to marry this exquisite woman is getting easier and easier to take. I look at her with as much sincerity and gravitas as I can muster. "Sweetheart, promise me you'll never accept any pills given to you at the studio—or anywhere else for that matter. And ignore anyone who tries to make you believe you are in some way wanting. You don't need to change a thing. Can you do this for me and for yourself?"

She blinks a couple of times at my intensity and answers softly, "Yes. I promise. Thank you for caring, Troy." This makes me wonder how her family treats her if my looking out for her welfare means that much to her. Perhaps her parents are overworked and worried about keeping their orchard running in the black. It's been a tough several years for many, many families around the country, and I know all too well that agricultural businesses have been hit hard by the Depression. I routinely send money back to my parents, not that I've ever mentioned it to anyone but Ollie.

Aside from this one intense moment, we have a great time together. Rosalie tells me more about her family's business and the relatively new Emmet Cherry Festival. It sounds like a popular event that began in 1935.

I have to ask, "Do you ever get tired of cherries?"

Rosalie laughs and answers, "Nope. I love them. We had to supplement our income by running a café too, though, so we didn't exist just on our cherry picking and selling. That wouldn't have kept our family fed due to the economic climate. It's still been lean for us, even with both incomes. My family works so hard, I felt rather awful leaving them, but I just had to try to make something better for myself than waitressing and cherry farming. Soon, I hope I can send them an even larger portion of my paycheck."

Atta girl, I think to myself. She does honor her parents as she should.

After living and working in Los Angeles for a while now, I know just how real and unaffected Rosalie is compared to most of the people I meet through work. She's like a breath of fresh air, and I hope her inevitable stardom doesn't do anything to change her. I want to keep her safe in a bubble and protect her from the hangers-on and the people who will try to take advantage of her. She's so beautiful, but in an effortless, natural way that you rarely see anywhere near the studios. I know from experience that people will want to take bits of her success for themselves by claiming to have discovered her, taught her how to dress, act, style her hair, and any number of lies and trivialities. I also know she will capture the hearts of movie-goers everywhere. She has this approachability you can't train anyone to have. You either have it or you don't.

"Do you sing?" I ask, thinking she might be another Judy Garland, but Rosalie looks at me and laughs. Not a polite little titter—a big belly laugh that makes me want to throw my arms around her and dance in the moonlight. She is unabashed in her reaction to my question.

"Absolutely not. No training whatsoever is going to fix my lack of a singing voice. I learned to mouth the words in church when people in front of our pew used to turn around and grimace at me. And at home, if I sang anything, it made our dog howl."

I can't help but laugh at her self-deprecation and wonder if it's really true. Her speaking voice is lovely and rich, but maybe she just can't carry a tune. Some folks are like that.

It's getting late, and we have another early morning tomorrow, so we reluctantly head back to the car. I can't resist taking her hand as we make our way toward it. We continue our conversation all the way back to her place and never seem to be at a loss for what to ask or tell about. When I pull up in front of the boardinghouse, I hop out and open her door, taking her hand again so I can hold it all the way to the front porch.

When we get to the front door, Rosalie turns to face me and holds her face up in what seems to me a clear invitation to give her a kiss. Not wanting to make assumptions, however, I whisper, "*I really want to kiss you right now.*"

"Then do it. I'd like to see if it's different than the one you gave me when you were acting." She gives me a saucy wink.

"Oh, Rosalie, there was very little acting necessary the first time I kissed you. The only difference is this one is ad lib instead of scripted, but the feeling is just the same." I seal her lips with mine, and a shock of elation goes through me. I wrap her tightly in my arms, and taste her lips, her tongue, and breathe her air like it's my very own. She gives a satisfied sound that's somewhere between a purr and a moan, and I hear music in it. Maybe she can't sing, but her voice and the sounds she makes stir my heartstrings more than any symphony or choir could ever do.

Motion at the door catches my eye, so I pull away to see the frowning face of the woman who must be the owner of the boardinghouse. She glowers at us for a second through the windowpane and then pulls the door open, grumbling, "I run a nice house here, you two. Stop with this public display and come inside, Rosalie. What are you thinking? Should I write to your parents?"

Instead of acting embarrassed, Rosalie gives her a sweet smile and says, "That won't be necessary; I'll be right in, Mrs. Vogel." She turns to me and says, "I had a wonderful time tonight, Troy. Thank you for a lovely evening. I'll see you in the morning."

"Right. I'll pick you up again at eight sharp." We still haven't arranged any car service for her—not that I mind. "Thank you for a terrific evening too, sweetheart." I turn to Mrs. Vogel and say as nicely as possible, "Evening, ma'am." And I'm off.

I can't help my goofy smile that won't fade all the way home. I relive the kiss and the feel of Rosalie in my arms over and over. Oh, I have it bad for her.

Chapter Thirteen

Ollie

I'm shocked at myself. Troy missed dinner and is late coming home, and even though I knew he would be, it upsets me. Even though we had that stimulating conversation about Rosalie and the remote possibility that we could all enjoy each other in a ménage, my realistic side says that's a crazy notion, and I'm probably going to lose the man I love. I haven't been able to write today because I've been in such a mental turmoil. I'm so jealous right now, I could die. This isn't like me. But...I've also never been in this situation before, so what do I know? I was so secure knowing Troy and I were committed and had our beautiful romance hidden from prying eyes. Now we're going to reveal our truth to someone who's a stranger to me. Maybe *he* feels he can trust her, but has he been blinded by her beauty and his need to be with a woman? And is he a pawn to the demands of the studio that might eventually lead to his own downfall? Or is he building a relationship with someone who could bring us all great satisfaction and joy? How far can I trust that to happen?

My thoughts are a swirling mass of ridiculous hopefulness and blistering pain. I need him to come home and look me in the eye.

I need to see my man. I need to feel his heartbeat next to mine and know it will always beat in sync with mine no matter who else he may lo...oh my God. I am not a selfish person. I'm not! If Troy needs this—and I know he does because I need it too...If we both need it, what will it take to get Rosalie to join us? Will she be appalled? Excited? Angry? Flattered? I need to see her with my own eyes. I need to speak to her and evaluate the possibility for myself. Troy and I are so different. What if she finds me too old? Too homely? Too literary and not exciting enough for a Hollywood star?

What if she rejects Troy because of me? What will that do to their careers? I cannot be the ruin of them both. Maybe I ought to pack up and head back to Ohio and lead a quiet life there—away from the Hollywood glitz and glamour. I'm not meant for public fame. I love my anonymity. That's why I've always written under a pen name.

I hear Troy coming home. I've been staring at my typewriter ever since Zelda and I had a nearly silent dinner a couple hours ago. At least he didn't stay out terribly late. Maybe he's not as crazy about her as he thought.

But then I see the look on his handsome face as he strides into my study. His eyes are bright and he's smiling like he knows everything is fine with the world. "Hello, Ollie. I missed you today," he tells me. How many times has he professed to miss me when he's off acting and doing the very thing he loves the most? Is he acting now? I need to stop this destructive thinking. Troy loves me. I know he loves me.

And now he's kissing me. I melt into his embrace, and the world is right again.

However...I detect a tiny scent of an unfamiliar perfume lingering about him. Apparently, I'm not the first person he's embraced today. My heart does a painful little jolt in my chest, and I pull away.

"Tell me all about her, my love. Are we going to survive this?" I hate the catch in my voice.

Troy steps back and blinks. "I thought we were looking forward to adding Rosalie to our relationship. What's wrong, Ollie? Are you having second thoughts?"

"I don't know if it's exactly second thoughts. I'm scared, though. There's only a small chance she'll agree to our plan, and if she doesn't, all sorts of bad things might happen."

"I know. Really, I do. So I guess we'll have to be extra convincing then. Shall we go upstairs and practice?" He gives me a flirty grin, and I'm suddenly putty in his hands once again. When Troy is here and one hundred percent with me, all of the scary ideas in my head float away like dandelion puffs on the wind.

"Yes, let's," I tell him. "I love you so much, Troy."

Chapter Fourteen

Rosalie

I'VE BEEN WORKING at the studio now for a few weeks, and I'm exhausted. Apparently, replacing Gloria with me slowed down production somewhat, so they're expecting long hours from everyone to make up the lost scenes. We've been working seven days a week, so I'm amazed at how people are keeping their spirits up. It's so tiring. Even though I'd love to lie down and sleep for three days straight, I tell myself to put a smile on my face and do as I'm told. I saw how quickly Gloria was removed from the cast, and since I'm still a nobody, I'm worried I could easily meet the same fate if I don't toe the line.

I have to be grateful for Troy through all of this. He makes sure they give us time to take breaks and have something to eat, even when the studio taskmasters would like us to be automatons. The director is at odds with anyone—like the wardrobe department—who monopolizes too much of our time, but then he's famous for making us sit around and wait for the lighting to be set up just right or the scenery to be adjusted, or any number of minutiae before he gets the cameras rolling. It's frustrating, but it's also exciting. I have no real reason to complain because this is what I've worked for, and I'm terribly grateful.

I get paid weekly now, although I understand that will eventually change. And the studio is paying for my acting classes now as part of my contract. The classes just add a bigger burden on my schedule, I'm afraid, but at least I'm not out of pocket for classes they make me miss when we need to have more retakes or someone messes up on set, or any number of things.

And now they tell us they're ready for us to start attending parties and events they send us to, so our evenings will be dictated by the studio as well. They recently alerted the press about my starring role in the newly named movie *Forever Yours*. Fortunately, I don't mind spending time with Troy in the least. He's such a gentleman, and he looks out for me like I'm the most special person in the world. One day, I was yawning on the set and one of the flunkies approached me with a glass of water and a pill he said he was directed to give me. Troy swore at him and told him to get out of his sight with his damn drugs and to never try that again. The flunky said, "I'm just following orders, Mr. Kingsley." But he removed the pill. I drank the water, though. The tenseness of the scene between the two men was enough to revive me. Then Troy handed me a peppermint and said they work as well as coffee for him when he gets tired. It seemed to help because all trace of sleepiness evaporated.

Troy and I have continued to find time to get to know one another, and he kisses me like I'm so special to him. My landlady had a stern talking-to with me about kissing in public, and she voiced her disapproval to the extent that she threatened to toss me out if I gave her boardinghouse a poor reputation for harboring "loose-behaving women" under her roof. I don't have enough money yet to move anywhere else, so Troy and I have been more circumspect.

He asked me why I hadn't moved into the Hollywood Studio Club when I came out here originally. They allow women to live there who are either employed by the studios or who are aspiring actresses actively enrolled in classes. I explained that they required references and a letter from my parents, who were unwilling to help me leave Idaho. Maybe now that I have a contract with Premier Works, the Studio Club would let me in without my parents' backing, but I'm alright living in Mrs. Vogel's boardinghouse for now. From what I've heard, the Studio Club also has strict rules, but I think Troy might draw an awful lot of attention if he were seen coming and going with me—even if it is well-known and lots of actresses get their start there. It's been called the place where Hollywood's good girls go. I can't deny it might be fun to meet more of the actresses who live there, but I'm not going to rock the boat right now. All too soon, I'll be moving into Troy's house anyway. I wonder what it's like.

He has spent a bit of time with me in my lovely new dressing room at the studio. It was assigned to me about a week ago after they finally got all of Gloria's personal belongings out of it. When we're not shooting, we've done a fair amount of smooching in there, and yesterday he encouraged me to take a quick nap, saying he'd send someone to come get me as soon as it looked like I would be needed on the set. That was a luxury.

The dressing room is quite comfortable and looks almost like a beautifully furnished apartment. I have a small kitchen that I don't have the time to use and a pretty fireplace—even though it's too hot to light one now.

Troy also has his own fancy dressing room that I've been in a few times when we had short breaks. It's always nice to get away from the hustle and bustle when we have the chance. The studio is a real beehive of activity all the time. It's fascinating to see the variety of jobs people do. Besides the actors and the director with his assistants, there are lighting and sound people, electricians, the camera crew, carpenters and painters for the sets, and of course the costume department. There is also a small army of pages and studio hands who scurry around fetching and delivering things. Then there are the behind-the-scenes folks who edit the film and accomplish all kinds of office jobs with the studio executives that I can barely imagine.

Troy's still chauffeuring me around, and I love that. I also love kissing him. He's the kindest, sweetest man I've ever met. Marrying him is beginning to sound wonderful rather than scary, and I'm so relieved. My only reservation about Troy is that he seems to be keeping something from me. The whole "don't *ever* talk about my living arrangements" thing has me a little on edge, even though he genuinely seems to care for me. I can't imagine what that's all about.

Tonight, we have our first public event, and we'll be getting outfitted here at the studio in our dressing rooms before we go. A gown and appropriate jewelry have been selected for me, and they will do my hair and makeup. It's enough to make me feel like a prize dairy cow getting primped and ready to show off at the state fair back home in Idaho. I hope they make me look like me. I have, as usual, no say in this. We'll be going to a fancy-pants anniversary party for one of the executives at Paramount. I hope that doesn't mean Gloria will be there. There's nothing I can do about it if she is.

A car is going to take us. This will be my first ride in a limousine, so I'm rather excited about that. Troy tells me it's all just part of the job, but he's happy he'll be escorting me and hopes I'll have some fun.

"You look incredibly beautiful," Troy tells me when he greets me at my door. "I'm going to be the most envied man at the party tonight because you'll be with me." He also looks divine in his tux, and I can't help feeling a thrill go through me as he offers me his arm and gives me a sweet kiss on the cheek.

"I feel like a princess tonight, Troy, and you're my handsome prince. I wish my parents could see us."

"It's a good chance they will if they read any magazines. Get ready for a lot of annoying flashbulbs pointed our way when we arrive. Your gown is exquisite."

"It was designed by Robert Kalloch, and I love it, but I feel a little like I'm masquerading as someone important."

"You're terribly important to me. And soon everyone will know your name as well as your face. Enjoy the anonymity while you can. You're going to lose it soon."

Ironically, the party is being held at the Beverly Hills Hotel where I worked until just recently. I wonder if any of my former coworkers will be serving, and if they'll even recognize me.

Troy was right about the photographers. They shout his name over and over and take innumerable pictures of us as we make our way in. I hope I don't have my eyes closed in most of the photos, and I wonder if anyone ever gets used to this. I don't hear my name shouted by anyone, and I also wonder how long that will be the case.

The party is in the Crystal Ballroom, and I've never actually been in it, so I'm glad I don't have to repress an automatic instinct to take orders or refill drinks. However, the waitstaff for this event seems to be made up entirely of men in formal livery. I wonder if waitresses were considered too common for the hosts. Who knows?

Over the next couple of hours, Troy introduces me to several famous actors and studio executives. I've been quietly propositioned twice, overtly once, had my bottom pinched, my breasts ogled, and I've been largely ignored by all of the women we speak to. A couple ladies have bordered on open hostility when they see the way Troy holds me close to him.

There are a few friendly women, though. I enjoy meeting John Packard's wife Sophie, for instance. She's gorgeous, several years younger than he is, and has a wonderful sense of humor. Maybe you'd need one being married to a famous director. I'm thankful when we sit down next to them for dinner.

"Are the men always so awful about propositioning women at these events?" I ask Sophie quietly.

"You're new, and they see you as a challenge," she answers in a hushed tone. "Once you've been around a while and they don't make any headway with you, most of them will back off. It would be far worse if you weren't with Troy, believe me. He's well-respected and a gentleman, so the men with good sense are leaving you alone." I can't help rolling my eyes at this, wondering, *This is good behavior?*

Sophie and I promise to make plans to get together for a luncheon date once the shooting of *Forever Yours* is over. It's nice to have a friend who understands what my life is like right now. She tells me she was an actress for a while, but she prefers being married and hopes to start a family soon, so she happily retired from acting.

As the evening progresses, Troy continues to introduce me as his "beautiful co-star," but he also adds, "and I'm proud to call her my girlfriend," much to my delight. The first time he did that, I squeezed his hand and watched his smile grow larger as he shifted his gaze to me. My feelings for the man are growing stronger by the minute.

We continue to socialize, doling out and receiving compliments as we make our way around the ballroom after dinner is over. My heart sinks a little when I notice Gloria is here, looking sour. She is on the arm of a man I don't recognize—not that I know too many people yet. She manages to convey pure hatred for me with a glare in her eyes that could blister the paint off a Ford, but she doesn't approach us or say anything. I'm relieved that we don't have to pretend to make polite conversation. I do catch her staring at me and whispering something into her escort's ear. He looks at her and laughs in a malevolent way.

I briefly wonder what she might have said, but then I force myself to put it out of my mind. This is my first Hollywood party, and I'm going to enjoy it. There is a champagne fountain, and the dinner was amazing. Naturally, everyone here looks gorgeous. I've never seen so much jewelry and so many designer gowns in one place in my life. Who am I kidding? I've never seen designer anything before tonight. Where I come from, everything was either homemade or from the Sears catalog.

We dance some, and Troy glowers at a smarmy man who attempts to cut in and dance with me by offering to tell me all about what he can do for me. My mouth opens to say something, but Troy glares at the man and says, "Get lost, Bane. She's taken. You'll have to find your own partner to bore. Somewhere else." And he whisks me away skillfully across the dance floor. It turns out Troy is quite the dancer, but I'm frankly a little shocked at how he spoke to Bane. When we're out of earshot, he tells me, "Stay clear of that man, and make sure you're *never* alone with him. He has a terrible reputation and doesn't mind who he ruins with it."

"Oh my," I say.

"I'm not joking. He's an agent who tries to poach clients, and he's a predatory wolf with women." Troy brightens immediately now that Bane has been left in the dust. "Are you about ready to call it a night?"

"As much fun as it's been, yes, please." I want to sleep in tomorrow until noon at least since we have a reprieve from shooting finally.

We find the host and hostess and thank them for a lovely evening and then head for the door. Almost as soon as we're outside, our limo driver arrives at the entrance. I guess he was looking for us since people are starting to leave. What a life, having someone at your beck and call like this. Back home, I generally used a rusty old bicycle to get around, and I've certainly never worn any fancy designer clothes or jewelry before. But most of all, I'm thrilled to be on the arm of the handsomest, sweetest man in Hollywood.

We slip into the plush seats in the back of the limo, and Troy scoots close to me, taking my hand. "I've had such a wonderful time with you, Rosalie." He looks at me with such fondness in his stunning light-green eyes. "I'm falling for you, sweetheart," he tells me, and my breath catches. No one has ever expressed any affection for me. I've been kissed prior to this, but it was never anything special. When Troy kisses me, it's a profound experience.

"I...um...feel the same way, Troy. You're the finest man I've ever known."

He looks relieved, and that surprises me a little. Who wouldn't fall for this man? But then he looks me in the eyes, and I detect more nervousness. What now?

"Darling, we finally have a day off tomorrow, so I was wondering if you'd like to come to my house for Sunday dinner. I'd like for us to get to know each other better away from the studio crowd. Also, I have that signed book for you that I promised weeks ago. Can you make it?"

"Oh! I...yes, I'd like that very much. Can I bring anything for supper?" Maybe we can have some real alone time at last.

He chuckles, "Definitely not. Zelda takes care of the meals, and you don't want to cross Zelda. She'll have the entire menu figured out to the last detail, and she would consider anything else an interference."

"She sounds...interesting." I try for a laugh. "Has she worked for you long?" I wonder if this Zelda is part of the big surprise at his house. I guess I'll find out soon enough.

"As long as w...I've lived in the house." He rushes to add, "How about if I pick you up at five? We can be casual, and if you'd like a swim, bring your swimsuit too."

"You have a pool?"

"Yes."

"Sounds lovely. Do you swim a lot?"

"Believe me, that pool is used all the time."

Hmm. Not exactly what I asked, but maybe that's how he stays in such good shape. I wonder when he has time to swim, though, unless it's at night. Or maybe Zelda swims in it all the time. Maybe she swims in the nude. If so, that would be something I'd keep quiet. I stifle a giggle.

All too soon, we're back at the boardinghouse. We stopped by the studio on the way here so I could drop off my jewelry with the security detail there. I'm relieved to be rid of it, truth be told.

Before we exit the limousine, Troy gives me a gentle kiss rather than a soul-bending one, and I wonder about that. I have so many questions about this man and his secrets. But he looks deeply into my eyes and says, "I'm so looking forward to seeing you tomorrow. Thank you for being your wonderful self and for making me the envy of all the men at the party tonight."

I try to be as silent as possible as I make my way up the stairs, hoping I'm not disturbing Mrs. Vogel. After removing my fabulous gown, I lie in bed with visions of all the beautiful people I saw tonight and feel warm in my heart because of what Troy told me about falling for me. I wish I could tell my parents to their faces how wonderful he is. Maybe I can visit them once the shooting is done. It sure would be nice if they could come to our wedding, but I'm not holding out much hope for that. They would have to leave the orchard and close the café, and they certainly don't have any suitable clothes to wear. I wouldn't want them to be embarrassed. I also doubt the studio would want to pay for a wedding in Idaho. Anyway, I'll see what I can do after we set a date.

Tomorrow is going to be wonderful. We'll have no schedule to follow for once and lots of time to be together— just us.

Chapter Fifteen

OLLIE

I'M A NERVOUS WRECK. I'm looking forward to meeting Rosalie, but I know how much rides on whether the two of us get along, much less whether we can find some kind of a spark between us. Troy keeps trying to assure me that he can't imagine Rosalie or me not falling for one other because he says we're both incredible, but...we'll see. I trust his judgment to a point, and he's been singing her praises for weeks now, but chemistry isn't something you can force. You either have it or you don't. And even if we do have chemistry, who's to say she'll go along with our crazy plan to have all three of us together at the same time? She'll probably run for the hills.

He left to go pick her up a little while ago, and I'm here

on my own trying not to turn into a jitterbug. Maybe if I try to get immersed in a little writing, I can forget my nerves for a while.

At least I know what Rosalie looks like now. Her photo was featured on the entertainment page of the Sunday paper this morning. There wasn't a lot of information about her—only that she and Troy are starring with each other in *Forever Yours* from Premier Works directed by the great John Packard. They expect a late fall release, so I'm guessing around Thanksgiving time. Rosalie is just as stunning as he described. Her full lips just beg to be kissed, and that figure of hers...a man could lose himself in bed for days with a woman like that. I can't wait to see if she's as beautiful when she's not professionally coiffed and made up.

Standing beside her in the photo is Troy, looking resplendent in his tux. They make a magnificent couple, and I can see why the studio would want to play up their romance. People are going to eat it up.

Before I can even get comfortable and start writing anything, I hear Troy entering the house sounding jovial and speaking to a woman whose voice goes through me like a lance. Low and almost raspy, she speaks from her gut in the way truly sexy women do. There is nothing kittenish about Rosalie, I can tell. I'm momentarily paralyzed with an emotion I can barely identify. Lust? Craving? I have a voiceless photo of a gorgeous woman and a faceless voice that is my own personal siren song, and my creative brain is putting them together for me rapidly. Oh, Lord.

I hear Troy making introductions between Rosalie and

Zelda, but our Zelda is typically spare with her words. She is barely civil, but that means nothing. She barely seems to tolerate Troy and me, even though she says she considers us family. She's a hard one to figure out. But Rosalie addresses the prickly woman with warmth and genuine concern as she offers to help her with anything to get dinner ready. Zelda refuses, which is no surprise. She hates in when anyone "butts in" on her domain.

I, on the other hand, am still sitting in the same position in my study and eavesdropping on their voices in the hallway. If I had any manners, I'd go out and greet them, but I'm mortified to say that Rosalie's voice has affected me so strongly, I'm as hard as a brick, and I'm sure I'd embarrass myself—as well as both of them—if I went shuffling out there like a pervert trying to ignore the tent in my pants. I would need to cover myself with the newspaper, and wouldn't that just look great if I hid my hard-on with the photo of them that I've been ogling? I need at least a few seconds to compose myself, so I close my ears with a sense of purpose and concentrate on what I've read about the aftermath of the Battle of Gettysburg. My imagination takes over for a few moments, and...phew! That's better. Well...for me at least. The fifty thousand soldiers who perished might disagree.

I still have my eyes closed in concentration as Troy leads Rosalie into my study, and when they fly open and I behold Rosalie for the first time, I'm struck dumb. She is so gorgeous, her photo barely did her justice. Her blue eyes sparkle with intelligence, and that mouth of hers could be my undoing. Her wavy hair looks like spun gold, and I want to plant my face between her luscious tits and breathe in her womanly scent. My jaw slackens, and I wonder how long it is before it occurs to me to stand up and politely extend my hand. She looks surprised to see anyone else in the house, so I take it Troy neglected to warn her of my presence.

"Darling, this is Robert Oliver, the author whom you admire so much. He has that signed book that I promised for you. And Ollie, this is Rosalie Channing, the woman to whom I am soon to be engaged."

"Oh! I didn't know we'd be joined by anyone else for dinner, but what a lovely surprise," she says as she grasps my outstretched hand. Her hand feels so perfect in mine, I don't want to let go. "Pleased to meet you, Mr. Oliver. I'm a huge fan of your books. It was such a sweet gesture for Troy to invite you here to surprise me." She looks a little puzzled, but there is also definite interest in her gaze. Her hand is soft and warm, and I suddenly have this insatiable urge to throw her over my shoulder and drag her off to bed. What has come over me? At least I can cross off *attraction* from my list of concerns.

"Yes, Troy is full of surprises. I'm delighted to make your acquaintance, Miss Channing."

"It's Rosalie, please."

"And you must call me Ollie like all of my best friends do." She blinks at me and stares right into my eyes until Troy breaks the spell.

"Would you two like a drink, or a swim, or both before dinner? Zelda says we have about forty-five minutes before it's ready, and she says it's so nice outside this evening, she'll be setting the table out by the pool anyway."

"I'd love to take a dip if you don't mind," Rosalie says enthusiastically, and I have to tell myself to calm down and not think about her in a wet swimsuit.

"In that case, I'll show you where you can get changed, and I'll go find myself a swimsuit as well. Ollie? Will you join us?"

"I wouldn't miss it for the world," I say honestly. Reaching over to my desk, I produce the novel I inscribed for Rosalie and hand it to her. "But first, here you go, Rosalie, with my heartfelt compliments."

"Oh, thank you! I've read the reviews that say it's your best one yet, and I can't wait to dive into it." She gives Troy a loving look and says, "It was really a wonderful gesture from you, Troy, to arrange this. I can't thank you enough. I've never met a famous author before, and," she smiles shyly at me, "this is the first of your books I've ever owned. I always had to wait for them to be available at the public library back in Idaho, and sometimes that seemed to take forever. This is a real treat."

"Well, hopefully this will be the first of many."

"Are you working on another one?"

I chuckle. "Always." I look at Troy. "Let's get changed, alright? We don't want to keep Zelda waiting to serve dinner. You know how she gets once she's given us a set time." That comment makes Rosalie look at me curiously.

"Are you here often? It sounds like you know Zelda well."

Great, now Rosalie probably wonders if I'm our cook's husband. I mean, Zelda is attractive, but she's made it clear that she doesn't want to have anything to do with men and is completely unaffected by our charms—not that I've ever been interested in her. This charade has gone on long enough, so I say, "Yes, I know her well, but I have no special relationship with her. You see, I live here."

Rosalie blinks her eyes a few times, and then her face brightens up as she says, "Oh! Now I see." She looks at Troy. "The big secret that I'm not supposed to talk about is that Ollie lives here, and he has a pen name and doesn't want people to know where he lives for privacy reasons, right? I'd never tell anyone." Then she looks at me with amusement and asks, "Since I've been sworn to secrecy anyway, do you mind telling me your real name? I find I'm rather curious."

She's caught me off guard, and even though it goes against my sense of propriety, I blurt out, "Robert Oliver Shackleton. I've never used Robert because that's my father's name, so everyone has always called me Oliver or Ollie. I dropped the Shackleton for an easy pen name for readers to remember since people wanted to call me Shackleford as often as Shackleton, even after they'd known me for quite a while. It was just too confusing." I certainly hope Rosalie doesn't give up my whereabouts to anyone. Soon this woman will have enough information about Troy and me to ruin both of our careers.

I need to stop babbling about my name.

"So you're roommates. Why didn't you mention that to me, Troy?"

"Um..." Troy doesn't have a good answer for that.

I blurt out, "Actually I'm the owner of the house." Persnickety of me, really. It's true if you look at the paperwork, but Troy paid for half. That was a rather mean thing to say, and I wish I could go back and edit it out of this conversation. Too bad real life isn't like writing a book where you can change things as you go until they feel right. I guess I'm feeling out of sorts because Troy kept her in the dark that I'd be here for dinner, and then he got all the credit for arranging a surprise for her. Just great. I couldn't possibly be jealous or anything, could I?

Troy gives me a narrow-eyed look and says, "Rosalie, let's get changed, and we can have this conversation out in the pool where we can cool off and then have a cocktail." He takes her by the arm and leads her further down the hall to a guest room. I head out and go upstairs to the master suite I share with Troy.

I'm in my swimsuit and heading out by the time Troy makes it upstairs to change. I don't know what to say to him as we pass one another, so I'm silent as I make my way out to the pool. On one hand, I want to give him grief for not cluing Rosalie in at least a little, and on the other hand, I want to kiss him senseless for introducing her to me. I've already swum my laps for the day, but as soon as I'm outside, I set my glasses on a table and dive straight into the pool. Swimming is always a good way for me to clear my head. But I only make it to the far end and back when I see Rosalie enter the pool area. She has a modest gossamer cover-up over her bathing suit, but her shapely legs are on full display, and I want to slide my tongue up one and down the other.

God, I'm so horny all of a sudden I feel like a feral beast. But then she opens her wrap and drops it casually over the back of a lawn chair and strides toward the pool. Her hips sway enticingly, and she's smiling right into my eyes. I'm standing in the shallow end of the pool gawking at her when Troy comes out of the house. His eyes are trained on her backside, and he licks his lips. I run a hand over my face wishing I hadn't had to leave my glasses off to swim. I can see, more or less, but I'd sure like more detail.

Rosalie sits down on the coping and dangles her feet in the water saying with a groan of pleasure, "Oh that feels good. I've been so hot all day."

I stifle my own groan, wishing she were saying that to me in bed. Reaching toward her, I ask, "May I help you get in and get wet?" I catch a glimpse of Troy stifling a laugh behind his hand. His eyes betray his feelings. He knows what I'm going through, and he finds it funny. I'm being tortured by this half-naked, exquisite creature, and he's snorting at me. Cruel bastard. He reads me like one of my novels; he knows me so well.

Then the showoff strides purposefully toward the pool and launches himself into the water with a smooth dive that makes him look like an Olympic athlete. He takes off at a fast crawl that shows off his powerful body. I'm the one who swims all the time, but he's the natural athlete, truth be known. He excels at everything he sets his mind to. He races to the other end and does a quick flip, returning to us just as rapidly to stand next to me, facing Rosalie. She and I haven't moved because we were too busy staring at him. I did, however, manage to grasp her hand again, so I'm calling that a win.

"Wow, that felt good!" Troy exclaims and flashes his signature cocky grin at us. The same grin that has movie-goers all over the country falling in lust with him. "Rosalie, darling, you're still sitting on the edge. Please come on in. It's just the right temperature."

She seems to shake herself mentally and smiles sweetly at him. She scoots forward and slides into the water. I'm sad to lose sight of so much of her creamy skin, but I'm also happy she looks so pleased with herself. "Oh my. You're right. You're so fortunate to have your own pool. My brother, sister, and I used to swim in our pond, and sometimes it wasn't all that nice because of the mud. We had to share the water with a few creatures too. The frogs and turtles were alright, but I wasn't so crazy about the snakes."

I have this ridiculous urge to make a crack about water snakes and showing her mine, so I squelch any further comment on the matter.

Rosalie shoots forward and glides like a water nymph toward the other end of the pool in a graceful breaststroke. And of course, thinking about that makes me want to stroke her breasts. I need to pull myself together.

"Stop drooling, you big goof," Troy breaks my concentration with a laugh. He lightly shoves my shoulder. "I told you she was something."

I sigh and say, "You've never been more on target in your life."

"Not true, Ollie. I was right when I told you I loved you. Nothing's going to change that. Even this incredible woman. I'm definitely falling for her, but my heart is big and has plenty of room for more."

If we were alone, I'd pull him into my arms and kiss the daylights out of him, but we're not ready for that kind of a revelation just yet in front of Rosalie. So we stand in the water and stare at her like two lovelorn puppies as she glides back toward us. Troy leans back in the water and floats a while with his eyes closed and a satisfied grin on his face and then asks, "Anyone else ready for a cocktail?"

Our answers are affirmative. Swimming is thirsty business. I opt for a beer, and Rosalie says she would like "A gin and tonic—light on the gin, please."

We keep a shelf of big, fluffy beach towels nearby, and he goes and grabs one, drying his hair and then working his way down his body, finally wrapping the towel around his waist, thereby showing off his muscular arms and chest to their best advantage. Because of his wet hair, he has a few droplets of water making their slow progress down his torso. I want to lick him. Then I glance at Rosalie, and I swear she has the same desire written all over her face.

Zelda has thoughtfully wheeled our bar cart out here with an ice bucket and plenty of alcoholic choices, so Troy busies himself pouring us all drinks. He also opts for a gin and tonic. I notice Rosalie watching him as his back muscles flex with his movements.

"Would you like to stay in the water or sit down on a chaise?" I ask, hoping she'll expose more of that body by lying in the sun until it sets.

My wish is granted when she heads for the stairs. Oh my, as she climbs out I see that her bottom is absolutely splendid. I want to squeeze her...I need to stop this!

"I think I'd like to sit in the last of the sun for a while. It's so perfect out here. How do you ever go indoors?" She selects a towel, squeezes the water out of her hair, and gracefully lowers herself onto a chaise longue. Apparently, she's not terribly modest because she hasn't tried to cover anything up. I like this.

Troy presents her with her drink and waves a bottle of beer in my direction, asking, "Ollie? Coming out or are you going to do more laps?"

I give myself a shake and climb out of the pool. As I take the icy cold beer from Troy, he gives me a saucy wink. I don't think he's upset about my comment earlier that the house belonged to me. I grab myself a towel and take the chaise next to Rosalie. Troy has already occupied the one on her other side.

As we sip our drinks and wait for dinner to be served, Rosalie asks me some well-crafted questions about writing, and I'm impressed with her insight. We start talking, and I find myself as attracted to her mind as I have been to her body.

All too soon, Zelda calls us to dinner. As soon as she serves us, she disappears back into the house, so she obviously doesn't want to join us. That's fine. She never contributes much to the conversation and has a pretty taciturn nature.

Troy and Rosalie keep me in stitches for a while as they recount some of the goings-on at the studio recently. There has been a rash of practical jokes played here and there, and everyone is trying to find the perpetrator. So far, whoever is doing it is skilled at deception. When they run out of stories to tell, I look at Troy and ask him with my eyes whether he's ready to tackle any of the unspoken, tough questions. An almost imperceptible shake of his head goes unnoticed by

Rosalie, but I don't miss it. I suppose he wants his girl to be completely comfortable around me before we expose our underbelly.

It's a little disappointing, but I'm sitting outside, eating dinner with two half-naked and totally gorgeous people. It's enough for now. In fact, I could get used to this.

Chapter Sixteen

ROSALIE

I COULD GET USED to this. It felt fantastic to take a dip in the pool. I'm still pretty confused about the living arrangements here, but I guess it doesn't matter if Troy has a roommate. I wonder where we'll have to move to when we get married though, since this seems to be Ollie's house after all. Too bad, because this place is terrific.

And speaking of Ollie, I thought Troy was unimaginably handsome, but Ollie is equally delicious. I should shield my eyes and stop staring at him because I'm Troy's girl, but Ollie is just...oh yum. He has bronzed skin, so I'm sure he spends a lot of his time out here in the pool, and his blond hair has that sun-bleached look to it that intrigues me. He's exceptionally tall—maybe six-foot-four or thereabouts—and his lean frame is beautifully muscled. I noticed how powerful his swimming strokes were as I was coming out through the patio. When he's wearing his glasses, they give him an air of sophistication and make him look scholarly, but his body makes me think of a large sleek, tawny lion.

I feel so strange and frankly guilty. I spent last night socializing with a hundred or so of the best-looking and most influential men in Hollywood, and not one of them aroused anything in me. I was with Troy, and he fulfilled all of my desires in a man. He's kind and smart, talented and generous, and he's so handsome it's hard to look at him sometimes. But one look at Ollie, and I want to curl up in his lap and ask him to read to me from one of his books.

I'm equally in awe of these men. Ollie's handsomeness doesn't detract from my desire for Troy, but I need to stop thinking about Ollie. That can only lead to trouble.

After we finish our dinner, we decide to change out of our damp swimsuits and back into our clothes (darn!) and head inside. I have noticed a few mosquitos flitting around, so it's no doubt a good idea, but I'm sure going to miss the view. I've never in my life been surrounded by so much delightfully naked male flesh. I don't know where to look.

As I'm putting my sundress back on, I think about how Troy and Ollie react to one another. It's clear the two men have a special bond. They don't just talk to one another, they *see* each other and project real affection in their gazes. I don't know what that means exactly, but it's nice they're so close, I suppose. Another thing hits me, however, and that has to do with the confidentiality agreement Troy was so adamant about having me sign. If we weren't going to be living here, why would he make such an enormous production about not revealing Ollie's author name to anyone? All they had to do was ask me not to tell anyone his pen name, and I'd have been happy not to spill the beans about it. Something's not adding up here. I need to ask some questions.

I look in the mirror and realize my hair is a little frizzy after my swim. It was worth it. I sweep it all up into a pony-tail and figure that will have to do. They told me to meet them in the living room where we can have after-dinner drinks. This is such a gorgeous, gated estate. I admire as much of it as I can see as I head out toward the largest area of the house.

When I slip into the room, the two men are standing together at a wet bar with their backs to me. Troy is pouring glasses of brandy, but Ollie has his arm around Troy's waist. Well, that's a bit odd, but then he moves closer to nuzzle Troy's neck, and I suddenly understand that all is not what I'd imagined. My heart speeds up, and I wonder if I'm going to pass out. I must make a noise, because both of them pivot toward me with shocked expressions, and Ollie looks as guilty as can be. I hear him say, "Oh, God, I'm sorry, Troy. I wasn't thinking."

Troy makes a beeline for me and takes me gently by the hand, leading me to a lovely couch where he makes sure I'm comfortable. I can feel that my cheeks are flaming red. Ollie approaches, looking embarrassed, sets a hefty crystal snifter of brandy in front of me, and sits down beside me—rather close, if you ask me. Troy sits on the other side and grabs my hand. Neither man seems to want to speak.

I take a swig of brandy, clear my throat and ask, "So, let me get this straight, guys. You two live here *together*, and you need me to provide you with a fake wife for Troy. How do you expect Ollie to fit into this scenario when people realize we're all three living here, hmm?" I don't project even an ounce of affection for Troy in my tone. I feel betrayed in the worst way, and I hope I can get through this conversation without crying. I thought he was falling in love with me! What a fool I've been.

"That's not what's happening at all, darling."

"I think you can skip the fake endearments, Troy."

"No. You *are* my darling, and I *am* falling for you." He hangs his head a moment and then looks up and into my eyes. "That's not really true. I'm not falling, I'm *in love* with you." I hate that I flinch and tears start to well up. But he forges on, "It's just not as simple a situation as you think. I've told people for as long as we've lived here that Ollie is my majordomo so his presence makes sense to the public. It's a large property, and having a household staff would seem right. But we own the house together, and the only real live-in help we have is Zelda. Obviously, Ollie doesn't work for me. As you know, he's a full-time writer. My feelings for Ollie in no way negatively impact my feelings for you. Please believe that."

I set my drink down with a plunk, and to my great surprise, Ollie takes my free hand in his. I swivel my head to look at him, and his eyes are full of concern. He has such beautiful brown eyes; I could get lost in them. What am I thinking? He's in love with the man I'm supposed to marry? What is going on here?

I turn back to Troy. "How could you agree to marry me, knowing full well there is someone else in your life who is this important to you? Are you in love with Ollie?" I'm afraid of his answer, but I have to know.

"Yes," he says simply, and my heart lurches in my chest.

I turn to Ollie and ask, "And are you in love with Troy?"

"I have been since the moment I laid eyes on him."

I jerk my hands away from both men. "Can someone call me a taxi, please?"

Chapter Seventeen

Troy

I NEED to fix this mess. I don't want to scare Rosalie away because I honestly have fallen in love with her. I know what love feels like because I've loved Ollie for so long. It's the same gut-wrenching, soul-rending feeling I get for him that I'm experiencing with Rosalie. It's like without them I can't take a full breath of air. The threat of losing my career pales to the thought of losing either of them, but I can't put Rosalie's career at risk before it even begins. I have to make her see that we must marry. If we don't, the studio will ruin us. But I also can't make Ollie give up what makes him so happy. Me.

And God knows, I can't give up Ollie. Even the thought of that nearly kills me.

"Rosalie, sweetheart, please don't run off. We need to

explain ourselves to you so you'll understand. We need you. I need you like I need Ollie. There is no either-or for me at this point."

"What are you saying? You want to marry me and cheat on me? With a man no less? Are you mad?"

"Only mad for you and Ollie. Believe me."

"*How can that be*?" she asks in a whisper.

When I'm slow to form my words, Ollie speaks up. "Rosalie, most men love women, and a small percentage of them prefer men. That's just the way of the world. But in this case, Troy and I were happily dating women until we met one another and fell deeply in love. It shocked the hell out of both of us because neither of us had ever looked at another man twice up to that point. But our connection was immediate and strong."

Rosalie frowns at him, not really getting why she needs to know any of this. "It's obvious you're playing a game with me, and I want to get out of here," she says.

Ollie gently takes her hand again and keeps speaking. "There are some people, like Troy and me, who can love a man and still crave a woman. We've spoken about it a lot recently, and we aren't minimizing our love for each other by being honest that we need the company of a woman in our lives to be completely happy. I've no doubt that Troy loves you, and having been the recipient of that kind of love from him for a few years now, I can tell you it's a gift from God. He loves unabashedly with his entire beautiful heart. Please don't turn him away because he also loves me."

I'm flattered by Ollie's words, but I'm not sure he's making things any better with Rosalie. Terribly perplexed, she asks, "What do you expect me to do with a husband who's in love with someone else? *Share* him?"

"Not just him, beautiful Rosalie. We could all be equal. Do you know what a ménage à trois is?"

She sucks in a breath and stares at Ollie a moment, then she turns and stares at me. "What?"

"It means—" I start to say, but she interrupts.

"I know exactly what it means!"

"Could you ever consider it? We'd be as discreet as Ollie and I have been for years. No one outside this house ever has to know. But we could make your life incredibly sweet together, dearest."

"How?" she asks in a choked whisper. Her eyes suddenly dilate, and I think we're making progress...maybe.

My eyes flick to Ollie, and I lean in to kiss Rosalie. At first, she stiffens, then she opens her mouth to me just enough for me to press my advantage. And when I do, she kisses me with equal ardor. I'm not surprised because I don't doubt her sincere affection for me. Ollie scoots closer and begins to kiss her bare neck. She probably has no idea how beautiful her long, slender neck looks with her hair pulled up like that, and I know Ollie can't hold back. I can sense his desperate arousal from here. He gently slides his lips down and across her shoulder. Rosalie lets out the tiniest of satisfied gasps before she pulls back from me and stands abruptly. She is visibly shaking.

"I...don't know if I can do this," she moans.

"You don't have to do anything you don't feel comfortable with," I promise her. "Ever. I know we've shocked you, and that was not our intent. We hoped you could get to know us both better and gradually learn about our circumstances, but I'm afraid you were too clever for us to hold back anything but the entire truth."

"I..." she stammers. "I don't know what to think. This whole notion of a ménage à trois sounds crazy. I need to get away from the two of you for a while and clear my head." She wrings her hands and begins to pace around the room. "I know the studio has us over a barrel, and I would never ruin your career on purpose, Troy. But how could I possibly say yes to this kind of arrangement? What would I tell my family?"

I notice that none of her worries stem from lack of interest, so I'm taking this reaction as a huge win. We have some obstacles to breach, but I see possibilities ahead. Ollie looks at me with understanding, and I know he sees this as well. "Darling, what would you say if I offered to bring you home after work a couple times a week and let you get better acquainted with Ollie? I wouldn't interfere. Or if you preferred me to be there, I could do that too. It's all up to you. We don't want to force you into any kind of arrangement that you're not one hundred percent happy with. As far as letting anyone know about it, we would still be Troy and Rosalie, the happily married couple, to the public. Ollie doesn't care about mingling with the Hollywood crowd. And once we're married, the studio might relax a bit on our scheduled public appearances."

She looks at Ollie with curiosity, "You don't mind being sequestered away in this big house by yourself all the time?"

He smiles. "I'm not alone all the time. I know it sounds a bit odd to everyone else, but my book characters keep me quite amused on a daily basis, and every other month I drive up to Santa Barbara for a weekend retreat with a group of authors. I have the privacy I need so I can work, I have Troy and his incredible love, and I have some fascinating, creative friends to share ideas with. So don't feel sorry for me. This is the life I've made for myself, and I'm more than satisfied with it. If you could become part of it as well, life would be perfect."

That was a darn good sales talk. I'll have to reward Ollie later with some extra affection. I look at Rosalie to see how she is affected by his words, and I see more confusion written on her face. What I don't detect, thankfully, is rejection.

"Darling, this is probably a lot for you to take in. Would you like me to drive you home and let you think about us? I can pick you up in the morning, and we'll talk more then, if you want."

She takes a deep breath, and her eyes dart back and forth between Ollie and me. "Yes, thank you. I think I need to sleep on this a while. Just let me go and retrieve my swimsuit, and we can be on our way."

"Don't even bother. We'll make sure it gets into the wash, and you can keep it here. It's obvious you love the pool."

"Oh, well, alright. I still need my purse and Ollie's book, though. I'll be right back."

As soon as Rosalie is out of earshot, Ollie grabs me and kisses me like he hasn't seen me in weeks. Once he steps back, he says, "She's incredible. How did you get so lucky?"

"Hopefully we'll *all* be lucky. I think she just needs to get used to the idea. She's been making eyes at you all evening with great interest, my handsome love."

"You think so?"

"Don't be so modest. By the way, did you ever find that possibly banned book you were hunting for?"

"I did. Having a publisher helped tremendously. I ordered two copies of it, so we can give one to Rosalie. You know...since she loves to read and all." He winks at me. "It ought to be here any day now. Ah, here is our lovely lady now. I'll say goodnight and look forward to seeing you again very soon, Rosalie." He approaches her and takes her gently into his arms. She looks momentarily shocked until it's obvious he's about to kiss her. Her eyes close and her mouth opens a little.

I have to say that watching my two favorite people in all the world kiss one another is incredibly arousing. Who knew? I can't restrain myself, so I join them, wrapping them both in my arms. I kiss Rosalie, then I kiss Ollie, and we hear her intake of breath at the sight.

Yes, indeed, we're making progress.

Chapter Eighteen

I CERTAINLY NEVER EXPECTED THE night I've had. I was expecting a nice, quiet, and hopefully romantic time with Troy, but it turned out nothing like that. When I first met him, it was a big enough shock to be ordered to marry a virtual stranger or I'll lose my budding career. Then it was a shock to realize that I was actually falling in love with Troy, even though our marriage was arranged like I'm the daughter of a duke instead of a cherry grower from Idaho. And finally, it was an even larger shock that Troy has a male lover, but he and Troy also love women. And how am I even remotely considering being a part of that? How did my life become so peculiar just because I wanted to move away from picking cherries and make something of myself in Hollywood? This is such a predicament, and I need to figure out how to handle it.

My first thought was that I could not imagine telling my parents about my life if I were to go through with Troy and Ollie's proposal. Of course, it's not like they're planning to visit; they never leave Idaho. I'm already the black sheep of the family for having ambitions outside of the town of Emmet. I've written to them about my part in *Forever Yours* and my contract with the studio. I've also begun sending them more money than I used to, but I haven't heard a word back from them. It hurts, but I suppose I don't have to worry about what they think of my lifestyle in that case. I'm absolutely on my own now, and I need to remember that. I just wish they'd write to me or communicate more than just cashing my checks. Right now, that's the only way I know they're alive. Maybe I ought to send them a photo of Troy and me together, although no doubt someone in that little town showed them the Associated Press photo from the other night. Imagine...a professional photojournalist took my picture, and it was shared all over the country. I can hardly believe it.

Two men. *Two* of them. And not just anyone, mind you. A well-known, popular actor and a famous author, and they both want me. I'm flattered and scared to death at the same time. I've never been with—in the biblical sense—even one man, so what am I supposed to do with two of them? My only experience up to now was with my high school boyfriend Jeff Barlow. I wasn't at all crazy about him, but at least I had semi-regular dates, and that kept me from dying of boredom. He was attentive and polite to me for a while, but such a brute—both on and off the football field—none of the other boys would come near me for fear of retribution.

Our relationship ended with a shock when Jeff had to quickly marry Eloise Marchand. It turned out that he had knocked her up late in our senior year. I guess I frustrated him when I refused to have sex with him, and Eloise didn't like me, so she probably didn't care that he had a girlfriend. Naturally, he went around telling all the other boys I was frigid—but I guess that was better than telling them all I was a nymphomaniac. In any case, his attitude and behavior sort of put me off men for a long time. No one in Emmet caught my eye anyway, and that's the truth.

When I met Troy, he was so refined and such a gentleman—which was a lot considering he was a farm boy from Ohio. It was like a whole new world of possibilities opened up to me. Little did I know that getting to know him was only the tip of the iceberg.

When both those Adonis-like gentlemen were kissing me, I thought I was going to burn up and crumble to the floor in a pile of ashes. And when they kissed each other as they were holding onto me...I have no words. How was that the sexiest thing I've ever seen? It made my body feel things I've never experienced before. It was like a warm tickle that started somewhere deep inside me and expanded outward.

I like it.

I want more of it.

I've always heard that two men lying together is a sin and illegal, but what Troy and Ollie have together is beautiful. They clearly love each other, so where is the sin in that? Doesn't the Bible tell us to love one another? How can any kind of love be sinful or illegal? Troy tells me that if his real relationship with Ollie were to be made public knowledge, he would most likely be arrested and lose everything. That's a good enough reason for me to keep my mouth closed about it. I would never do or say anything to harm those lovely men. But do I want to go so far as to effectively marry both of them?

My head is swimming.

Speaking of swimming, those men in their swimsuits… well, what a sight. I could have that every day if I agree. If I don't agree, I see only heartache ahead for all of us.

Does that mean my mind is made up?

I have no idea.

Maybe I could give it a little bit of a try. Spend more time with Ollie like they suggested, but I'd feel strange without Troy, I just know it.

Oh, for crying out loud, I need to make my head quiet down and let me get some sleep. We're shooting a big scene tomorrow, and I need to be on my toes, not in cloud-cuckoo-land.

Chapter Nineteen

Rosalie looks tired and tense this morning. I pray she isn't going to make an announcement that breaks my heart. I don't want to push her too hard, but I have to know.

"Darling?" I ask quietly. "Have you thought about what Ollie and I suggested last night?"

She lets out the most undignified snort I've ever heard come out of such a lovely creature as she swings her head my way. Her eyes are clear at least. They don't appear as if she's been crying or anything awful like that.

"Troy, how can you even ask that? I've done nothing *but* think about it. My head is spinning, and I barely slept last night." Then she does something that might be good or bad. She reaches for my hand and grasps it. Fortunately, we're sitting at a red light. The light turns green all too quickly, though, so I have to extricate my hand and shift gears with it.

I glance at her questioningly and then look back at the road. Traffic is pretty heavy this morning.

"I would like to spend more time at your house and get to know Ollie better. He seems wonderful, and I can see that you love him. Despite the way I was raised, that doesn't bother me at all. I think it's splendid, actually. Your love for Ollie and his for you is beautiful to me, and I've decided it makes more sense to trust you than run away from you." A thrill pulses through me at her words. Our cockamamie plan might just work! Oh, that would be...everything.

"I wish I weren't driving right now because I'd like to kiss you so hard, you wouldn't believe it. You really mean it, sweetheart? You might want to give us both a try together?"

"I, uh...yes. I think so. The alternative seems horrible. I'm afraid I'd lose you, and we could potentially lose our jobs, and...well, all of that sounds like a fast road to hell, if you ask me." I hope she isn't choosing us because it's the least offensive way to move forward, but she stills my fears when she goes on to say, "You have to understand that I'm not at all experienced with men. One at a time is more than enough for me, but two at once? I have no idea how to handle that. I'm not scared, but I am in the dark. *Way* in the dark. I haven't ever..."

"We'll help you."

"You'll help me," she murmurs to herself. Then her head snaps up. "Does that mean the two of you have done this together before, with another woman?"

Her tone is tense, so I quickly dispel that worry. "No,

never! I've never been in love with a woman before you. I just meant that we'll take good care of you and guide you. Ollie says he has some reading material you might enjoy on the topic of living as a ménage à trois. I haven't seen it yet, but he says it all sounds quite beautiful and ah...stimulating." What a strange conversation to be having on the way to work. As I pull up to the studio, I compose myself and pull through the gate, attempting to look normal. I may have to take a moment before exiting the car because thinking about having Rosalie *and* Ollie has caused some expansion in the lumberyard.

"Darling, do you mind if we table this conversation for later? When we get inside, I'll call home and let them know we're both going to be there for dinner. I'm sure Ollie will be thrilled. But for now, I need to get myself...uh...in check a little before we face anyone." I indicate the tent in my pants with my eyes, and Rosalie turns crimson.

"Oh! Of course. So, um...how do you...like the wallpaper the set designers used for the dining room? I find it a little garish, don't you? I do like the furniture, though, especially the chairs."

Atta girl, talk to me about something boring. She goes seamlessly from set design to an unattractive pair of shoes they're making her wear, then she chatters about how angry Packard was when a grip tripped over a light stand and ruined a take that was going well, and in minutes we're ready to step out and face the studio. I can't help but clasp her hand as we walk inside, and I murmur in her ear, "My God, I love you."

The look she gives me is the sweetest sight in the world.

"I love you too, my dear handsome man."

Glory hallelujah.

Chapter Twenty

THAT WAS the best news I've had in years. Troy called to say he's bringing our lovely Rosalie home tonight, and she has maintained an open mind. Our truth didn't scare her off.

I thought I was the luckiest man alive when I met Troy, but this? Incredible.

"Zelda!" I call out as I float happily toward the kitchen. "We'll have company again tonight for dinner."

"Hmph. So is Troy bringing home another actress?" she snaps at me in her usual disagreeable tone.

"Not at all." I can't help smiling at her despite her grumpiness. "He's bringing home Rosalie again. She seemed to like you, and I forgot to tell you she asked us to relay that she loved your cooking. You know, they're going to be married soon, and she'll be moving in."

"Huh. News to me. Are you moving out?"

"Heavens no."

Zelda narrows her eyes at me. "Okay. Well, lunch will be ready in two hours, and I'll plan to make something nice for dinner." She turns her back on me and heads into the pantry. I have been dismissed. She's never much company, or very enthusiastic about anything, but that was downright pleasant of her. Maybe she's taken a shine to Rosalie too.

I try to settle down and get some writing done, but my emotions are running too high to concentrate. If this new way to live works out well, it could be beyond my wildest dreams. I plunk away on my typewriter somewhat aimlessly and end up pulling out sheet after sheet of paper I've made messes of. I doubt my editor would be able to make any sense of what I've written, so I crumple the current fiasco into a ball and toss it toward the wastebasket where it bounces off the edge and hits the carpet next to three other duds. Not dredging up any inspiration, I pace around, go for another swim for no good reason other than restlessness, have a light lunch outside with Zelda who is her typical taciturn self, and then take a shower. After I'm dressed again, it will still be a few hours before Troy and Rosalie get home. See? I'm already mentally moving her in. I try once again to write something coherent. It's simply not happening for me today, and that worries the dickens out of me.

The phone rings, but I'm too preoccupied with obsessing about my writer's block and fantasizing about Troy and Rosalie to answer it. After three rings, the noise stops, so I assume Zelda picked up. I have no trouble forgetting about it as I dream up possibilities that I certainly cannot add to my current manuscript. I don't write erotica; I write mysteries.

So where are they anyway? My stomach gives a loud rumble right before Zelda raps lightly on the open study door and tells me, "Dinner's ready, Ollie. It's in the kitchen."

"What? Why? Where are Troy and Rosalie? Weren't they supposed to be here by now? I was so...ah...engrossed, I forgot what time it was."

"Troy called hours ago and said he and Rosalie were being sent to some swanky party at the Brown Derby. He sounded pretty put out, if you ask me. I meant to tell you, but I was in the middle of interviewing a possible new maid and forgot. Sorry. The last one quit because her husband got a better job in Santa Ana, and they're moving, and the commute to get here would be too far on the bus. Anyway, Troy said they'd try to be home for dinner tomorrow."

I attempt to swallow my irritation at this turn of events and clomp out to the kitchen behind Zelda. She's made a nice dinner for me—lamb chops covered in a delicious minty sauce, fresh vegetables, and buttery new potatoes, so I can hardly be cross with her. I should have answered the damn phone myself. I attempt to make small talk with Zelda for a while but finally give up. I thank her for dinner and grab a bottle of brandy to take back to my study. When Troy still isn't home at eleven-thirty, and I've had enough brandy, I give up and go to bed. I barely wake up when he climbs into bed an hour or two later. He snuggles up to me and wraps an arm around my waist.

He must be exhausted because I can tell he's sound

asleep in less than two minutes, and I doze off again right after that. The studio is crazy to be running him around like this for publicity stunts when he still needs to be working some days for nine or ten hours straight.

No wonder the studio encourages actors to use so many drugs to stay awake and go to sleep. I'm just thankful Troy hasn't been tempted.

In the morning, I'm shocked to see that Troy is still asleep at eight. I gently shake his shoulder and ask, "Are you alright? Shouldn't you have left to get Rosalie by now?"

Troy's eyes are bleary when he grumbles, "Packard doesn't need us until one today. He's shooting some crowd scenes, and he wanted to give us a rest after the couple of weeks we've had. He's not usually so understanding, but I think he's either developing a crush on Rosalie, and he wants her to be happy, or Packard's wife may have told him to lay off of Rosalie and not push her too hard. Sophie has dropped by a few times to say hi, and I like her as a friend for our girl."

I smile at his calling Rosalie "our girl" and nod sagely, saying, "It pays to have friends in high places. Go back to sleep. I'll get you up in time to shower and have lunch." I give him a quick kiss and head out to the pool. I hope this doesn't mean Packard will feel compelled to keep them late this evening. The man must want to go home to Sophie sometimes too. I hear she's quite the looker and is as shrewd as her husband.

Outside, I take off my glasses and step over to the pool. It's then I catch a strange flash shining out of one of the tall trees beyond our perimeter privacy wall. I stare for a moment, but with my eyesight, I can't make out anything, so I figure it was just an odd play of sunlight on leaves—over as quickly as it began. Forgetting about it, I dive into the pool and begin my daily regimen. It feels so good to stretch my muscles and fill my lungs with fresh air.

SEVERAL DAYS GO BY, and I manage to get back into writing somewhat more successfully. I'm also able to spend some time on my own with Rosalie and get to know her better, but it's not enough—especially considering how wonderful I've decided she is. I want her here all the time.

One afternoon, I find myself wondering if having a new lifestyle—albeit one of my absolute dreams—makes me too complacent to write. I ponder this question a while (instead of writing) until I hear the security gate chime at the end of the driveway. Glad to have something to do, I head outside to answer it.

A tired looking deliveryman thrusts a clipboard through the gate and asks me for my signature. Then he hands me a box that is heavy for its size, and I realize I've hit the jackpot —it's the ménage books I bought. What perfect timing! I thank him, and he probably wonders why I'm so eager, but I turn and sprint back toward the house. Then I spin around and run back to the gate again, hollering to the guy who's just now stepping into his truck, "Wait. Wait!" He gives me a quizzical look, so I reach into my pocket and hand him a sizeable gratuity. "Sorry, I was preoccupied. Thanks again."

"Anytime, mister." He tips his hat at me with a smile. "Enjoy whatever that is in that box, and thanks for the tip. It helps a lot, but most people aren't that kind."

I know how hard the guy must work, and this horrible Depression has people in a bad way across the country, so I'm glad to be generous when I can. I make my way back to my study once again, quickly slice open the box, and behold the Holy Grail. As soon as I see it, however, I realize this is not a book Rosalie can take back to her boardinghouse in case anyone sees her carrying it. It's rather unfortunate that it's not still in its original French, but Rosalie and Troy wouldn't understand it that way. I carefully peruse my bookshelves looking for just the right thing and discover the book is almost exactly the same size as *Rebecca*. I remove both dust covers and place *Rebecca*'s jacket onto the ménage book. I laugh, wondering how Daphne du Maurier would feel about this and think to myself what an interesting book it is she wrote. I know I could have used one of the dust jackets from my books, but I didn't want to give Rosalie the wrong idea with false advertising. I also know that doesn't make any sense, but I guess I'm more proprietary about my own work.

Then I sit down to read and read. The first time I saw it, way back when, the book was in French, but I find my comprehension is even better this way. Anyway, my command of that language is rusty now. My grandparents and sometimes my mother used to speak to me in French when I was younger, but it's been too long now. I think I originally found the book in my grandparents' library, so I wonder about them a little. Eh...if they ever partook in ménage, I say good for them. Maybe my desire to make this work is something I inherited from them.

What a thought.

This book is mesmerizing despite its unimaginative title *Ménage à Trois*. It was interesting when I first read it years ago, and I remember chuckling about it a little but also finding it arousing and sensitively written. But now that I can try to put myself in the place of one of the participants... well! It's a whole new matter entirely. The book is written in sections—each one having a different coupling (or should that be a tripling?) of participants. It's erotic fiction, but it is also extremely explicit in its descriptions. It begins with two women and one man, and that sounds like fun, but there are parts of it that seem somewhat improbable. Still, I study it carefully, paying more attention to their attitudes than what they are actually doing physically. The next section is three women, and I just speed read through that because it has no bearing on us, and I'm not able to relate to this section at all, not that it's poorly written or anything—it's just missing some important appendages. Then three men—again, not something that would ever particularly pique my interest because I would hate to share Troy with another man, but I browse through it to see if they come up with anything Troy and I have neglected when we make love. We've covered pretty much all we've been inclined to do (and able to do with just the two of us), and that makes me happy.

Finally, the author settles in on two men and one woman, and I've struck gold. I peruse this section three times, taking in all of the positions and activities. I can't wait for Troy and Rosalie to get here so we can discuss this. I'm positively vibrating with excitement at some of the possibilities. Then it hits me that Rosalie might not be ready for immersion into this text quite yet. I'm eager, but I've had lots of time to think about it, and I'm far more sexually experienced than I imagine she is. I guess a slow approach is always a good bet.

Chapter Twenty-One

Rosalie

Now that I've made my mind up about moving forward with Troy and Ollie's plan, it seems as if there is a conspiracy to keep us all apart. I've been shooting the scenes I don't have with Troy for days now, and unless he can manage to have lunch with me or find me in my dressing room for five minutes, the only time I've seen him is when he picks me up in the morning. I've had to work late, or he's had to work late, and that keeps us apart in the evenings, despite our wish to spend time together with Ollie. I've been driven home by studio drivers when Troy isn't around and briefly considered having the driver take me to Troy's house so I could have some time with Ollie. But I was worried about studio gossip and winding up looking terrible if I drove to his place when Troy wasn't home.

I finally take matters into my own hands and take the bus that gets me closest to the guys' house and have Ollie pick me up at the bus stop. I also don't want to answer questions at the boardinghouse about why some strange man is driving me somewhere instead of Troy. I have a good couple of hours with him until Troy comes home exhausted but delighted to find me there. We have time for some lovely kissing before he completely fades and has to go to bed. Ollie puts me in a taxi, prepays the driver, and goes back to tend to Troy. I love how Ollie cares for Troy that way. I also appreciate that there was no contact between us until Troy showed up. Our visit was just getting-to-know-you stuff before that. My plan to join Ollie this way is so successful, I manage to do the same thing a few more times—and I wish it could be even more often. My feelings for him grow exponentially—he's such a bright, articulate, and affectionate person.

Last night, Troy and I were able to attend a party together instead of working late, but it was a stifling, noisy affair, and some blowhard dragged Troy away from me to talk about something he said was important and private. Troy looked worried about leaving me, and he should have been. This left me cornered by a man from one of the lesser studios who spent the whole time yammering on about how important he was and ogling my bosom. I couldn't get away from him because he would stand in front of me blocking my passage each time I took a step. Finally, Troy got rid of the windbag and rescued me, taking me by the arm and saying we needed to leave. He was also fed up with the guy who wanted to talk nonsense to him about possibly leaving his—

actually *our*—agent Moe. I guess I should have been more assertive about sticking close to Troy, and we may have both been happier.

The time we had together in the limo was equally unsatisfying because I fell asleep on the way home. I didn't mean to, but exhaustion hit me pretty hard. Last week, the studio added ballroom dancing lessons to my schedule for when I'm not needed on the set, and it's wearing me down to a frazzle. I need to look as confident and graceful as Troy when we dance, though.

Another reason I'm so worn out is that we've been having a somewhat early Santa Ana wind condition all week, and the heat has been unbearable at 102°. It's hard to get comfortable enough at night to sleep well.

Tonight, I'm less than thrilled because we've been directed to attend a United Artists movie premiere together. It's funny how the excitement of attending a Hollywood function wears off pretty quickly when you're forced to go no matter what else you have going on in your life or how much energy you have left after a long day of work. I hope Troy and I will be able to carve out a little alone time finally, even though I know we'll be surrounded by hundreds of Hollywood bigwigs. I understand that United Artists, unlike the other studios, funds independent projects, and they've had some great success with several of them. They treat each release with high hopes that the public will embrace the movie, and it will make them lots of money.

It's heavenly sitting in the limo holding hands with Troy, but he's afraid of ruining my makeup and hair if he kisses me before we have our pictures taken together. It's wonderful how thoughtful he is that way.

"It feels like we've barely seen each other," he tells me. "I've missed you terribly."

"I know just what you mean. It feels like ages since I've been able to get over to your house after work," I tell him and check to see that the privacy screen is raised. Even knowing it's closed, I ask softly, "How does Ollie deal with it when he doesn't get much time with you?"

Troy gives me a sweet smile and tells me, "We make sure to make the most of the time we have. And don't forget—we have all night together no matter what. We just wish we could have you with us as well."

I blush, but I feel that thrill of excitement pulse through me at the same time. I am so curious about how our future living arrangements will work out. *If* they'll work out.

"Rosalie, how would you feel about getting through the swarm of photojournalists when we first get to the premiere, answering a few of their questions, and then sitting way in the back of the theater? Once the movie gets going, we can slip out and leave. If anyone should ask, we can say you developed a severe headache—or we can say that I did, if you prefer. I've heard this movie is expected to be a flop anyway, so we won't be missing much. Once we're seen together, our part is pretty much done. I promised Ollie I'd really try to make it home at a decent hour, so we can have the driver take us back to the studio and then I can drive you to my house as soon as we get there. Zelda can feed us, and we can have the rest of the night to spend with Ollie for as long as you want. This sounds better to me than a lousy movie, another noisy party, and missing Ollie. He's been dying to see you again anyway."

"Yes, please, to all of that," I tell him and snuggle closer. "I won't mind staying at your place late since we have tomorrow off finally."

"Terrific. He's terribly anxious to show you that book anyway, and I'm in the mood for some quiet time with the two of you."

"Oh! He has that book?" I suddenly feel jittery over and need to look away for a moment. Maybe I'll want to read it alone. "Would Ollie be offended if I wanted to look at it by myself at first?"

"He'll be fine, no matter what you decide, but I have to warn you, he's pretty enthusiastic." Troy gives my hand a squeeze and winks at me.

Just before we exit the limo, Troy lowers the privacy screen and asks the driver to stick close by. "I think we'll want to leave in about thirty minutes," he says.

"Yes sir, Mr. Kingsley. Whatever you need, sir."

As expected, not only is it as hot as Hades out here, the flashbulbs are blinding, and if I have to fake a headache, I can't imagine anyone disbelieving me after this experience. Reporters hurl questions at us, and mostly we just smile and wave, but Troy knows when to stop and whom to speak to. We get through the gauntlet in less time than I expected, and I didn't have to do or say much. The press still isn't exactly sure what to make of me. I'm a new actress starring in a big role, but Troy has a huge following. He gets the attention, and it's fine with me. I just smile a lot and try to look decorative, as I've been instructed to do.

Also, as expected, the film isn't very good, and it's miserably hot in the theater. The acting is heavy-handed and the story unimaginative. I wonder how the filmmakers got it funded by United Artists. You never know in this town—could be a relative with connections, someone needed to repay a favor, or someone bestowed "favors" of a more physical nature. I shudder to think of that.

When I begin to yawn, Troy nudges me and whispers, "*Ready?*"

"Absolutely," I grumble with a nod, trying to keep from rolling my eyes.

We're on the end of a row, so our exit is seamless and quick. There don't seem to be any photographers skulking around in the lobby, so we walk swiftly out the front door of the theater and straight into the limo.

"I'm so relieved, it's ridiculous," I sigh to Troy when we're safely on our way, and he's ripping off his jacket. I noticed a few cars lined up behind ours, so I guess we weren't the only people who had plans to leave early. There must be a lot of imaginary migraines going around tonight.

When we reach the studio, Troy gives the chauffeur a hefty tip and thanks him. I'm sure the driver is glad to have some free time now that his work is done for the night, so it's unlikely he'll go blabbing that we cut out early. He's probably anxious for a cold beer. We hurry in and change out of our formal wear, Troy makes a quick call to say we're on our way, and finally we're going to see Ollie. Together at last.

As soon as we get back to Troy's house, Ollie meets us at the door and sweeps me into his arms. I'm delighted when he kisses me breathless while Troy stands by grinning. I can't find it in me to cut the kiss short. Instead, I simply relax and enjoy Ollie's style of kissing. He's a little different from Troy, but not one iota less appealing. When he finally steps back, he stares into my eyes with unmistakable heat for a couple seconds and then grabs Troy so he can kiss the daylights out of him too. Each time this happens, I'm mildly shocked at how much pleasure I feel watching the two of them kiss. Does everyone feel like this? I somehow doubt it because then everyone would want two lovers.

Ollie leads us in, and I expect him to pull out my chair at the dining room table. However, we remain standing while he says, "I know you're both probably starving by now, and Zelda made a lovely supper for us."

"So formal," Troy says with a laugh, eyeing the beautifully set table with crystal, fine china, and glowing candles under a sparkling chandelier. He looks at me and says, "We generally eat in the kitchen with Zelda."

"But this is a special occasion," Ollie says with a twinkle in his eye. "We have lots to talk about and plenty to celebrate, so I thought this would be a nice change." He looks at Troy and asks, "Have you proposed yet to our beautiful Rosalie?"

"Not yet. Rosalie and I know we're getting married, and we're both happy about it, but the studio wants to dictate when and where I'll pop the question. I assume it's supposed to be in a very exclusive and yet public place for maximum effect. And they want it timed just right with the release of our movie." He's happy and resigned in equal measures.

"That sounds like what they would want," Ollie answers, but then he does something highly unexpected. He positions himself in front of Troy and me, taking our hands in his, and drops to one knee. "Rosalie, Troy, I have found in the two of you the fulfillment of all my wildest dreams. I have loved you, Troy, with all my heart for years now, and Rosalie, I can see a long future ahead of loving you, even though we haven't known each other a long time. I know Troy's heart, and I know he loves you deeply the way he loves me, and that's good enough for me to know my affection for you, which is already strong, will grow and grow. We can't do this legally, but in spirit and in our three hearts, will you both marry me?" He produces a small box from his pocket, and in it we see three platinum rings. Each has an emerald, a brown topaz, and an aquamarine, and in each ring, the center stone is different. "They are as close as I could get to the color of our eyes, and they represent us. If anyone thinks it's odd you're wearing these on your left hands, we can all pretend we're Scandinavian and wear them on our right hands. So, what do you say?"

Troy and I answer, "Yes!" simultaneously, and yet I still wonder whether I've lost a little bit of my mind for agreeing to this. The men are so thrilled, however, I find myself caught up in their joy as we kiss and hug one another over and over.

"Ollie, this is so sweet of you. How did you find these gorgeous rings?" I ask.

"I had them specially made, and it was a real challenge to get the various gemstones to match one another in size and color. I wanted them to represent us as equals."

"Well, I love them, and I'll be proud to wear your ring," I say and kiss him once more for good measure.

Troy has had tears in his eyes since Ollie dropped to his

knee, and he hasn't said a lot. I'm afraid he's a bit overcome, the sweet man.

Finally, we sit down to dinner. Zelda quietly brings us a bottle of chilled champagne and a lovely meal of chicken sautéed with mushrooms and artichoke hearts. It looks every bit as good as what I used to serve people at the Beverly Hills Hotel, but now I actually get to taste it myself. I love it, and I'm impressed that she could pull together a delightful meal like this with hardly any notice. I'm enchanted with the way our three rings sparkle in the candlelight. Ollie's glowing with an inner joy, and once again I tell myself I'm the luckiest woman on earth.

I hope I can always feel like this. But how secretive will we need to be? And what if someone finds out? Will our love be our ruin?

Chapter Twenty-Two

TROY

IF I LOVED OLLIE BEFORE, it's nothing like how much I love him now. He has accepted and embraced Rosalie like the three of us were always meant to be. His enthusiasm is infectious, and I feel the weariness of the past weeks seeping out of me to be replaced with a glow of joy. Of course, it could be bubbles from the champagne we're toasting ourselves with over and over, but I choose to think that the love inside of me is expanding, and I can feel it. How could I be so lucky? Rosalie could have turned out to be a stuck-up actress who's all full of her own importance, but instead she's sweet and kind. She's beautiful inside and out, and the best part is, she's falling for Ollie. I see it happening to both of them.

"Troy tells me you also have some reading material for us," Rosalie says, looking a little coquettish with pink cheeks.

She dips her head and peers up at him through her eyelashes.

"I absolutely do, and your copy is ensconced in a public-friendly dust jacket proclaiming it to be Daphne du Maurier's *Rebecca*. I wanted you to be able to leave it on your nightstand with no one asking any questions."

Relaxing, she laughs and asks, "What if someone wants to know anything about *Rebecca*?"

"Have you read it?"

"Certainly. Who hasn't? It's a wonderful story and so cleverly crafted."

"Then tell them what you know but just don't offer to show them any passages. And tell them you can't loan it out until you're finished." Ollie gets a good kick out of this. "You can switch my real copy back into the cover if you ever want to loan it out. But I don't suppose you have too many people wandering through your bedroom at all hours."

"No, just my friend Daisy now and then. But she *is* the type who might be nosy enough to pry."

"You can lock your room when you're not there, can't you?"

"Yes."

"Then I suppose you're safe. Besides, you'll want to bring it back here and discuss it with Troy and me soon enough."

Rosalie's face is pink again, and I'm getting excited just thinking about discussing the content of the book with them. "Do you have any favorite parts, Ollie?" I ask.

"Indeed I do, my friend. The fourth section is actually the only one that pertains to us, but the other three are also explicit and might be interesting to you two. I won't say to skip them, just to pay closest attention to part four." He turns to Rosalie. "Please, dearest, don't be nervous about all of this. We don't expect you to do anything you're not completely comfortable with. And we expect to go slowly as we get to know one another this way. It's going to be new for us as well."

Rosalie sits up as straight as a ramrod, raises her chin, and asks, "What are your positions on pre-marital sex?" She looks at Ollie and then at me. There's a sparkle in her eye, yet she still manages to look serious.

Ollie's jaw drops a little and then he recovers quickly with a wolfish grin. "Rosalie..." he growls at her. "I'm a huge fan of several positions."

Rosalie gasps, "I wasn't referring to..."

I interrupt, "My position is that I'm one hundred percent on board for it, personally, but this is, as Ollie says, completely up to you, sweetheart."

Rosalie tries to suppress a smile, but she bursts out laughing. "You two are precious. You're such gentlemen, it makes me love you both more and more, but I personally don't see the need to wait for marriage. After all, we don't even know when that will be unless the studio would like to clue us in." She sobers suddenly and adds, "That's not to say I relish the idea of getting pregnant right now. We have a movie to complete, after all."

"We can be careful with that," Ollie says with a firm conviction. I'm not as convinced about the effectiveness of modern birth control practices, but we can certainly try hard not to be reckless. At least we both managed to not get anyone else pregnant up to now, and neither of us was celibate before we started our relationship. But I suppose if we're *both* planning to have sex with Rosalie, it just ups our odds that she could become impregnated. God, the studio execs would blow their tops if that happened. They have ordered more than one young woman to have an abortion, and I certainly wouldn't wish that on her. I shudder at the thought.

"Rosalie, darling," I ask, "perhaps that's something we ought to discuss before we go any further." I clear my throat. "What is your position on having children eventually? Do you want them or…?"

She looks deeply into my eyes, then shifts her attention to Ollie, then back to me. "I have always wanted a family. And I love children." I shouldn't be at all surprised at her answer. "I'm several years older than my twin siblings and took care of them a lot to help my mother after they were born. I loved it. As they grew older and were so wrapped up in each other, I haven't stayed as close to them as I'd have liked. Our age gap was too great to have a lot in common when we were in school, but being a mother is definitely something I see for myself." She takes a deep breath. "But not quite yet. My career is just on the precipice of becoming something I can be proud of, and I may never get any chance like this again with such a great movie script and a terrific co-star." She smiles sweetly at me. "I have to do everything in my power to make sure I do it right." Ollie and I are both nodding at her as she asks, "How do the two of you feel about children?"

I look at Ollie with a smile, and I see his handsome face glowing with happiness. "Troy and I have discussed this," he says. "And the only downside we saw in our relationship was the lack of possibility for children in our future. If someday you're ready, it would make us extremely happy men. We have a lot of love to give, you know. There is no pressure on you to quit your career and pop out ankle biters as soon as you and Troy are married, but we can discuss it when you're ready." He looks back and forth at us and adds, "Oh, the beautiful babies we could have. Just imagine."

"So," I say, "I guess it's settled then. We all want children, just not this soon. And we'll do our best to see that Rosalie doesn't wind up in the family way until we decide we're all ready." We're all finished with our lovely dinner, so I add, "Would you both consider cooling off in the pool tonight? I'm rather hot and need a cool down." Then I add in a sultry —I hope—tone, "Bathing suits are optional. We'll have to turn some lights on so we don't trip and fall getting out there, but we do have the tall privacy wall."

"I vote for naturalism," Ollie says with a straight face. "It's all the rage in Europe, I hear."

"Cooling off does sound nice," Rosalie says enigmatically. "I assume I can get changed again in the guest room?"

"If you like. Your swimsuit is in the top drawer—if you need it. And extra towels are by the pool. We'll meet you outside." Ollie is already getting out of his seat. I know he won't run upstairs for a swimsuit. Sure enough, he's heading for the patio door with an eager expression. Then he makes an about face and goes to the kitchen instead. I hear him thank Zelda for the wonderful dinner and tell her we're all finished.

Chapter Twenty-Three

ROSALIE

MY HEART IS RACING like crazy right now. I've never been totally naked in front of a man before, and now I'm considering doing it in front of two of them. If I wear my swimsuit, will they be disappointed in me? Will I be disappointed in myself? Or will they think I'm too brazen if I forgo the swimming attire? They've been clear all along that the pace we go is all on me. So now what?

I sit on the edge of the bed and take off my shoes. No matter what, I need to get undressed. It's whether I choose to cover up again that's important. I stand and slowly undo my blouse. I shuck it off and unzip my skirt. Now that I'm just in my underthings, I am still hot, and the pool water sounds wonderful. Slowly, I remove the rest of my underwear and carefully fold everything, laying it all out on the bed.

Now totally naked, I open the top drawer and find my swimsuit and cover-up, just as I was told. My nipples harden as I look at the silky robe and scanty swim attire. I feel a nervousness in my tummy that reminds me of the excitement I get when I'm kissing the men. I understand it's arousal, and it's a glorious feeling. I remember what their bodies looked like glistening in the sun, and I long to touch them.

Two naked men are no doubt waiting in the pool for me. Two. Men.

Resolutely, I grab what feels like flimsy armor and put it on.

I'm ready.

Chapter Twenty-Four

OLLIE

TROY HAS THE BEST IDEAS. We've been out here a few times in the buff when it's been too hot to sleep at night, but the idea of doing this with Rosalie was a stroke of genius. We both quickly shuck our clothes in the patio, grab a stack of towels, and head for the pool. I leave my glasses on this time, though. I don't want to miss anything, and I'm certainly not interested in swimming laps after eating a big dinner—and with such wonderful company. Oh my God, the water feels wonderful.

The yard lighting out here is dim, but we can see well enough because there is a generous moon tonight with no clouds. The air is still stifling hot with the constant blowing of the Santa Ana wind. At least the air moves, and it's not humid the way it often was when we lived in Ohio.

Troy and I are standing in the shallow end of the pool when the door opens. We turn to see Rosalie silhouetted in light from the house. She closes the door, and all I can tell is she's wearing that gauzy thing she had on over her swimsuit the last time she swam with us.

Slowly, she prowls her way to the edge of the pool—hips swaying as her shapely legs bring her closer and closer to us. She's barefoot and has her hair up in a ponytail, showing off her graceful, elegant neck. No one says a word. As she stops at the edge of the coping by the pool steps, she undoes her belt and lets her robe fall open. My breath catches in my throat. She did it. I want to shout, "Brava! Well done, you wonderful, beautiful creature!" But I stare at her in reverence instead. Slowly, slowly, she pushes the robe off her shoulders and lets it cascade down in a colorful puddle on the tiles.

Rosalie is gorgeous in her clothes, but out of them, she is a goddess.

We simultaneously reach up and offer her our hands as she steps into the water and makes her way down the steps to us. Her hand is hot in mine. Hot and smooth. Soft like the silk she discarded. As she submerges more and more of her body, she lets out a satisfied groan, and I feel myself reacting to the sensuality of the sound.

"Oh, this was the best idea, Troy. I'm so much cooler now," she says in that low, sexy voice of hers. She seems to have been created solely for the purpose of carnal delight the way she looks tonight in the moonlight.

I can't wait to pull her into my arms and bestow on her a kiss so deep, she'll feel it in her soul tomorrow. So I do just that. She tastes of champagne and lust. Oh, my Rosalie.

What are you doing to me? I suddenly want to rut and mark her as forever mine. But she is not just mine, is she? She was Troy's first, and I need to keep that in mind. But I was also Troy's first. Oh, we're going to have some fun with this new reality of ours. As I kiss her, Troy wraps his arms around both of us, and one of his hands slips between Rosalie and me where he's stroking her glorious breast. His knuckles are simultaneously stroking my chest, and I love it all.

Rosalie isn't shy about her kisses. She battles my tongue with hers, and I love it. She applies pressure when I let up and nips my lips now and then. I'm fully hard now, and I feel her naked body rubbing against me. I don't know how conscious she is of her actions because I'm sure she's inexperienced, but her instincts are spot on. I'm about to explode from being so excited. Just as I fear I'll embarrass myself by coming all over her from just kissing, she pulls away and turns to Troy. She keeps her arm wrapped around me though, seeming to need the contact as much as I do.

He takes her lips, and the two of them get lost in one another. I crave maintaining contact, so I bend down and find her breast with my mouth. She lets out another sexy little sound when I suck her nipple into my mouth. Her reaction is so strong, she has to stop kissing for a moment just so she can catch her breath. She relaxes finally with the sweetest smile on her face that I've ever seen. But then she goes back to smooching with Troy, and I begin to stroke both of their bodies wherever I can reach. The contrast is wonderful and amazing. Troy is hard, slightly furry here and there, and infinitely familiar. I've explored every inch of his glorious physique over the years. Rosalie is a new delight.

She is soft and smooth, fit, and ever so feminine with her curves. Touching them both like this in the night air and the cool water is like a smorgasbord of contrasts and wonders— all for me.

We go on and on like this, alternating the kisses equally. When Troy and I kiss each other, I feel Rosalie's gentle touch on my cheek as she murmurs, "You're both so wonderful." Her body is pressed up to both of us, and I burn for both of my lovers. I want more and more from them, but I cannot let myself get carried away. Rosalie needs to set the pace.

And just as I think that, I feel a hand that is definitely not Troy's exploring my erection. I look down and see that she is doing the same to Troy. She's not grabbing us, just stroking as if to get an idea of our contours. We're quite similar in our endowments, and we are both circumcised. I close my eyes and relish her caress. Her touch is soft, but not tentative. I press into her to let her know she can use more pressure, and she seems to understand immediately. Her response is to gently wrap her hands around both of us and stroke us up and down.

"Is this alright?" she asks.

Troy lets out a growly moan, and I break away from kissing him long enough to say, "It's perfect." Then I go back to kissing my man. This night is turning out to be one of the best of my life. I can feel Troy tensing along with my arousal and know we're both going to come in her hands unless we stop. I just don't know how far to take this, so I pull away and ask, "Troy, don't you think Rosalie would like some attention now?"

He grins at me and pulls away. Grabbing a large, folded

towel, he places it on the edge of the pool like a cushion. Then he turns and takes Rosalie by her waist and hoists her out of the water, setting her gently onto the soft towel. "My God, you're gorgeous, sweetheart. Ollie and I want to admire you and pleasure you, if you'll allow it." He encourages her to open her legs and begins to slide his hands up her thighs.

I'm about to combust, thinking about getting a taste of that glorious lady-garden when we suddenly hear a strange sound over at the side of the yard accompanied by a flash of light. It sounded like splintering wood, a lot of rustling, and a man's voice hollering, "Ow, damn it all to hell!" My blood runs cold, and I leap up the steps and over to the privacy wall. It's too high to see over, so I go back and grab a sturdy lawn chair to drag over. I climb up onto it just in time to see some creep running away toward a car parked at the curb. He's limping pretty badly, and he's carrying something in his hand that partly reflects the moonlight. I hope he broke his stupid leg.

Troy is right behind me asking, "What can you see, Ollie? What happened?"

"Apparently some asshole has been spying on us. I need to put on some clothes and go check it out, but he's long gone now. There's something in the bushes by the wall, though. It's too dark to tell what it is."

"Dammit. I'm going to go call Jack Cramer and see if he has any advice or, since he's a lawyer, he must know a private investigator. I certainly don't want this getting back to the studio." He grabs a towel, wraps it around his waist, and storms into the house.

After climbing down off the chair and dragging it back to

its normal location, I see Rosalie has wrapped herself up tightly in one of the big towels. She's shaking like a leaf. I wrap my arms around her, ignoring my own lack of attire for the moment, and say, "I'm so sorry this happened."

She tries for a laugh, but it sounds like a muffled sob. "That was a real killjoy, wasn't it? I heard what you said to Troy. Do you think someone followed us home after the function tonight? If so, they were pretty sneaky about it, especially since we went to the studio before coming here."

"Could be, or it could also be that they want photos of Troy for some reason and already know where he lives." Then I think about the weird light I saw once in the tree beyond the wall and add, "I don't think this is the first time he's been here. Or someone has been here at least—maybe not this dunderhead. Come on, let's get ourselves dressed."

Once I'm decent, I grab a flashlight and head out to the exterior of the wall. I find there is a wooden crate stuffed back into the bushes. There are broken branches in the bushes, and the ground isn't level, so anyone who tried to balance there on a box like it was a stepstool had to be a lamebrain. The crate has a large hole in the top where it caved in under the weight of our Peeping Tom. On closer inspection, I can also see that the jagged wood is bloody and has a chunk of what looks like skin attached to the sharpest point. *Good*, I think to myself. I train my light around the exterior of the shattered box and spot something that tells quite a story. It's a burnt-out flashbulb. It might be time to call the police, but not without discussing this with Troy and Rosalie first. I leave everything just as I found it and head back indoors.

Rosalie is dressed in her skirt and blouse again. She's sitting by herself in the living room looking ashen. I can hear Troy's voice coming out of the kitchen where he's speaking to someone on the phone, but I can't make out the words. I go sit next to Rosalie. "Would you like a brandy, dearest? It makes me feel better sometimes."

She leans into me and says, "No thanks. Just hold me. I'm so worried for you and Troy right now. Do you think that was just some random wacko, or was someone taking photos?" She certainly gathered the gist of things in a hurry, and it's typical that she's less worried about her own embarrassment for having been caught stark naked with two men. Her reputation is also on the line here.

"I found a flashbulb, so I'm afraid there may be pictures. If he took more than one, I don't know how we missed seeing the flashes."

"Ollie, we were all pretty occupied with our own dealings, and I don't know about you and Troy, but I certainly had my eyes closed a time or two. It all felt too good to keep them open."

"Yes, there's that. I just hope he was too far away and it was too dark for his camera to register much more than a dark blur. I can't imagine we'd be recognizable from that distance at night, even with a flash." A very grim-faced Troy heads our way. I fill him in on what I found outside, and he tells us, "Jack knows a PI, and he's sending him over right away. Can you deal with him, Ollie? The less he knows about us, the better because it's just one more person who could potentially spill the beans to the wrong person. I'll take Rosalie home, and maybe I'll be back about the same time as he gets here. Can you slip back into your majordomo role for one more night?"

"Absolutely. You know I can do that. I'll say I was here in the house, and you two were swimming when you heard the commotion by the wall. You wanted to get Rosalie home, and you'll be back right away."

"Alright. The guy's name is Ray Falco, and I told Jack to explain to him about the privacy gate." He takes Rosalie—not before I give her a sweet goodnight kiss—and she thanks me for a wonderful evening and for the ring.

She admires it on her hand. "We're married in spirit, for sure, Ollie."

It's so easy to fall for this woman.

Now I sit and wait for Ray Falco to show up. I'll have to go out and open the gate for him when he arrives. Grabbing a book, I try to read it to stay calm, but I'm reading the same page over and over and have no idea what it says.

It's the best and the worst night ever.

Chapter Twenty-Five

TROY

WHILE I DON'T WANT Rosalie to feel like I'm giving her the bum's rush, I want to get back to talk to the PI. After making sure she's doing alright, I give her a deep kiss I hope she understands is from my heart, walk her to her door, and ask, "Would you like to come back to the house and spend the day by the pool tomorrow? Suits on this time?"

"That sounds wonderful, Troy. Thank you."

It's going to be another scorcher, so we won't be good for much else, I'm afraid. The studio hasn't given us an assignment for where to show up. Of course, they could do that at the drop of a hat.

"I'll see you at eleven then. Good night darling."

I hurry back to the house to find a strange car parked in the driveway. It didn't take the PI long to get here. I rush inside to find Ollie leading the guy outside. They both have flashlights. Ray Falco has salt-and-pepper hair that is unfashionably long, and he wears it combed straight back from his face with no part. He's a handsome, no-nonsense kind of guy with a somewhat hooked nose and strong chin. His eyes are tawny brown and have an alert look about them. I have an instant respect for the man and feel as if he already knows a lot about me just because we're breathing the same air.

His handshake is firm, and he looks directly into my eyes. Jack Cramer said Ray Falco was the best, and I can see why he'd think so. I hope Ray can help us.

I follow them out to the scene of the...not a break-in exactly...more like the scene of the crime?

Ray kneels down, inspects the ground around the splintered crate, and looks at the discarded flashbulb and bloody wood. He pulls out a camera from the case he's carrying and takes photos of everything, then asks to be taken back in to see the pool area.

There, he paces off the distance from the shallow end of the pool to the wall where the intruder was and laughs quietly. He looks up and says, "Well, guys, I can say one thing about this man. He was certainly stupid. He might have gotten something on film at that distance, but without extra lighting, the quality of the image would be pretty bad. And from your description, it sounds like he shot the photo at the same time his rotten wood gave out, so the camera would have moved too much. He might have gotten lucky, but the odds are poor."

"What about during daylight from one of those trees

behind the wall toward the deep end of the pool?" Ollie asks, and I frown at him.

"What's that all about?"

Before Ray can answer, Ollie continues, "A couple of weeks ago, I was coming out here for my morning swim and saw a strange flash of light coming from the tree back there. I'd taken off my glasses to swim laps and couldn't see very well, so I immediately chalked it up to sunlight on the tree leaves or something. Then I forgot all about it until this happened tonight."

"Were you by yourself?" Ray asks.

"Yes."

"Okay, well, how about if I come back in the morning and we can take a look around the entire perimeter of your property? It sounds like you've possibly had a visitor more often than you realize. Have either of you been aware of anyone following you from place to place, or has anyone strange posed as a deliveryman or anything like that?"

"Not to my knowledge, but I'll be sure to keep an eye out for someone tailing me now," I tell him with a shudder.

"I've only seen one delivery guy recently," Ollie says. "But he was legit. We'd have to ask Zelda if she's had anything strange happen."

"Who's Zelda?"

"She's our live-in cook and estate manager," Ollie says and immediately looks sick to his stomach.

Ray squints his eyes at Ollie and says in a flat tone, "I thought *you* were the estate manager."

"I...uh..." Ollie looks at me. I give him a tiny nod, and he looks back at Ray. "We have a complete confidentiality agreement with you, right?"

"Yeah."

Ollie sighs. "I don't work here; Troy and I own this house together. We've been...um...*partners* for years, but now he's getting engaged to his co-star, and she replaced someone for the lead role in a major movie."

I speak up, "If you're looking for someone who's angry with us, you might want to look closely at my previous co-star, Gloria Dumont. The studio tried to paint her a rosy picture about replacing her by getting her a leading role in a movie at Paramount instead. Gloria saw it as a total insult, though. She's pretty vindictive and hates Rosalie for taking her part away."

"Well, well. The plot thickens. I'm glad you told me because this will certainly help my investigation." He looks around and says, "Will Zelda be here tomorrow?"

"She's here now but probably asleep. She'll definitely be here tomorrow," I tell him. "So will Rosalie. I had to take her home before Mrs. Vogel, her landlady, got huffy about her being out too late. The old bat would like to impose a curfew on her residents, even though she has no power to do so, but she can be so unpleasant, we just make sure Rosalie gets home by midnight when she can. We sometimes have studio functions that run late, so we've been trying her patience." Then I add, "I'm thankful to you for coming out so late to talk to us about this. I'm worried for Rosalie's safety as well as her reputation."

"Why are you worried about her reputation if you have

plans to marry? It makes sense she'd be spending time with you. And it's nobody's business if she spends the night here."

"True," I say. A cold chill runs down my spine as I add, "But it's less usual for a young woman to be spending romantic time with two men at once."

To his credit, Ray doesn't flinch. He just nods like he understands completely. "Yeah. So your possible photos are somewhat incriminating then. I get it. That ought to be a different kettle of fish, but in this town...you'd be surprised what I've seen. Anyway, I'll get out of your hair now and see you tomorrow. How's one o'clock?"

"Sounds good."

"You also might think about hiring some security for your property. I can give you some names tomorrow."

After Ray leaves, Ollie wraps me in his arms and says, "My emotions are all over the place. I feel so great about you and Rosalie on one hand, and on the other hand I'm scared to death that this entire relationship is going to blow up in our faces, and we'll lose everything."

"We'll do our best to make sure that doesn't happen," I tell him. "Come to bed and let me make you feel better now. And also, thank you again for the rings and for accepting Rosalie with open arms. You have no idea how happy you make me, Ollie. If this all gets out in the open and we manage to stay out of jail, I'd still be willing to give up my career to be with you and Rosalie. We can just move on to the making-babies part of our lives. Maybe we can move to a more secluded place away from prying eyes. Do you know of anywhere around Santa Barbara you'd like to live?"

Ollie kisses me and says, "We can think about that later. I love you so much, Troy. You're perfect in every way."

To show him my deep affection, I drop to my knees as soon as we close the bedroom door and suck him off like there's no tomorrow. Then he turns around and orders me to fuck his ass until I explode inside him. We're noisy and messy, and it's fantastic. The only thing missing is the taste of Rosalie. But that will come in due time—unless we're arrested for "crimes against nature" before then.

We absolutely have to be careful.

Chapter Twenty-Six

Rosalie

I HAD a hard time getting to sleep last night, despite being exhausted. I feel so violated, knowing some creep was taking photos of us—not only all three of us sharing an intimate moment together, but in the nude! It took so much courage for me to drop that robe in front of Troy and Ollie, and now this disaster comes to light. I tried to act strong for Troy because he seemed to feel terribly guilty about what happened—not that he had anything to do with our being invaded by a Peeping Tom.

As soon as he left, I burst into tears and hurried to my room before anyone caught me in that state and started asking questions. I know Daisy, for instance, would see my level of distress and immediately assume I'd broken up with Troy. I get the feeling she might not be too upset about that.

She's been acting more and more jealous the more time I spend with him after work. I try to be as nice to her as I've always been because she is my friend, but between her petty jealous remarks and Mrs. Vogel's growing antagonism, I can't wait to get married and move out. The sooner, the better.

I might also look into getting a room at the Hollywood Studio Club if we're not going to marry soon. I think I'll have more in common with those women. I bet John Packard would write me a recommendation. I hope I can afford it, though, because I don't want to cut back on the money I send home to my family now that they're getting used to my larger checks. I'll start making inquiries about it tomorrow. I don't think it's a good idea to call anyone from the boarding-house, just in case someone overhears me.

I spend the early morning doing some chores like laundry and cleaning my room. I'm a tidy person by nature, so there isn't much to keep me busy, and finally I sit down to wait for Troy to come get me, and I pull out the new book Ollie gave me. I skip all of the parts about multiple partners that don't match our configuration, and my gracious, what an education it is to read about two men and one woman. I had *no idea*. Now I wish I'd skipped the chores and spent all of my morning on this book. My head is full of mental images I can barely comprehend. It's almost time for Troy to arrive, so I slip the book under my pillow and head downstairs. Ollie's dust jacket idea was a good one, but I'm not sure it will be enough; if anyone were to ask me about *Rebecca* at this point, I don't think I'd be able to fake my way through a discussion without blushing.

Well…at least the ménage book took my mind off our intruder for a while.

Dressed in a light cotton sundress with my hair already up in a ponytail to combat the heat of the day, I am thrilled to see Troy arriving at the door the moment I hit the ground floor. There's no one else around to say goodbye to, so he takes my hand and whisks me off to his car. I feel like such a lucky woman each time I see his handsome face and think to myself about how he loves me and I love him.

As we drive toward the house, I ask, "Would you mind if I used your telephone when we get to your place, Troy?"

"Go right ahead. Is there a problem? You look a little worried."

"No, not really. I wanted to call the Hollywood Studio Club and see about moving there. They may not even have any openings, but I'm pretty sick of Mrs. Vogel and her bossiness as well as Daisy's snide remarks. Breakfast was a pretty unpleasant meal this morning between my landlady's dire warnings and Daisy being tiresome."

"I thought Daisy was your best friend."

"We were friendly, but I think the green-eyed monster has taken over her personality lately, and I'd like to be around more understanding women if it's possible. But this also depends on when you and I are supposed to get married. Can we ask for some details about that? I don't want to be tied to a lease somewhere that I'll have to pay even if I'll be moving out as soon as we get married."

"That all makes sense. Would you like to swing by the Studio Club right now and take a look? I bet they could fill you in on what they have available."

"Oh! Well, sure. That sounds like fun actually. Do you know where it is?"

"Yes."

A few minutes later, we're parked and walking into a lovely building with three impressive arches at its entrance. It's quite beautiful and makes my boardinghouse look like a flophouse in comparison—not that it is. It's always neat and clean, and the residents are respectable. Several pretty young women are coming and going, some on the arms of men. There is plenty of activity inside, and we can hear singing and chatter coming from various directions. Troy gets a lot of looks from the ladies who obviously recognize him from his movies, and there is plenty of whispered conversation while staring at him, but no one's willing to bother us. Asking around, we finally find an office where we can make inquiries about the place.

"Good morning," Troy says and flashes his dazzling smile at a lady sitting behind a desk with a nameplate saying she is Mrs. Markham. "I'm Troy Kingsley, and this is my co-star Rosalie Channing from Premier Works Studio. Rosalie is interested in seeing about getting a room here." It was nice of him to start with this because only women who work in the movie industry can live here.

Beaming at Troy, Mrs. Markham tells us, "Yes, I believe I've seen pictures of the two of you together, Mr. Kingsley. The rent is fifteen dollars a week for a private room and eight dollars for a shared one. The residents get breakfast and dinner and access to all of the facilities." The woman seems to prefer to address Troy rather than me, and this makes me a little miffed. It's not as if he's paying for me, nor would I expect or want him to. But my ears perk up when she says, "Normally, we have a long waiting list because we're so sought after. However, we have one vacancy right now that is going to be available only until January fifth. It's a long story, but one of our residents has paid through the end of the year to secure her place, but she has to be out of town for a while. You could take her room temporarily, but she is coming back, and we've promised her she won't lose her spot. As soon as she's back, you'll have to leave. It's one of the private rooms."

"Do I need recommendation letters?"

She simpers at Troy. "I assume Mr. Kingsley is willing to vouch for you."

"I am." He turns to me. "Have you paid your current place in advance?"

"I just pay her each Monday for the coming week, that's all. I could move out anytime actually, but, Troy, this is twice what I pay now for a private room."

He nods sagely and turns to Mrs. Markham asking, "May we see the room and some of the rest of the facility?"

"You may both tour anything on the ground floor, but no men are allowed upstairs. You would have to wait while Miss Channing visits the upper floor."

"Alright. I have to ask, ma'am. Miss Channing will only be here to sleep and eat breakfast and will often have her dinner elsewhere. The current renter of the room has paid you in full—even though she's not here to eat at all— wouldn't it be more equitable to charge Miss Channing the shared room fee? You're already double-dipping on the rent if you let her in."

I like his style.

And then Troy adds, "And a temporary stay is all Miss Channing needs, so this works out nicely for her as well. How many other young ladies in Hollywood do you think would jump at the chance to move in here and leave that quickly? Hmm? My guess is only those with no job and no other options. Miss Channing has a seven-year contract with Premier Works, so you know she's good for the money." He leans closer to Mrs. Markham, and I can practically hear her heart pounding as he murmurs, "Now, please don't repeat this because it's not public knowledge yet, but Miss Channing will be getting married soon—to me—so she won't need to stick around for very long. I can trust you, can't I?"

She'll probably tell everyone she knows before the day is over, but she blushes and says, "Of course. Your secret is safe with me. Congratulations."

Troy turns to me and says, "Darling, this decision is yours to make. You go up and take a look at the room while I wait down here, and then we have to get back to my house soon so we won't miss our appointment with Ray."

I have no idea who Ray is, but Troy has me thinking this is a great idea. So I look at Mrs. Markham and ask, "Can you rent me the room for eight dollars? If so, I'd like to see it and no doubt sign the lease or agreement or whatever you have."

Excited and softened up by Troy's juicy gossip, Mrs. Markham agrees, "Yes, under these conditions, I suppose eight would be fine."

Since you're double-dipping, it's a great investment, lady.

THE ROOM LOOKS GREAT, and the facilities are top notch. I love it here. Lots of friendly women smiled and said hello, both when I was upstairs on my own and downstairs with Troy. I think I'm going to love this experience.

I write them a check for four weeks.

"Can you drive me back here tonight after I pack my bags?"

"Absolutely. I love to see the beautiful, carefree smile on your face." Then he leans in close and says softly, "Just be careful about reading '*Rebecca*' around everyone. And be sure not to leave it anywhere." He winks at me and kisses my cheek. No one gasps at our public display of affection.

What a relief.

AFTER LUNCH and an exhaustive meeting with Ray Falco, who turns out to be the private detective Jack Cramer recommended, I'm ready for a cooling swim. We all head out and float around leisurely for a while, and I tell Ollie all about moving into the Hollywood Studio Club. It's then I realize I have yet to confront Mrs. Vogel about moving out. This confrontation sort of spoils my enjoyment for the rest of the day, so I ask Troy if he wouldn't mind taking me home so I can deal with it sooner rather than later.

"You don't need to wait around for me to pack, Troy. I can call a taxi to get me over to the Studio Club when I'm done."

"How long will it take you?"

"Oh, maybe twenty minutes, tops. I don't have much."

"Then I'll sit in the parlor and wait."

"You're so good to me, Troy. I'll hurry then."

"Darling, I'd do just about anything for you, especially after the way I've complicated your life."

"Well, maybe you have, but only in the best way."

As I expected, when I return downstairs with my belongings, Troy is being interrogated by a very crabby Mrs. Vogel, and Daisy is standing in the doorway with her mouth hanging open. She really needs to stop making that fish face, and she also needs to mind her own business. She jumps a little and turns toward me when I announce, "Pardon me. I'm ready to go now, Troy."

Daisy's face turns red, and she verbally attacks me with, "So! We're not good enough for you now that you're a big ol' movie star and all? Well, lah-di-dah, *Miss Channing*!" She says my name like it's a bad word. Instead of waiting for a response, she sweeps past me, bumping my shoulder hard, and stomps up the stairs with the grace of a Holstein.

Mrs. Vogel also turns to me and says in a grumpy voice, "You certainly need some lessons in manners, young lady. You didn't give me any warning you were planning to leave, and now I need to find another tenant right away."

"I apologize, Mrs. Vogel, but the rental agreement was only week-to-week, and I'm all paid up until Monday. You never said I was to give you advance notice that I'd be leaving. Here are your keys." I hand her the keys to the front door and my bedroom. "Thank you for everything."

She sniffs and frowns at me. "Furthermore, I think you're making a big mistake moving into that place with all those loose women over there. Your parents won't be pleased."

"My parents haven't asked or cared about what I do since I left Idaho, and the Hollywood Studio Club has a wonderful reputation and stricter rules than you have, so I think you're misinformed about the tenants." I look at Troy and ask, "Are you ready to go, darling?"

He stands and takes my suitcase as Mrs. Vogel directs her last shot at me. "If I were you, I'd never trust an actor. You mark my words: your life will be a shambles if you do this."

She's still carrying on as I close the front door behind us.

Chapter Twenty-Seven

I HATE this feeling of helplessness that fills me with guilt.

We had our meeting with Ray a couple of days ago, and although I'm sure it embarrassed the heck out of Rosalie, she handled herself with dignity befitting a queen. She was polite and forthright with her answers and didn't flinch when Ray asked her what she planned to do.

With her chin held high, she looked him straight in the eye and answered, "Today I'm moving into a better living situation until Troy and I can have our wedding, and then I'll move in here to be the wife of these two fine men."

I probably looked like a lovesick fool in front of Ray, but I felt awful that I hadn't been able to help Rosalie move into her new place or even go and see it. I have to keep my distance in public. I'm falling in love with this delightful woman, and it kills me more and more each day to be unable to declare and demonstrate my love for Rosalie and Troy out in the open. What is so wrong with love? Just because we don't fit the norm doesn't mean we're doing anything against society. We're not hurting anyone, corrupting anyone, or making spectacles of ourselves, and yet here we are—breaking the law by loving.

I have to think Ray was being a little nosy when he asked her that question. But maybe it's somehow pertinent to his investigation. He knew about our arrangement from Troy and me, but maybe he felt he needed to hear it from Rosalie as well.

When he and I walked the perimeter of the property outside the privacy wall, we found cigarette butts in the lawn and a spot under a tree where the tall grass was all smashed down as if something heavy had landed on it. We thought the snoop had fallen out of the tree, but that's just an educated guess. When we looked up, we also saw a large broken branch, so it was a darn good guess.

I've never seen our gardener smoke, and he's meticulous about making sure everything looks perfect, so the butts had to be from someone else. It made my skin crawl to think someone has been out here spying on us more than once. Also, they were Lucky Strikes, so that didn't give us much to go on: they're the most popular brand of all.

But now that I think about it, our gardener ought to have cleaned up the butts, and I'm surprised he hasn't. The grass looks way too long, and it's odd he would leave a dead branch in a tree like that. I wonder if he's even been here lately. I'll have to check with Zelda about that. I might give

Ray Falco a call too and let him know I find that a bit curious. I have no idea what the gardener's name is. I hope that doesn't mean I'm some kind of elitist. I just don't have any interaction with the man. I do keep tabs on the pool guy at least because I don't want to be swimming when he shows up to work.

I find Zelda in the kitchen and ask, "Do you know what's happened to our gardener? There were cigarette butts in the yard, a large dead branch, and the grass needs mowing. Doesn't he usually work a couple days a week?"

She gives me a blank look for a moment and then says, "I hadn't noticed, but now that you mention it, he hasn't been here for a while. I better give him a call."

"Thanks, Zelda. I'll be in my study if you find out anything."

Hours go by. Troy and Rosalie are working, but they'll both be here for dinner. Apparently, she's fitting right in and making new friends at the Hollywood Studio Club. Troy's presence there is a popular attraction for the other women, according to Rosalie. She finds humor in it and thankfully doesn't see any reason to be jealous. She also told me Troy seems oblivious to some of the more "energetic" flirting, and that gives her the giggles. Troy's such a gem. He's completely in love with us, and he's not going to be swayed by another pretty face.

I'm just wrapping up a scene in my current manuscript and almost ready to quit when Zelda politely raps on the open door. "Ollie? I spoke to the gardener finally."

"Oh? What did he say?"

"He says you called and fired him a couple of weeks ago."

"What? Of course I didn't do that."

"I know, and that's what I told him. He was terribly relieved because he always needs money for his family. He promised to come by tomorrow and spend extra time doing everything that's been building up. I said we'd pay him double for his extra time because I know he'll need the money. That's alright with you, isn't it?"

"Of course. What else did he say about this supposed call I made to him?"

"He just said Mr. Shackle*ford* was very insistent that we didn't need him anymore and that you planned to do the yard work from now on."

"Hah! Well, I think I'd know my own last name. Sounds to me like someone was making sure they'd never be seen by a worker on the property. I think I need to call Ray Falco and report this to him. I wonder who on earth did this."

Troy and Rosalie arrive home for dinner a bit earlier than usual, and they're all full of smiles and kisses for me. There's an air of jubilation surrounding them, so I ask, "What has you both so excited?"

Grinning ear to ear, Troy says, "We only have a couple more short days of shooting for *Forever Yours* now, so I've been given strict orders to propose to Rosalie this coming Saturday night. We have dinner reservations at that new place, Romanoff's, and we'll be seated in one of the most select booths in front where we have the most visibility. The studio has hired a photographer to capture the event, and their writers are working on a proposal script. I was told I could veto anything that sounded wrong to me, but that I wasn't supposed to suddenly go off-script because of nerves or something. They don't even realize this is something we all want tremendously. I'm so happy!"

"This is great news! Congratulations, you two. And Romanoff's—wow. I've heard nothing but rave reviews about that place. You're lucky you have the studio making arrangements for you because I understand people wait for hours to get a booth, and reservations are booked way in advance. I wonder how much Premier Works had to spend to get it done. You know they must have greased someone's palm in a big way, even though the restaurant will get great publicity from this."

"I'm so excited," Rosalie says, looking radiant. "They also said they're planning an early December release and want us to get married on Christmas Eve. Doesn't that sound beautiful? A Christmas wedding. The only possible downside I see is that there are a few other high-budget films that will have premieres in December—like *Gone with the Wind*—so I hope ours doesn't get lost in the shuffle."

"I wouldn't worry about that, dearest. Troy is a huge box-office draw, and when people see the two of you together, they'll go crazy for you both. You're both far better looking than Clark Gable and Vivien Leigh."

Rosalie gets the giggles and adds, "I'm the lucky one. I've heard Clark Gable has the worst breath ever because he smokes like a chimney and has false teeth!" She gives a shudder and looks lovingly at Troy. "Kissing you is always wonderful."

Troy smiles and adds, "The release of *Gone with the Wind* is another reason they're making such a splash about our romance and upcoming nuptials. Everyone loves a great Hollywood love story, so we'll be a major topic of discussion, and everyone will want to see our movie." He looks into Rosalie's eyes. "The public always buys into these manufactured love affairs, but just wait until they see a *real* one unfold."

I don't have it in me to burst their happy bubble by discussing the issue with the gardener, so I decide to wait to tell Troy about it in the morning. Instead, we uncork a lovely bottle of champagne and sit down to another one of Zelda's amazing dinners. Apparently, she likes dining alone just fine because once again we're seated in the dining room with candles and flowers decorating the table that is only set for three. I know Zelda has her own friends—including a special girlfriend somewhere—and she doesn't like to be in the middle of us when we're in a particularly romantic mood, so it's fine.

Our dinner is filled with laughter, and for some reason we all find things to toast about throughout the meal. Troy starts by wiggling his eyebrows with a salute to "sexy threesomes," and that makes Rosalie blush.

Then I raise my glass to "custom-made, extra-large beds" which makes her splutter and blush even more deeply. I explain to her, "Troy and I are both so tall, commercial mattresses aren't very comfortable for us together. So we had this one made when we bought this house. It was worth every penny."

"Ollie still likes to snuggle, so it's really only important when the weather's hot like it was during the Santa Ana," Troy explains.

Rosalie has a faraway look like she's trying to come up with something, then her expression brightens, and she says, "Cheers to cooler nights! I look forward to lots of snuggling when I move in here."

After a few more toasts, I ask, "Do you know where you're going to have your wedding ceremony?"

"Oh, yes!" Rosalie answers with stars in her eyes. "The Packards have volunteered their house for the ceremony and reception. I guess it's an amazing mansion in Bel-Air. I didn't realize that John Packard is one of the richest men in the movie business. And his wife Sophie is so down-to-earth. She's just lovely, and she's going to be my matron of honor, can you believe it? She's going to help me decide on a wedding gown. The studio says they'll make it, but we'll come up with a design I like first. She has impeccable taste, so I feel as though I'll be in good hands."

"My darling, Rosalie, I would be proud to marry you in a potato sack, but I'm sure you will be the most exquisite bride this whole town of beautiful women has ever seen," Troy says, and he takes her hand. Then he turns to me and asks, "Ollie, will you be my best man? I don't want you to be uncomfortable for any reason, but I want you by my side. I need to have you close so that when Rosalie and I make our vows to each other, we will also be saying them to you in our hearts."

"Do you think I can carry it off without giving away my feelings?"

"Everyone looks emotional and gets carried away at

weddings, so if you tear up or look at one or the other of us lovingly, people will just think you're happy for us. You can even dance with Rosalie, and no one will think anything of it. Just keep the kissing to a minimum until later." He gives me a wink. "And if anyone asks about our connection, we'll just say you've been my best friend for years."

"If you think I can pull it off, I'll be honored to do it." I did not see this coming. Best man in Troy's wedding.

Wow.

Chapter Twenty-Eight

Troy

It's still relatively early, and even though the Studio Club has a strict midnight curfew that can only be broken with permission for such things as nighttime film shooting and related work issues, I think we have lots of time to enjoy ourselves in a private way. As of yesterday, we have two guards who patrol the perimeter of the property, so the likelihood of another Peeping Tom episode is remote. The guards have been told nothing about us. They were hired to discourage and report anyone who is snooping around or trying to sneak in. It's comforting to know they're out there, but, even with them, I won't chance nude swimming anymore with my two lovers. We are only meant for each other's eyes. It sure was fun, though, until we were so rudely interrupted.

"So, my darlings, is anyone besides me craving a return to the carnal delights we started the other night before we were invaded? I'm sure we could have the same kind of fun in a more private setting."

"Well, yes, I think I'd love to have you show me your fancy custom-made bed," Rosalie says with a flirty smile. She sips her champagne.

"Too much talking. Let's go," Ollie says. He stands abruptly and grabs Rosalie's hand, propelling her out of her chair and leading her to the stairs.

"I'll just go thank Zelda for the meal and let her know we're finished. See you upstairs," I say, trying not to laugh at their eagerness. I'm ecstatic at how well Ollie and Rosalie suit one another.

When I get to the bedroom, my two perfect partners are sitting on the edge of the bed and kissing. Ollie's fumbling for a zipper on the back of Rosalie's dress. I clear my throat and say, trying not to laugh, "Front buttons, Ollie. It's a blouse."

He pulls back and, always the eloquent one, says, "Uh, oh, yeah, right." Rosalie starts to undo her own buttons with a shy smile, but he gently pushes her hands away and says, "No, please let me."

"Zelda says to come back down and enjoy her fresh apple torte once we're done with our shenanigans. She made a special caramel sauce for it that has brandy in it or something. She seemed a little miffed we took off so fast after dinner," I tell them.

Ollie looks at me with flat eyes and asks, "Can you please not talk about Zelda right now? I'm sure whatever she made was lovely, but you're in danger of killing the mood here."

"Sorry. Just reporting what she said." I know he's not really mad; he's teasing.

I sit down on the other side of Rosalie and remove her blouse now that the buttons have been freed. I also undo her brassiere and slide it off her shoulders. Ollie's attention goes straight to Rosalie's perfect breasts, and I fear his eyes will pop out. I reach around and cup one breast while Ollie takes the other.

Rosalie makes a happy little whimper and shivers. I'm positive she's not cold as she says, "Come on, you two. I don't intend to be the only one who's getting naked here."

Making a split-second decision, I stand and pull Ollie to his feet. We practically tear each other's clothes off as we kiss frantically. Ollie's kisses are deep and ferocious where Rosalie's are gentler and sweet. She has a wild streak too, however. I've seen glimpses, and I intend to cultivate it.

In less than a minute, Ollie and I are completely naked, and we both turn to Rosalie. Her face is almost level with our dicks, and she shocks the hell out of me—and probably Ollie as well—when she grabs us both by the hip and drags us toward her. She buries her face into my body, rubbing against my lower belly and even lower than that. Her hand reaches around and strokes my buttock, and I see she's doing the same to Ollie. She shifts her face over to him, like she's feeling him with her face and smelling the essence of his body. I know that scent so well. He is all masculine and a little spicy where I tend to have more of a musky aroma, according to him. We're both fully hard, and

Rosalie likes that. I am beginning to wonder what she's going to do when—"Oh God, Rosalie!"—she grabs my erection and takes the tip into her mouth. I sure did *not* expect that.

"Is this the right way?" she pulls back and asks. "I don't want to do anything wrong here."

Ollie laughs and tells her, "There is no wrong way. I'm sure Troy loves what you're doing. It's pretty obvious because his eyes are rolling back in his head."

I laugh at him and say, "I wouldn't go that far, but Rosalie, dear, you're doing great." I'm so hard, I ache for relief.

She gives me a few licks with her clever little tongue, making me jump, and then she creates a lot of suction with her mouth. She pops off and immediately shifts to Ollie, saying, "Your turn," and winks up at him. I step behind Ollie and rub myself in his butt crack because I know he gets aroused by that. He groans as his hips jut forward involuntarily, and this action shoves more of his dick into Rosalie's mouth. She sputters a little and looks up at him with wide eyes, then she smiles around her mouthful and goes to town on him. Our Rosalie. She's so perfect. I know this is her first time, but she's stroking and sucking like she's done this hundreds of times before. She has a gifted mouth and great instincts. I'm so proud of her, it makes me happy, and that makes me rub harder with my dick on Ollie's ass. I want to be inside one of these people so badly. I'm sure Ollie does too.

Just when I think Ollie is going to come in her mouth, Rosalie pulls off and asks, "Which one of you handsome men is going to take my cherry? Hmm? Because I'm anxious to see what that's like."

"Are you one hundred percent sure you're ready, sweetheart?" I have to ask, even though just the thought of quitting right now might actually kill me.

"As long as you can manage not to get me knocked up, I'm as ready as I'll ever be."

Ollie's chest is heaving, and he's almost ready to explode, but he looks at me with the tenderest expression and says, "You need to do the honors, my heart. You found Rosalie first, and she'll be married to you."

With a similar look of absolute adoration, Rosalie regards Ollie and says, "You are in no way in second place for me, Ollie. I love you, you know. I love you both equally."

"As it should be," he tells her. "And I love you too, but the fact is he will be your true husband…"

"Only in the eyes of California law, but not in my heart. You know I love Troy deeply and without reservation, but I want you to know you are the same to me."

I'm not about to argue when Ollie has given me the go-ahead to be Rosalie's first, and she clearly doesn't mind who does it. My heart melts even more for these two, but I have to let go for a moment and reach for a couple of things in the bedside drawer. While I'm doing that, Ollie removes the rest of Rosalie's clothing and positions her on her back on the bed.

Ollie takes this initiative to make certain Rosalie is ready for me. He covers her body with his and kisses her passionately. Then he makes his way down her body, kissing and fondling her lovely breasts, lavishing both with tweaks and nips. She's squirming and moaning in the most delicious way by the time he lowers his face to her lady parts and spreads her legs. "Look, Troy. Our beautiful Rosalie is all pink and slippery for you, but I think I can get her even wetter."

"Please do," I say with a chuckle. God, how I want a taste of that.

Rosalie gasps when Ollie slips a finger inside her and rubs in and out. "She's so tight!" he exclaims. "Rosalie, you're perfect." He continues to slide in and out and lowers his mouth over her stiff little nub and gives it a lick. She nearly comes apart as she jerks off the bed for a second.

"Oh, wow," she pants. "Do that some more!"

"Come on, Troy. Join me in here."

I scoot next to Ollie and caress one of her breasts, intending to slip a finger inside Rosalie alongside Ollie. But I'm afraid we might hurt her if she's that tight, so I pull back and grab for the tube of K-Y jelly I got from the drawer. I squeeze a little on my finger and reach past Ollie's hand, saying, "Raise your knees, Rosalie."

As soon as she's spread open with her knees up, I slip my hand beneath Ollie's and find her backdoor opening. Ever so gently, I push the tip of my finger inside and fall in love with the surprised noise Rosalie makes—that starts as a gasp and ends as a purr. Encouraged, I press in deeper and begin to slide in and out in the same rhythm as Ollie. It's crowded in here, but he manages to continue tonguing her clitoris until she's writhing and her legs begin to shake. It's then I see him suck her nub into his mouth, presumably continuing to lave her with his clever tongue. And that does it. With the most glorious sound ever, Rosalie comes, shaking and nearly convulsing with spasms of bliss.

"Ohmygod, ohmygod, ohmygod," she chants with a strangled voice. It's the most beautiful sight ever and more exquisite than the finest symphony.

"She's definitely ready for you now," Ollie tells me, supremely satisfied with himself. He spies the K-Y jelly and gets a mischievous look on his face. I wink at him, and he breaks into a huge smile.

Still breathing a little heavily, Rosalie looks at us with curiosity. She watches with full attention as I slip the condom on. "Does that really work?" she asks.

"If I'm careful to pull out at the right time, and it doesn't break," I explain. I reach for the jelly and slather some on myself. "You can only get this stuff by prescription, but it works much better than Vaseline because the petroleum jelly breaks down latex. K-Y is water-based, so it's become quite popular. Anyway, it will make things more comfortable for you for your first time."

She frowns slightly and asks, "So you keep it around for deflowering virgins?"

I shake my head, but Ollie bursts out laughing. "No, my love," he tells her. "Troy and I use it all the time for our various activities. Men don't self-lubricate as well as women."

"I guess I have a lot to learn."

"Remember to tell us to stop if anything is too much for you. We'll be as careful as possible." I desperately don't want to hurt this precious woman, but I'm dying to get on with things. I lean down and begin kissing and caressing until she relaxes beneath me. I reach down and stroke her again until she's making happy noises once more, and I take that as my cue. I line up my dick with her entrance and rub her with the head for a moment. I feel her relax even more, so I begin to push inside. She seems to be doing well, but she suddenly gasps.

"Are you alright?"

"Yes! I think that feels amazing. But it feels bigger than it looks, and it looks huge."

"Keep going, Troy. Take her all the way," Ollie says in a strangled voice, but it's then I feel him plaster himself to me and begin to play with my hole. He's using plenty of the K-Y to get me ready for him.

This is going to be incredible. One finger inside me becomes two, and then just as I'm ready to make the final push into Rosalie, he rams his cock into me. This forces me into Rosalie, and she and I let out matching "Oh!" sounds.

"Are you doing alright?" I ask her in a shaky voice.

"Never better," she proclaims. "This is...I...God, I love this!" Her eyes are gaping at the sight we must make.

Ollie has a firm grip on my hips, but he relaxes a moment to let Rosalie and me catch our breaths and adapt to our invasions. Her eyes are wide, but she smiles and asks, "Is Ollie inside of you while you're inside of me?"

I nod and try to gather my wits about me, but Rosalie says in an almost reverent tone, "How perfect. You're both making love to me this way at the same time."

Finally, when I'm able to talk coherently, I say, "You'll soon discover that Ollie loves to have his way." I think it's time to start moving, but Ollie is about a second ahead of me. His hands on my hips begin to push and pull me in and out of Rosalie as he does the same inside of me. I am beside myself as I choke out, "Ollie, you have absolutely no idea how beyond perfect this is. Rosalie is tight and warm and feels divine squeezing me, and you're hitting me in the perfect spot. How do people manage with just one lover? This is heaven on earth." I kiss Rosalie and say softly, "Thank you, my perfect love, for allowing both of us to cherish you this way."

Ollie speeds up our in-and-out action and begins to shout incoherently—possibly about how good everything feels and how much he loves us both—but it's honestly hard to decipher.

I continue to stroke Rosalie and feel her tensing as she begins to pant, and then I see the moment when another orgasm overtakes her. Her eyes close and her muscles grip me in a pulsing vise. It's transcendental. Seconds later, Ollie gives a mighty thrust and pours his jizz into my backside, and I'm absolutely done for. My orgasm hits me like a tornado, and I try to muffle my shout of rapture, but I simply cannot hold back. Nothing, I mean *nothing* in the world can compare to this!

We all land in a heap as Ollie slides out of me, but I grab the end of the condom and hold it tightly as I pull out of Rosalie. "I'll be right back," I tell my perfect lovers as I leave to get rid of the prophylactic. I quickly wash my hands and clean up before heading back to them with a warm washcloth. I tend to Rosalie as Ollie slips into the bathroom to clean himself up. He hurries back, and we all end up in a snuggly pile of arms, legs, spent bodies, and lots of kisses and murmured words of love.

"Will it always be like this?" Rosalie asks sleepily.

"Do you have any pain?" Ollie asks. "I hope I wasn't too rough."

"No. It stung a little for a moment, and then it felt wonderful. I still feel all warm and fuzzy throughout my entire body. Don't you?"

"Women's orgasms are much better than men's," he announces sagely. "Physically, it's more fleeting for men. But I feel love for both of you in my head and my heart."

"Ollie researches everything," I tell her with a sleepy chuckle. "What time is it, Ollie? Can you see the clock?"

He grabs his glasses and says, "Ten forty-five. There's plenty of time before our lovely lady needs to be back. Let's just relax a bit, and then we can get dressed and have a bite of Zelda's creation so she doesn't get her feelings hurt."

In a soft, low voice, Rosalie tells us, "This was a lot more wonderful than I ever expected. I've had girlfriends tell me for years how terrible their first time was. They must not have been in love, or they had lousy boyfriends or something. You two are perfect." She yawns and closes her eyes. I promise myself not to let her sleep too long. The last thing we need is for her to get in trouble at the Studio Club. I'd love to make love again, but I don't want her to be too sore. We'll have to pace ourselves.

Chapter Twenty-Nine

Rosalie

I feel different inside. Do I feel like a true woman at last? Maybe. Can people tell? I wonder if I'm exuding something in the way I talk and move that lets everyone know I've experienced something beautiful and profound that other people take for granted. After all, everyone has sex.

Maybe it's my imagination. No one's treating me any differently, that is except for Troy, who is more loving than ever. I haven't seen Ollie yet. Troy tells me he's been floating around the house on a cloud like a lovesick fool though, and Troy says this with pride—not like he's teasing Ollie.

It amazed me just how much pleasure those men were able to give me. It was fabulous, actually. But beyond my own physical rapture, the joy I felt when I saw them pleasuring each other was incredible. I've never imagined anything so sexy in my life. I simply can't understand how or why two men together seems to threaten people so much and how it could possibly be illegal. But since it is, I'm going to have to be extra careful about what I say regarding home life in the future. I love them so much—I cannot be their downfall.

We've had a couple of very busy days and evenings at the studio, even though I was led to believe things would be winding down, and our days would be short...Hah! We had a couple of retakes to do for some technical reason, but we finally finished shooting *Forever Yours* late this afternoon. The ending is terribly romantic, and John Packard had to tell Troy to tone it down a couple of times while we were doing the final kissing scene. He finally said, "Okay, you two. I can see there isn't much reasoning with you. We'll let it go for now; however, if the censors get itchy about your obvious passion, we'll have to reshoot it. And that's going to be a pain in the ass because we're setting up the scenery for the next movie in the morning." He's probably just kidding around because he's a total perfectionist when it comes to his directing, and I doubt he's actually worried about the censors. If he didn't like the way we did things, my limited experience has shown that he would never "let it go for now."

When he finally utters the words "That's a wrap!" I feel an overwhelming sense of accomplishment and relief. But it only lasts a moment. About five minutes later, Packard calls us over, takes some papers from one of his assistants, and hands them to us. "Good job, both of you. Here's the next script," he announces. "See you for rehearsals at nine tomorrow." He lumbers away with three flunkies following in his wake.

I blink at Troy and ask, "Is this normal?"

"Is what normal?"

"Do they always just hand you a script and expect you to start up the next day? Like this? No time off?"

Troy barks out a laugh and says, "Yes, quite normal. A studio is run like a production line. Time is money, so they want to work every possible minute. The film is now in post-production, and we'll be expected to start acting on the next project. I have never even been consulted as to whether I'd like to play the character they give me in the next movie. Welcome to being a contract actor.

"We'll also have to do more public appearances to promote the movie, so get ready to be tired. And be prepared to answer the same questions over and over about working with John Packard and me. The nosier people will ask personal questions you don't need to answer. Just smile at them, look beautiful, and deflect. Anyway, let's take a look at the script together, shall we?" He opens the packet and grins. "Hey, look at this! It's a Western called *Wild Horses*. Did you tell them you could ride?"

"Oh, um, I may have mentioned it to someone—I forget who. But I remember saying my family has horses back in Idaho. They're an easy way to get around in the orchard, and they pull wagons too. What about you?"

"Yep. Like any typical farm kid, I rode our horses. We also have a very glamorous mule who we call Bunny because she has the largest ears anyone has ever seen on a mule, and she loves carrots. She has quite the personality."

"Aww! This is going to be fun, Troy. I hope we get to ride a lot. Horses though—not mules."

"Don't count on it. The studios hate it when their stars get injured, so if we get to ride at all, we'll probably do close-ups and that sort of thing. But any galloping around the countryside will be done by stunt doubles."

"Hmm. How sad. Oh well, I'm always happy to be around horses no matter what."

"Atta girl. At least we'll probably be acting outdoors a little instead of always in the studio. Anyway, we're done for the day unless you have something I don't know about. We can head home." He lowers his voice to a whisper. "I think Ollie is pining for you."

"Oh, I have a fitting for the dress I'm to wear for our special dinner this Saturday, and I need to meet with Sophie Packard and the designers about wedding gown ideas. Sophie also wants me to see their house so I can get an idea of what the ceremony will be like. She's invited me to have dinner there, and she said she would get me back to the Studio Club after we're done. John has some meeting to attend, so it's just going to be the two of us."

Troy feigns a crestfallen frown. "You're planning a wedding and choosing a gown, and I haven't even popped the question yet." He sighs dramatically.

"I'll just have to trust that you'll still want to marry me in two days." I lean closer and whisper in his ear, "*And after the other night, I doubt you'll have a change of heart.*" I kiss him sweetly on the cheek and start to pull away, but he grabs me around the waist and plants a big one on my lips. Somewhere in the distance we can hear a sharp smart-alecky whistle. I feel his lips curling into a smile, but he keeps kissing me anyway.

We're still kissing when the distinct clatter of high heels approaches at a steady pace. "Oh, you two are adorable," Sophie says. "Can you give her up for one evening, Troy?"

"Well, I don't know. Last night, she had to stay at the Studio Club for dinner because of some function there. I think it's a female conspiracy to keep us apart."

"Oh, you'll manage, big boy. After you get married, she'll be all yours."

Troy and I exchange smiles. That's not exactly so, but who's complaining? We'll both be sharing each other, and we wouldn't have it any other way.

"Alright, darling. Have fun with Sophie and be sure to get home on time. I'll pick you up in the morning as usual. I guess I'll find something to entertain myself with tonight. Maybe a book."

I laugh and whisper, "I bet you will. Study hard." I turn to Sophie and say audibly, "Shall we go over to the design department now?"

Troy gives me one last kiss, and we're off.

The dress for Saturday is incredibly beautiful. It's a champagne-colored satin gown designed by André Durst that drapes deliciously over my curves in an alluring manner and makes me feel terribly feminine. There isn't much to worry about fit-wise except for the hem, so that only takes a quick measurement.

Then we look at some fashion bridal magazines together and discuss designers with a young woman who works for the studio. After neither of us acts terribly interested in anything, she says, "If you don't mind me saying, I think a lot of these gowns are overdone. You're so beautiful, Miss Channing, you don't want to be overshadowed by a dress that is just too much of everything. I see you in something more elegant and simpler than these." She takes a sketchpad and begins to draw.

"I couldn't agree more," Sophie says with authority. "We don't need ruffles and poofs for you. Maybe some lovely beadwork, but a simple silhouette."

"Yes, I can see that." We stand spellbound as my dream gown gradually appears on the sketchpad. "Oh, this is perfect! What do you think, Sophie?"

"I think our young lady here has an incredible future as a designer. This is genius."

"I'll have some fabric and bead samples for you to look at in a couple of days then. Thank you both for the compliments. I love my job so much, and I'm thrilled the studio has tasked me with this project." She laughs, "Also, it will get me out of sewing calico dresses for *Wild Horses*. Anybody can do that."

"Will I be wearing those?"

"I assume so," she says. "We were directed to order several bolts of the stuff."

"Oh well, I'm sure the movie will be fun anyway, even if I have to wear a feed sack." I need to look over the script tonight before I go to bed. "Maybe I'll actually be a dance hall girl and get to dress in lace and feathers."

"Eh, maybe," Sophie says with a shrug. "Are you ready to go?"

"Yes." I turn to the designer and say, "I can't thank you enough for your input...?"

"Irene."

"Thank you, Irene. I'm looking forward to working with you. You really are quite a talent."

Sophie leads me out of the studio and into the parking lot. She heads for the most amazing car in the lot, and when I gasp at its beauty, she says, "It's a BMW 327 Sport Cabriolet. Packie gave it to me for my birthday. It's cute, isn't it?"

"Is it ever! I love that you call him Packie instead of John."

She shrugs. "He's never looked like a John to me. My icky former employer was named John, and I had to get over that before even accepting a date with Packie."

"He sure has excellent taste in birthday presents. This is gorgeous," I say as she pulls open the rag top. It's a light blue with midnight blue trim convertible and has elegant, curving lines and shiny chrome details. The fancy grill on the front is spectacular and fun. The interior is all black leather that looks soft and, well...simply perfect. I want to stroke my hand over its glistening surface, but I don't want to look like too much of a rube—even though in truth I probably am compared to Sophie.

As if she can read my mind, Sophie says, "Being married to Packie is a far cry from working the five-and-dime counter in Festus, Missouri." She beams at me. "I *had* to get out of there."

So much for thinking she had some fancy upbringing. She's a lot like me. "I completely understand. I picked cherries and waitressed in Emmet, Idaho my whole life. Coming to California was like reaching the promised land in lots of ways." Then I add, "So you're a small-town girl too. I knew there was a reason I liked you so much."

We climb into the car, and she takes off. The breeze feels wonderful, and the sun is setting, so the sky is vivid pinkish orange and purple. I smile so much, my cheeks are aching pleasantly. I'm feeling positively giddy until Sophie breaks the mood.

"Don't turn around and look, but someone has been following us since we left the studio gate."

Chapter Thirty

ROSALIE

"CAN YOU SEE WHO'S DRIVING?"

"Unfortunately, I can't. There are two people in the car, but that's all I can tell. Their headlights went on as soon as we got going, and that makes it too hard to see into the car with just my mirror."

"What should we do?"

Sophie grips the steering wheel grimly. "I'm going to continue on home. We have a guard at our gate, similar to the studio's, so no one can come in at will. But if they speed by us, try your best to see the license plate, can you?"

"I can do that." Troy and Ollie are going to be so upset when they hear this. I'll need to call them when I get to the Packards' house so they can alert Ray Falco. I can't figure out why anyone would want to follow us.

Sure enough, after winding through neighborhood streets with them on our tail, we reach the Packard estate. Sophie stops and waits for an employee to open the gate for her. As we wait, the driver pauses a moment and then zooms past us. I can see their yellow California plate with black numbers and call out, "G9 21 79," hoping that together we can remember it long enough to write it down.

Sophie pulls through the gate and immediately asks the guard for a pencil and paper. She writes down the plate number and thanks him profusely. Then we make our way up to the house. Frankly, it's more of a castle than a house. My jaw drops.

"Some place, huh? Packie had it built a few years ago, and it's supposed to look like a French château. I think it's a bit much, but he gets a kick out of it. We have ten acres and heaven knows how many rooms to take care of, so the staff is pretty big. I think you'll like the formal ballroom for your reception. We can do the wedding ceremony in the grand salon in front of the fireplace. It'll be gorgeous all done up for Christmas." She looks at me seriously and adds, "Look, sweetie, if I'm ever overstepping, just say so. I don't want to take over your plans. I just know how hard Packie pushes his actors, so I know you have a lot on your plate. If I can help, I'm here for you, but I don't want you to think I'm being bossy. I also want to say that I love to plan parties, and I'm darn good at it." She gives me a saucy wink as we step out of the car in front of the house. She hands her key to a uniformed man and says, "Thanks, Otto. I won't need the car again tonight, but Miss Channing will need a ride back to the Studio Club after we have dinner. We'll say nine o'clock."

"Yes, Mrs. Packard," he says. "I'll be ready with the Rolls."

She nods to him then looks my way. "I want to give you enough time to read through that script you have clutched in your hands, so I'm not going to keep you here too late," Sophie tells me as a servant opens the front door for us. "Come on, through here. We'll have a cocktail, and then I can show you what I'm talking about with the rooms. I hope you're famished; our cook is amazing."

As we cross the threshold into an impressive foyer, I say, "Sophie, I need to tell you that I don't see you as being bossy or overstepping in any way. I'm used to simple country church weddings and barn dances. Putting on the type of event that's expected from the Hollywood crowd is clearly beyond my expertise, so I can't thank you enough. I just hope you don't think I'm leaning on you too much."

"Nonsense. I love it. And you're the sweetest, most genuine woman I've met since I got here, so we need to stick together. There are a lot of pretenders and users in this town, and it's refreshing to meet someone who can be a real friend. Now, what do you like to drink?"

We get comfortable for a while in a relatively small sitting room overlooking the grounds behind the house. This room is cheerful and colorful and less formal than the rest of the house I saw as we made our way here. Sophie explains that it's her favorite room, and she had full say in how it was appointed. "It's where I come to read and relax," she says. A servant brings us our cocktails and a plate of delicious little canapés, some of which are covered with caviar and hard-boiled eggs. I've never tried caviar before, and I must say I could develop quite a taste for the salty burst of flavor.

"We'll want to discuss the menu for your dinner at some point, but I think we'll need to sit down with the cook and her staff. There's plenty of time for that part. I want to make sure the setting is going to work for you first. Ready?" I know she's only giving me the illusion that I have a choice because the studio is actually covering this for their own benefit. But since she's so nice, and this place is like a dream come true, I'm not about to argue for a simple wedding on the beach or anything like that. The idea makes me laugh inside.

I'm all kinds of relaxed after a refreshing gin and tonic, but suddenly I remember my need to call Troy. "Sophie, would you mind horribly if I called Troy for a moment? I need to tell him about the driver who was tailing us. He'll want to know right away."

"Sure, you can use the office phone. Over here."

She leads me to a gorgeous, paneled room with a desk the size of a yacht, and then leaves me and closes the door, saying, "I'll be back in a couple of minutes." I look around for a moment and see two Oscars sitting on the credenza behind the desk. I smile at that as I sit down to make my call.

"Hello, Zelda, this is Rosalie. May I please speak to Troy?"

"He's having his dinner."

"Yes, I understand, but this is something he'll want to hear. I'll only take a moment of his time." Good grief. She's such a gatekeeper for these men, even from *me*.

She grumbles something and drops the phone with a clatter. *At least she's a great cook*, I tell myself.

Soon Troy is on the line. "What's up, darling, is everything alright?"

"Well, I'm not exactly sure. I just wanted you to know

that someone followed us all the way here from the studio and then sped off when we got to the guard at the front gate."

"Did you notice anything about the driver or the car?"

"It was a black Ford, which isn't all that unusual. We couldn't see the driver or passenger clearly, but there were definitely two people in the car. Can you let Ray Falco know? I have a very strange feeling about this."

"Yes, I'll call him right away." He takes down the license plate number. "How are you getting home later? Do you need me to come get you?"

"No, I'm fine. Sophie has a driver for me, and you need to relax and get some sleep. I'll see you in the morning. I love you and—" I'm about to say, "and Ollie," but Sophie takes that moment to knock politely and open the door again, so I'm sure glad I closed my mouth. That's just the kind of slip of the tongue I'm afraid I'll make sometime. "Good night, Troy."

"Thanks for letting me know. We love you too. Be careful. Good night."

Sophie's assurance that the grand salon will look fabulous decorated for Christmas is absolutely right. It's a large room with an extremely tall ceiling. The fireplace is an enormous marble affair with a splendid painting over the mantle. I don't know a lot about art, but even I can recognize the signature, which reads *Renoir*.

Sophie explains to me where they always put a fifteen-to-twenty-foot Christmas tree. "We like lots of candles and greenery, and there will also be poinsettias all over the room to give it a festive look."

"Um, what's a poinsettia?" I have to ask.

"Oh, sorry. They're a lovely, rather large, deep red flower with dark green leaves. The Ecke family has been doing a huge marketing scheme to get them into households over the holidays because they bloom well in December and are so vivid and Christmassy. The Eckes' business actually originated here in Hollywood, but now they have a huge flower ranch down in Encinitas—a town in north San Diego county. They've sent us hundreds of plants because of the Christmas parties we throw, and they also work with many prominent people in the entertainment business to get the word out where it's visible. They're terribly clever, but the fact is their flowers are wonderful. They send potted plants rather than cut flowers, so they last a long time. We can order more from them this year for the ballroom too. You'll see how great they'll look."

She points out where we can have a string ensemble for the ceremony music and arrange the seats for the guests, and she assures me they have plenty of chairs in storage. I guess their entertaining must be pretty extravagant.

"Let's see the ballroom now, alright? Are you feeling comfortable with all of this?"

"Oh, um, yes. It's all so...amazing. It's so far from what I'm used to, but it seems wonderful."

"Great. I'd much rather invite people to a wedding than just a regular Christmas party. This is going to be so much fun, Rosalie!"

As we head in to see the ballroom, I come to a frozen stop. Who on earth has a ballroom like this in their *house*? It's incredible. There is an enormous crystal chandelier hanging in the middle of the room and crystal and gold sconces around the room on the walls. The dance floor is all gorgeous gleaming parquet, and another incredible fireplace adorns the wall on the far end of the space. The ceiling is a detailed fresco of dancers in beautiful costumes. I've never even conceived of anything like this.

"We'll have a swing orchestra here since that's all the rage now," she points out. "We'll have to see who's available to provide the music right away. And the dinner tables will fit around the perimeter of the dance floor." She goes on and on talking about linens and place settings, servers and table decorations. "We'll have a festive red and green theme with lots of sparkly gold accents and plenty of candles," she assures me.

I'm getting positively dizzy.

"Oh dear. I'm overdoing it for you, aren't I?" she says finally and gently takes my arm. "I'm sorry. This is all stuff I've become accustomed to, and I forget how it affected me at first. I understand how you're feeling. It's all a bit much, isn't it?"

I smile, but it's wobbly, and I try not to embarrass myself with the tears that threaten to overflow. "Sophie, I never in a million years thought I'd see anything like this in real life. I just don't know what I could possibly do to repay you for this."

"Repay me? Are you kidding? I'd pay you to let me do it!" She laughs, and it's such a beautiful, carefree sound, my nervousness vanishes. I have to believe her. What an incredible friend to have found.

"So how long will your family be staying in town?"

"Excuse me?" My family?

"Oh, sorry, I'm making assumptions. Won't they be coming to the wedding?"

My joy deflates a bit. "They don't know about it yet. I mean, no one outside of the studio actually does know. But I ought to write to them before they read about it in the newspaper. I just wanted it to be official, but I seriously doubt they would leave their business. I might offer to send them train tickets, but I'm almost positive they won't come."

"Oh! I'm so sorry."

"Yes, well, they won't answer any of my letters. They do cash my checks though, so I know they're still alive."

"Um. Wow. That's pretty harsh."

I shrug. "They were furious with me when I left, and I can't change their minds apparently, even by showing them that my life is terrific and I'm making a success of myself. They know I'm seeing someone special, and they also know I'm not waitressing anymore because I'm the star in a major movie. But they haven't responded to any of that news."

"Sounds like jealousy to me."

"Maybe. I'm pretty sure they would have seen at least one or two pictures of me with Troy in the newspaper by now. And I'm positive they already knew who Troy was because of his movies. But whatever their reasons are, whether it's jealousy or they're still angry with me for leaving, I have to say, it stings." This is the first time I've acknowledged the pain aloud, and once more, I find myself blinking back tears.

Sophie's expression is understanding. She reaches over and pats me on the shoulder briefly before taking a breath and surveying the room once more. "Well, it's their loss, I promise you that. This is going to be a spectacular party."

I laugh despite myself, grateful yet again for my new friend.

Sophie smiles. "Let's go have dinner. I'm starving. We won't worry about them right now."

Dinner is incredible, so I'm looking forward to discussing what we can have for the wedding reception. However, it's getting late, and I do need to read the script for tomorrow's first rehearsal. Wedding plans can wait for another day. I thank Sophie profusely for having me over and showing me what I can expect. She gives me a big, warm hug and sends me off with Otto in their Rolls Royce. The car is so plush and quiet, I find myself nodding off, only to awaken when Otto stops and opens my door saying, "Miss Channing, we've reached your destination." He reaches in to help me out of the car and then walks me politely to the door.

A couple of other women arrive about the same time as we do, and I see them eyeing the Rolls and the uniformed chauffeur. One of them winks at me, but they don't say anything until we're inside and the front door is closed.

"Wow, honey, you really know how to travel!" one of them says with a laugh. "What was that all about?"

"Oh, um, that was Otto. He's John and Sophie Packard's chauffeur. I just had dinner with Sophie."

"Impressive," her friend says. "How do you know them?"

"I'm working on a couple of movies with John Packard, and Sophie is my good friend."

"Wow!" They both say, and one of them asks, "What are you doing in the movies?"

"Oh, I'm...um...starring alongside Troy Kingsley."

"So you're the lucky duck who replaced Gloria Dumont. We heard about that."

"Yes," I extend my hand. "I'm Rosalie Channing."

They both introduce themselves, and we talk for a while. They seem nice, but I have to excuse myself. "I'm starting a new film tomorrow, and I need to read through the script tonight. We'll chat some more another time, I hope." I can feel their eyes on me as I walk up the stairs, and as soon as I turn the corner, I hear excited whispers from below. I have to bite back a smile. They seem almost starstruck, and it's a strange new feeling.

I guess it is pretty impressive. It's amazing how normal all of this is beginning to feel to me, though.

It's a far cry from picking cherries in Emmet, Idaho.

Chapter Thirty-One

THE READ-THROUGH GOES WELL, and I'm happy to have Rosalie at my side. I've always enjoyed acting, but with Rosalie, my enthusiasm for it has reached a whole new level. After lunch, we rehearse a couple of scenes, and then—surprise of all surprises—we're told we can take the rest of the day off. I know just what I want to do and give Rosalie a look I'm certain she understands. We're going to be doing several outdoor scenes, just as I predicted, so I say, "I think Rosalie and I will head back to my place and work on our tans by the pool. We'll need to look like people who are outdoors a lot."

"Right, and the makeup artists aren't ever any help with that," Packard answers with a wink. "Go relax for the day and have a great time at dinner tomorrow night at Romanoff's. Your reservations are at eight, and Jimmy will be there with his camera. They'll have chilled champagne for you as soon as you have a seat." Then he smiles and chuckles, "Don't forget your lines, Loverboy. Or the ring." He turns to Rosalie and says sternly, "Be sure you say yes, or it'll be all of our jobs that go up in smoke." He's trying not to grin.

Winking back at him, she says in a saucy voice, "As if I'd refuse this wonderful man."

WE GET to my place in record time, and I nearly drag Rosalie into the house where I call out for Ollie. Completely surprised, he appears shirtless, barefoot, and in his dry swimsuit from sitting out on the patio by the pool.

"You're home early!" he beams at us. "I hauled my typewriter outside to do some writing because the day is so gorgeous, but it's a great pleasure to see you both." He makes a beeline to Rosalie and traps her in his arms, bestowing a searing kiss on her. He's clearly spent a lot of time outside today because his tan is a lovely bronze and his hair looks as if he's been gilded with sunny highlights. He's so beautiful with Rosalie in his arms. If I don't get out of my clothes—mostly my pants—soon, I'm going to feel pretty strangled. Together, they look like a golden treasure that is all for me. I sidle up to them and horn in on the kiss. As I lock lips with Ollie, Rosalie steps back and gives a satisfied sigh. She's staring at us with great interest.

I pull back a little and ask softly, "Rosalie, are you ready to make love to Ollie today?"

"Absolutely, but I want to see the two of you together too."

I feel a small shiver run through Ollie, and his face has an expression like a kid being presented with an ice cream sundae. He pulls Rosalie back into his embrace where she rubs her face into his chest with a happy little hum.

"Mmm, you smell like sunshine, Ollie." She moves back and looks up at him. "I've read some more of the ménage book, and I have some ideas of what looks particularly interesting to me, but I think the two of you men know more about this than I do just because to me any kind of sex is new. I might need a bit of instruction."

I can't help relishing the thrill that goes though me hearing Rosalie's ready acceptance of three-way sex. She's so ladylike and proper in everything, but she's obviously excited about something I imagine would have most women shying away. I think having her get to know us both without introducing physical relations right away was a very good thing. All she really knows is sex with two men. Weren't we clever? I have to laugh inside at that a bit. And I can't help asking, "What sounded particularly interesting to you, dearest?"

"Hmm. I loved what you two did last time, where you were making love to me, and Ollie was inside of you. That was exciting. I'd love to see you in the middle the same way, Ollie, and I'd also like to have the experience of being in the middle of the two of you."

Ollie's grin is enormous, and his eyes light up. "I think, darling, that Troy and I should stick to your first idea for now —not that I'm trying to be selfish because it's extremely pleasurable for a man to experience that configuration. It's just that you might want to work up to that position for yourself."

"I agree," I tell them. "Let's not rush things. There are many things we can do."

"Well, then let's get busy, guys. I want to experience more of...everything."

A few moments later, we're all in the bedroom and we're naked. I feel like the luckiest man alive to have my two golden lovers, and I barely know what to do first. Everywhere I look, something is alluring, and I can't wait to stroke it, hump it, or kiss it. Ollie is obviously eager to be inside Rosalie, so I grab a condom for him as well as the tube of K-Y jelly and set them on the bed. Per Rosalie's request, I drop to my knees in front of Ollie and take him into my mouth. He lets out a huge sigh of approval, and I see out of the corner of my eye that Rosalie is squeezing her legs together and plucking at her nipples. God, I love an eager woman. She is so *not* shy.

"You're both so perfect," she breathes, her eyes glittering with arousal. "Is that how you like it, Ollie? Do you like Troy sucking so hard on you? What about his teeth? Do they ever hurt or get in the way?"

Ollie's having a somewhat difficult time articulating right now, but he croaks out, "I like uh...teeth. It enhances. He's careful."

I finally decide to slow down on Ollie, as much as I'm enjoying this. I want Rosalie to be able to have him make love to her, so I quit sucking and hand him the condom. "Sweetheart," I say to Rosalie, "why don't you get on the bed on your hands and knees and position yourself so you can see in the mirror over there? I think you're going to like this position, and you'll also be able to watch."

She does just as I asked as Ollie quickly pulls on the condom. He climbs onto the bed behind her and grabs her by the hips. He positions his face in her bottom and begins to lick her lady bits. One of his hands locates her clitoris and manipulates it while he's licking and savoring her folds. Rosalie is shocked, judging by her loud gasp and wide eyes, but soon she's panting and saying, "I never imagined *this*. It feels so *naughty*. But...oh my God. Don't stop!"

I slather my fingers with lube and begin to prep Ollie's hole for my exploration. He's alternately squeezing and relaxing around my finger, so I can tell he's enjoying the attention. I prod him carefully with one, then two, and finally three fingers, and his moans become increasingly louder. The moment I slide in the third finger, Rosalie shakes with a hard orgasm. Her eyes are squeezed shut, so I tell her, "Open your eyes, darling. I'm going to enter Ollie now, and he's going to enter you. You don't want to miss seeing it."

She looks satisfied and sleepy, but that changes immediately when Ollie slides himself into her doggie-style. "Oh, yessss," she exclaims. "I like that sooo much."

His hand keeps a steady pressure on her clit, and she's still twitching with aftershocks.

"Keep watching," I order, and I slide into Ollie's relaxed hole. Ahh, he feels so good as he clenches around me. I meet eyes with Rosalie in the mirror, noting her wide-eyed look of curious delight.

Ollie tosses his head back when I hit his prostate and cries, "Yes, oh yes!"

Rosalie's expression changes as we find a rhythm. With my efforts behind him, Ollie is shoving in and out of her at a swift pace.

"I love this so much!" she cries, and then adds, "And I love you both so much. Oh, I feel it happening *again*. Ollieeee!"

Ollie looks positively out of control. His hips are being pounded into Rosalie, and as I pull back, I pull him with me. "It feels incredible, Troy. You're hitting me just right at the same time Rosalie has a death grip on me. It's like the best feeling in the world. Oh...ohh!" he grinds out a growl and shivers with an orgasm like I've never seen from him before, and believe me, we've had some great sex together over the years. I'm so happy, I let my own orgasm barrel through me as I hang on tight to Ollie's hips. I growl out a sound like I've also never heard from myself before.

This kind of sex is ridiculous. It's so amazing it ought to be illegal.

Oh. Wait. It is.

Fuck.

Chapter Thirty-Two

Ollie

I quickly grab the end of the condom and start to pull out of Rosalie. But the thought runs unbidden through my brain that a pregnancy would actually be an exciting and happy occurrence. I know Troy, and especially Rosalie, would need to be on board with the idea, but I certainly would welcome it. Well...it's something we can talk about one of these days. We need to get them married first, I suppose.

No sooner do I think this than I see the devastation of the condom as I extract it from Rosalie's body. Either this one was faulty or our combined efforts were too much for it, and we sprung a leak.

"Uh oh." I can't believe this.

"What's the matter, Ollie?" Troy asks.

"Look." I show him my deflating member with semen dripping from the end of the rubber.

"Uh oh."

"What's going on, guys?" Rosalie asks in a small voice.

"We've had a malfunction," I tell her. "Maybe you need to douche or something."

Rosalie gasps and says, "I don't have anything for that. Now what?"

"Is this your fertile time?" Troy asks. He frankly doesn't sound any more worried than I am. In fact, his pupils are wide, and he's looking more aroused than ever at the thought of my seed inside her. I wonder if it is the inborn masculine need to procreate that has awakened in us.

"I honestly have no idea. How would I know?"

"You need to figure out the last time you menstruated and count the days from that." Then, in true farm-raised fashion, he goes into a lengthy discourse about it, making Rosalie look worried until he decides that from her answers, she's probably in good shape to not be knocked up this time. We all go get cleaned up and pull on swimsuits. We decide a swim sounds good, then a cocktail, and whatever Zelda has prepared for our supper. The idea of an unwanted pregnancy is forgotten.

I hope Zelda made something out of beef. I'm ready for some meat.

Chapter Thirty-Three

Rosalie

I HOPED I would be able to spend some time with the guys at their house on Saturday, but it turns out the studio has booked a pre-engagement manicure and pedicure. Afterward, I'm in need of a nap after a bite of lunch. I have an extra-long trip to the hairdresser, and then a makeup artist comes to the Studio Club to get me ready. My dress is delivered, and it's time to go. Glamour is serious business.

Romanoff's has a strict dress code, and since this is a special night for Troy and me, we're in formal attire. Troy looks extra handsome in his tux. "I had it specially made for tonight," he tells me when I compliment his dapper looks.

"What's Ollie up to tonight?" I have to ask. I'm so sad he has to stay home by himself.

"Oh, he's alright. Don't worry about Ollie. He's still

walking on air about yesterday," Troy tells me with a wicked grin. He's a little extra-gleeful, but I chock it up to the coming performance.

We arrive at Romanoff's right on the dot of eight o'clock, and we're led to our booth by the owner of the restaurant himself. Troy asks me to sit on the side of the booth that faces the bar area. I don't think anything of this until Troy sits next to me and shifts his eyes toward the bar. I follow his gaze and catch sight of a familiar, beautiful man with blond hair, striking eyes, and a bright smile.

"*He's here!*" I whisper. I had to catch myself and not blurt out anything someone might hear. I'm so delighted to see Ollie, also dressed in a tux and looking debonaire. He barely raises his glass to me and winks, then schools his features into a bland look. He can't give anything away, but I can imagine that it's both exciting and frustrating for him to be here. Then I notice something else. The bar is fairly crowded with people waiting for booths, and several women are giving Ollie the eye. He's ignoring all of them.

Troy takes my hand and says in a low voice, "He's been planning this for weeks as a surprise. He came early so he'd get just the right seat to watch us. Don't you just love him? He's the best man I've ever known."

"I do love him, and I love you so much, Troy. How did I get to be so blessed?"

Before Troy can respond, a waiter appears at our table with a bucket of ice and a bottle of champagne. With much flourish, we are presented with crystal coupes of bubbly. I see a man enter the door with a fancy camera in his hand,

and I know it's time. Troy raises his coupe to me and says, "To our love."

I grin from ear to ear, gently clink glasses with him, and take a sip. It's delicious. Troy slides out of the booth on his side and stands before me in the aisle. Is it just me, or is there really a hush that goes through the entire restaurant as Troy gracefully drops to one knee? I steal a glance at Ollie and see that he's staring at us, spellbound. He's also drinking champagne.

Troy reaches into his pocket and pulls out a robin's-egg blue box and says in a clear voice that was trained for the stage, "My dearest Rosalie, I love you more than words can express. When you came into my life, I felt complete for the very first time. Your kindness and loving nature melted my heart, and I knew right away that I wanted to be *forever yours*." He winks at me, and I immediately realize why John Packard didn't want Troy to forget his lines. He wanted to advertise his movie in a subliminal way with a captive audience. It makes me want to giggle, but I keep a straight face. As the cameraman starts taking photos, Troy goes on to say, "You are not only the most beautiful woman I've ever seen, you have the most beautiful heart. I would like more than anything to live out all my days with you at my side as my wife. Rosalie Channing, will you marry me?" He opens the box to present me with a gorgeous, sparkling Tiffany-style solitaire in platinum. It's incredibly beautiful, but not anything compared to the love I see reflected in Troy's eyes. The studio might think this is all a setup, but I know how much we love one another.

All I can say to him is, "Yes, Troy. I'll marry you." And I watch him slip the gorgeous ring onto my finger.

The room erupts in applause and cheers. Troy stands and pulls me to my feet. We kiss as the flashbulb goes off again. People all around the restaurant raise their glasses to us. Everyone loves a love story.

Don't they?

Chapter Thirty-Four

Ollie

I can see how happy Troy and Rosalie are. They aren't acting; it's completely real. I join everyone and raise my glass in salute to them, smiling broadly as people are cheering and chattering about the happy couple.

But then I hear some slurred grumbling from the guy sitting next to me at the bar. I wasn't even aware the seat was filled; I was so engrossed in watching my two lovers. But it's overly crowded in the bar because it's Saturday night, and this is the hottest place in all of Los Angeles. I had to get here early so I'd have the best seat to watch Troy propose. Of course the seat by me is occupied.

As I turn to the man, I hear, "What a pitiful shpectacle. He's only marrying that little floozy because people know he's a homo, and he wants to look reshpectable. Makes me sick. Perverts like that need to be locked away where they belong." He's obviously pretty liquored up, but his bloodshot eyes are shooting daggers at the happy couple.

I shiver, and my stomach threatens to purge my champagne right in this guy's face. "What did you say?" I ask in a voice I'm trying desperately to control. I hope it's noisy enough in here that he can't detect that it's shaking.

The guy has a sneer on his face that makes him look like he smells dog shit on his own shoe, and he snarls, "You know the actress Gloria Dumont? Well she's a good...uh...*friend* of mine. That ashhole Troy Kingsley got her fired from *Forever Yours* so he could get this younger broad hired in her place. Gloria shmelled a rat and hired a guy to watch him, and the guy says he has some pretty incrim...incrimible...incriminatin' photos. Serves that pansy Kingsley right, if you ask me. Gloria's a great actresh and deserved the part." Then he burps and says, "She's also a great lay." He laughs like it's the funniest thing in the world and sways on his barstool.

Burning rage sears through me, and I clench my fists, telling myself I cannot pound them into this idiot's face, no matter how much I want to. I'm suddenly afraid I'm about to vomit, so I signal to get the bartender's attention, then toss some money on the bar. I beat it out of there like my ass is on fire and puke beneath the tree out front. I need to get home and call Ray Falco as soon as possible, but my vision is clouded with anger and fear. I hope no one saw me get sick; it would hardly say much for the cuisine of the finest restaurant in town—even though I was only there to drink. I quickly make my way down the street and climb into my car.

My nerves are shot. I'm driving too fast, and I realize that on some level, but my need to get to a phone clouds my judgment. Traffic thins the closer I get to home, but something runs across the road right in front of me, and I slam on the brakes and swerve to miss it. My car jumps the curb, and I smack into a tree.

Pain.

Everything goes black.

Chapter Thirty-Five

TROY

I'm confused when the maître d' brings a telephone over to our table just as we're finishing dessert. With an apologetic expression, he announces, "I'm terribly sorry to disturb you, Mr. Kingsley, but the lady on the phone insists this is an emergency." He plugs the phone into a jack next to the booth.

Lady? Emergency? I immediately think of my family back home in Ohio, but they don't know I'm here. I look questioningly over at the bar and realize I was so caught up with Rosalie, I hadn't noticed that Ollie left. I pick up the receiver and say, "Hello?"

It's Zelda, and she sounds awful. "Troy! It's Ollie. The police showed up and said he was taken to Cedars of Lebanon after crashing his car a couple of blocks from home.

The cops said he was in and out of consciousness when they found him, but he was muttering something like, 'Call Ray,' until the ambulance took him. It sounds pretty awful, so you need to get over there right away!"

On hearing her words, my vision goes black for a moment, and my heart pounds so hard my chest hurts. I have to haul in a deep breath before I can respond. "Yes, thanks, Zelda. We're on our way." I'm sure glad we have a driver because I know I'd probably crash too, I'm so scared.

The absolute horror of possibly losing Ollie slices through me like a Samurai katana.

"Sweetheart, we need to go *now*. Ollie's in the hospital, and there's more. Let's get out of here." I signal the waiter and pay the check, grab Rosalie's hand, and we practically run for the door. A few people try to stop us to offer their congratulations, but I can barely muster up a smile for them. Rosalie is slightly more poised and thanks them graciously but tells them we have an emergency to attend to. I tug her out the door, hoping she won't trip in her high heels. We don't need another injury.

When we get to the limo, I make sure the privacy screen is closed before I tell Rosalie what happened. Her eyes are filled with tears as I explain what I know—although it's not much. I'm worried to death about Ollie, but apparently, I also need to get in touch with Ray Falco.

I just wish I knew why.

As soon as we arrive at the hospital, I make sure Ollie has a private room. I'd have him moved if he didn't. When we finally find him, my poor Ollie looks like a mess. His face is bandaged, and he has two swollen black eyes. The nurse tells us he broke his nose by smacking the steering wheel when he crashed. "He was given anesthesia when the doctor set his nose, and he's on pain medication now, so he might not be able to talk for a while. He's lucky he still has all of his teeth. You two might want to go home and get some sleep and come back in the morning."

"We are not leaving him," I tell her with conviction. "But, Rosalie, you better go call the Studio Club and explain there was an emergency, and you won't be back until sometime tomorrow. If they kick you out for missing curfew, you can just move in with me and hang anyone who objects. I'm done following everybody's damn rules."

The nurse ignores my fervor and says, "Visiting hours end in twenty minutes anyway, sir—"

"And, as I said, we're *not* leaving. We're not bothering anyone, and Ollie will want us here when he wakes up."

She glares at me a moment. She's probably used to actors and studio people who throw their weight around by now since this is where they all come when they need hospitalization. The ambulance driver probably could tell where to take Ollie by the neighborhood where he crashed and his expensive tuxedo. She turns to Rosalie and orders, "Come with me, and I'll show you where you can make your call." Spinning around, she marches out.

As soon as the two women are out of the room, I grab

Ollie's hand and lean over him. "Are you awake? Can you hear me, Ollie?"

His eyelids flutter, and he moans unhappily. "Yeah."

"I'm so sorry you're hurt, Ollie. How are you feeling?"

"Like I was hit by a train. Everything hurts."

"You'll get better soon." I stroke his hand because it's a part of him that doesn't look too bruised. "Can you tell me why I need to call Ray Falco? The police said you were muttering about it when they found you."

He sighs and winces like breathing is painful. "Asshole at the bar. Said Gloria hired someone to watch. There are photos. Call Ray. People know. Gloria's talking."

My blood runs cold with this news, but I ask, "How did you crash your car?"

"Going too fast cuz I was so mad. And scared. Almost hit a raccoon, I think. Swerved but caught a tree instead. Sleepy now."

"Oh, Ollie." I want to hug him, but I'm sure anywhere I touch him would hurt.

He doesn't say anything else, so I continue to hold his hand until Rosalie comes back.

"Darling, I need to make a call to Ray. Is the phone in a private area?"

"Yes. There's a private booth if you go out to the right and around the corner. You'll see it." She takes my vacated chair and holds Ollie's hand in my stead. "Did you talk to him?"

"Yes, a little until he went back to sleep. He's going to be alright. I'll be back in a moment; I need to make the call as soon as possible."

Ray's phone rings several times before he picks up, and he sounds sleepy when he grunts, "Falco."

"Ray, it's Troy Kingsley. I'm at the hospital with Ollie, who was in a car crash and got pretty banged up. He was muttering something about calling you when the police found him. I was able to determine from our conversation that the photographer was hired by Gloria Dumont, and she probably also had something to do with the car that followed Rosalie and Sophie the other night. Can you look into it? Some guy at the bar where Ollie was having a drink was shooting his mouth off about us and thinks he knows something about me and Ollie. Gloria must have blabbed to him after seeing some photos. I don't know the particulars of their conversation, but Ollie was extremely upset. Oh, and it doesn't sound as if there was another car involved in his accident. He was avoiding a raccoon."

"I still doubt any photos that jagoff took could be incriminating, Troy. So maybe the photographer just told her what he saw, claims to have photos, and she wants to sound important. That's the good news. The bad news is she wants to sound important and has started talking. So we need to make her shut her yap."

"Well, um...yes, but..."

"Don't worry. I'm not going to shoot the bitch. I'll come up with a plan."

"That's a relief. No one needs to die or go to jail forever; they just need to shut up."

"On it." And with that, he hangs up on me. I feel marginally better, but I don't even know why.

This night sure started out better than it ended up.

Chapter Thirty-Six

Pain. Everywhere. Was I run over by a bus? Where are my glasses?

The sun is up, judging by the light filtering through the window shade. I blink, but it doesn't do much to clear my foggy vision. I can see, however, that I'm flanked on either side by Troy and Rosalie.

Troy is slumped over my bed and sound asleep in a chair. Boy, is he going to be stiff when he wakes up. Rosalie has climbed up and laid down on the bed next to me. She's snuggled up beside me, and her delicate hand is resting on my stomach in what looks like a protective pose. I feel warm inside knowing they stayed with me. I feel their love for me as they sleep, and I'm sure they're exhausted, but I also know I desperately need the bathroom.

I'm just about to wake Troy to help me get up when the door opens and a cheery young doctor marches in, saying, "Ah, good morning, Mr. Shackleton. I'm Dr. Bixby. I see you have company." He chuckles. "How are you feeling this morning? Are you ready to get out of here and go home?"

His voice wakes Troy, who sits up with a grimace—not surprisingly—and Rosalie, who stirs more slowly, but looks mildly confused. She too sits up, and her lovely gown is wrinkled. She's barefoot, and her makeup is smudged. She still looks magnificent to me, though. She shakes the cobwebs out of her head and retreats from the bed to the adjoining restroom. I hear the water running. Now I really, really need to go.

"Good morning, Doctor. I don't remember meeting you," I say, but my voice is raspy, and I don't recognize it.

"That's understandable. You were in and out of it when you arrived. You had a nasty collision involving your steering wheel and your face. The good news is we examined and x-rayed everything that looked bruised, like your ribs, and nothing besides your nose was broken. You were a very lucky man. I set your nose, and when the bruises and swelling go down, you should be back to normal. It's gonna take a few weeks, but you'll be fine. I'm sure you have plenty of aches and pains right now, however."

Rosalie returns looking fresh-faced with no makeup and gives me a smile that I wish I could see more clearly.

"Any questions?" the doc asks.

"Yeah, where are my glasses?"

"All of your personal effects are in the closet, but everything is pretty bloody from the massive nosebleed you had. I don't remember seeing glasses, so it's possible they flew off when you cracked into that tree, and they're still in the car. You might want to check there. The police can let you know if the car has been towed somewhere."

I nod, but the motion makes my face hurt. "Thanks. I need the bathroom," I croak.

"Fine, I'll get you a prescription for pain pills and write up your discharge papers. You can be out of here after your breakfast. You'll need to have a follow-up appointment, so I'll include my office number."

I'm already sitting up with Troy's help as the doctor exits the room. And when I shuffle back out of the bathroom, I have a tray of breakfast waiting next to the bed. It doesn't look anything like Zelda's meals, but I'm surprisingly hungry, so I sit back on the bed and pick up a piece of toast. Ugh. It hurts to chew. I set it down and reach for a bowl of oatmeal. That tastes disgusting, so I try the coffee. Yuck. "Troy, can you help me get dressed so we can go home?"

By the time the painstaking process of getting my clothes on is complete, a pretty, young nurse comes flouncing into the room. She stops dead when she sees Troy. "Wow," she gasps. "You're even better looking in person!" Then she blushes crimson and looks down. "Sorry, Mr. Kingsley. We're instructed to be polite to our celebrities here, but you're the most famous one I've seen since I started to work here."

"It's fine, I don't mind being called handsome," he says with a laugh. He looks a lot more relieved than what I remember from last night, but there is still an air of tension about him. My memories of last night are foggy, so we need to talk.

The nurse hands me a small sack that must contain my pain pills and a stack of papers. While I sign a few things, Troy heads out to call for a driver.

After what seems like an eternity, the nurse finally maneuvers me out the front door in a wheelchair as I'm flanked by Troy and Rosalie. It's still early enough that there aren't a lot of people milling around, but a couple of photographers are standing outside the entrance. When they see Troy and Rosalie, the flashbulbs immediately begin to go off. I have to shield my eyes, and I notice Rosalie is holding her small beaded handbag in front of her face. What vultures they are, preying on people who are stressed. They start bellowing stupid questions at Troy about why he and his fiancée are coming out of the hospital in the morning in formal wear. And who is this man with him in the wheelchair? Did Troy hit him in the face? He ignores every one of them. Apparently, the news of his engagement is well known already.

The attention from the photographers is annoying, but—not to sound full of myself—if they also knew who I am, it would probably be ten times worse. Thank heaven for pen names.

The driver is fortunately already here, so we can escape immediately.

On the way home, we drop Rosalie off at the Studio Club so she can change into more comfortable clothes. Troy plans to get me situated and tells her, "I'll be back in a couple of hours to get you."

My poor beat-up car is right where I left it, slightly wrapped around a tree. I'm lucky it wasn't a huge tree, and

I'd used my brakes before hitting it. I still shudder when I see the damage. Troy asks the driver to stop for a moment, and he gets out to inspect the interior of the car. He fishes around a while and then straightens up and heads back to us. My glasses and set of keys are clasped in his hand. Thank heaven for small mercies.

Now all I want is a bath, clean clothes, some of Zelda's cooking, and a nap.

Troy insists on helping me get cleaned up, and Zelda presents us both with fresh-squeezed orange juice, fluffy, cheesy omelets, coffee that tastes like coffee, and fresh cinnamon Danishes. She may be grumpy sometimes, but Zelda is a jewel.

I head back to bed after eating and wake up hours later sandwiched between Troy and Rosalie.

I love this.

It occurs to me that I'll have to let my people know I might miss the deadline for my next book by a few days, but I can't get too worried about that today. I drift back to sleep.

Chapter Thirty-Seven

Troy

Several days go by, and I try to spend as much time at home as possible, but work makes that nearly impossible. Since the marketing for *Forever Yours* is on the upswing, Rosalie and I are making the rounds of parties and interviews. After working all day, we have to dress up in designer clothes almost every night and make happy statements about how wonderful it is to work together on such a fabulous project, and how excited we are to be getting married. That's not hard, because Rosalie is a dream to work with, and I do love her with all my heart. But answering the same inane questions over and over is trying. We'd both rather be home with Ollie.

Ollie is recovering just fine. I'm over the initial panic from the possibility of losing him, but I'm still not sure what's going on with Gloria Dumont. I haven't heard any nasty gossip, and if it were floating around, I'm sure I would have by now. I also have no idea who bent Ollie's ear at Romanoff's regarding how I'm a law-breaking pervert bound for hell.

I'm more and more in awe of Rosalie. She's far better than I at smiling when someone asks rude or probing questions. She deflects when I bristle, and she's a consummate lady about it. One such memorable question was, "I understand you used to serve meals at the Beverly Hills Hotel. You must have been propositioned a lot by important men since you're so pretty. How many times did that make you hopeful you'd get a better job?"

Her answer was, "Thank you for calling me pretty, but no one propositioned me, and I like to think that was because of the way I handled myself. Like all the ladies who work there, I stayed professional and did my job. I was very happy there and felt lucky to work in such a nice establishment as the Beverly Hills Hotel."

Another one that got my hackles up in the worst way was delivered by a drunk studio exec at a party. "We hear you were raised on a cherry farm, Miss Channing." That made him guffaw for some reason. "Has Troy plucked your cherry yet?"

Rosalie looked past the man and answered vaguely, "I'm sorry, I must have misheard you because that sounded like a rude remark, and I'm sure your mother raised you better than that. I see someone I need to speak with, if you'll excuse me." She strode away and I followed her while suppressing the urge to sock him right in the kisser. She can make her own jokes about her cherry, but no one else can.

It's late on Friday when we get summoned to Harry Walken's office. I can't help but wonder why the president of Premier Works needs to talk to us now. We barely have enough time to get dressed for the event we're attending tonight. As we head over that way, Rosalie asks, "Are we being sent to the principal's office? You weren't cutting class again, were you, Troy?"

She's making light of this, but I know she's worried. I'm shaking in my boots. And I do mean boots. We're shooting a Western after all. Rosalie and I are going to be able to do some riding next week, I'm told. Yippee ki-yay!

We make our way through the spiderweb of hallways until we get to Walken's office, and he's all smiles as he says, "Come in, come in! Have a seat. Whiskey? Scotch? What would you like?"

"Oh, thank you, but just water for me," Rosalie replies politely. "We have a function to go to pretty soon, and I need to keep my head so I don't say anything silly."

"I'd love a beer, if you have any," I answer. "I might just let Rosalie do all the talking tonight." I wink so Harry knows I'm kidding. I hope we can get through what he wants to say quickly. And I hope it's nothing bad, but after what Ollie heard, I'm not so sure.

Walken hands Rosalie a glass of water and me a chilled beer, and I take a long swallow before he sits down again and says, "I'll cut right to the chase since it appears you have plans tonight." That sounds ominous, but he's all smiles. "I've been hearing a lot of chatter about the two of you." I take another gulp of beer, and Rosalie's hand has a white-knuckled grasp on her glass. "I know we've thrown you two into some tricky situations and requested that you marry when you barely knew one another. We've had a few situations in the past where the actor and actress have caused a bit of a stink about that or turned out to already be legally married to someone else—unbeknownst to us." He takes a sip of whiskey, and I wonder anew what he's going to say. "I just wanted to thank you for the terrific work you've been doing together and say that I'm grateful to know that you're making your situation easy on everyone around you by keeping a positive attitude. Packard was delighted with the work you did together on *Forever Yours*, and the clips I've seen make me agree with him thoroughly. So with that in mind, I'd like to let you know that we've planned an extra-special honeymoon trip for you, and we've decided to let you take a full week instead of a long weekend. We're booking you a bridal suite on Waikiki Beach in Hawaii. I haven't been yet myself, but I understand it's idyllic and relaxing. I think you've both earned it. Now get out of here and get ready to dazzle some more people with how great looking you both are and show them a little of what to expect in the movie. You've become wonderful advertising for us."

I can see the tension draining out of Rosalie as she smiles and thanks Walken for the thoughtful trip plans. "I've never been anywhere besides Idaho and California, so a trip to Hawaii sounds fantastic. Thank you so much, Mr. Walken."

"Call me Harry. Now go have a great night."

I shake his hand and thank him before we head out to get dressed.

The leftover stress makes me jittery as I tie my tie several times before I can get it right. I hope I can calm down pretty soon. A night with Rosalie ought to help, but I wish we could both be home with Ollie instead.

THE EVENT IS TERRIBLY CROWDED, stuffy, full of overly perfumed, cigarette-smoking women and cigar-smoking men, and I feel my lungs tightening up. I haven't had a problem with my asthma in years, but I know enough about the signs to know I need to get out of this room *now*. I grab Rosalie's arm and say, "Darling, I can't breathe. We need to leave."

"What's going on, Troy?" She speeds up to match my stride.

"Asthma," I choke out. It's starting to feel worse and worse. "Hospital."

Once again, we pile into the limo, and Rosalie tells the driver to get us to Cedars of Lebanon quickly. Yet again, I'm so glad I wasn't driving us. I know Rosalie can drive, but she's more at home on a tractor than in a fancy Mercury. The driver double parks at the emergency entrance and runs to grab a wheelchair. By the time I'm seen by anyone, I'm in terrible distress, and I'm horribly embarrassed about it. I'm glad Rosalie is here for moral support, but I'm mortified to have her see me like this.

After an injection of epinephrine, I can breathe tremendously better, but now I'm dizzy, and my heart is racing, so I still feel pretty terrible. I get a prescription for pills and a serious lecture about having the pills with me at all times from the doctor. He tells me to go home and take it easy for a few days because it was likely that stress set me up for the attack triggered by the stuffy room. I agree with him but know I can't avoid stress all that well. He also tells me to lay off the booze because that can make things worse.

At least we're done for the night with a good excuse.

Sitting on the beach in Hawaii is sounding better and better, even though that's still weeks away.

I sure wish we could get rid of the stress brought on by Gloria's actions, though. I hope Ray calls soon with some answers for us.

Since it's relatively early, we elect to go back to our house instead of dropping Rosalie off at the Studio Club. We can all relax together for a while.

Chapter Thirty-Eight

Rosalie

I CAN'T EXPRESS how scary it was sitting in that limousine watching Troy struggle for his next breath. I wanted to breathe for him, but all I could do was hold him and try to get him to relax. I forgot he told me he'd had trouble with asthma when he was younger, but I realize now it was much worse than he was letting on. It's a wonder he hasn't had more attacks with all the stress he's been under—worrying about Ollie and the nonsense with Gloria Dumont. What a horrible person she is! I love Troy so much and seeing him gasp for air was a sobering experience. At least now he understands he hasn't outgrown it like he thought, and he can try to take better care of himself.

The chauffeur drops us off, and Ollie is delighted to see us. He's looking much better, but he's still sporting two black eyes. He says the aches and pains are much better now. I hope he's not just trying to act stronger than he is.

We tell Ollie and Zelda about our party and hospital adventure. He looks pale as we recount the tale. Well, pale except for around his eyes. As soon as we're done with the story, Zelda disappears.

My men. They're so special to me, and I love them so deeply. We all sit down in the living room with glasses of fresh lemonade, and I tell them, "You've both given me quite a fright recently, and you better cut it out." I smile to soften my words. "You're going to make me wrinkled and gray haired before my time if you keep it up." I kiss Troy and then Ollie and tell them, "I love you both so much. Please don't get sick or hurt anymore."

Right then, Zelda comes into the room and sets a tray down on the coffee table. It's laden with three large servings of peach cobbler topped with ice cream that she knows we all adore. "I thought you all looked a little peaked, so please —eat." It's times like this when she shows us her true heart. She worries about these guys too.

"Thanks, Zelda!" we all say as we reach eagerly for spoons and our bowls, but she's already leaving and just waves her hand in the air like she can't be bothered by sentimentality or even basic manners. She's an enigma.

"How is your heart feeling now, Troy?" Ollie asks. "Has it slowed down?"

"It's much better, and I'm not lightheaded now. I'm definitely not sleepy, but how would you both like to go *lie down* with me for a while after we finish stuffing ourselves?"

"I hope it doesn't bring on another attack," I say with a cautious voice.

"It won't. I'm all filled with adrenaline now. But what did you think I was implying, Rosalie?"

I snort. "Exactly what you *were* implying. You can't fool me." I give him a sultry look and add, "The doctor didn't give you any cautions though, and he did say regular exercise would be good for you." I turn and ask, "Ollie, how are you feeling?"

"Fit as a fiddle." He takes an extra-large mouthful of cobbler, swallows, and grins. "As long as I don't have to use my nose for anything but breathing."

So we finish up our delicious confection and head to the bedroom. Clothes fly off in record speed because we haven't had much time for fun lately. I still think we need to take it a little easy tonight, no matter what these guys say.

Ollie gets to me first and carefully angles his face so that his nose is out of the way before he gives me a soul-shattering kiss. Troy comes up behind me and kisses my neck while he caresses my breasts. He's already hard, and I relish the feel of him rubbing against my bottom with his substantial erection. I feel Ollie's growing in front of me, and it gives me a deliciously naughty idea. I stop kissing for a moment, and say in a low voice, "I've been studying my so-called *Rebecca* before I go to sleep at night, and I'm anxious to try what you both said I needed to wait a while before we did. I'm quite comfortable with the idea now and want you both inside me finally. Can you do that for me, my loves?" Just asking that question makes me all jittery inside—in the best way possible.

"That's a wonderful idea," Ollie croons at me. "Troy?"

"If the lady is willing, I'm all for it. Just let me get the K-Y." He goes to the drawer and asks, "Ollie, do you want to help get Rosalie prepped?"

Ollie gives a shiver and looks at me with hunger. "That sounds like fun. Rosalie, lie down on the bed so Troy and I can stretch your pretty hole. One of us needs to get a dick in there."

I gasp and my face flames red, but I'm so excited, I flop down face-first on the bed and spread my legs. Whether I'm eager for them to begin or I'm covering my blush, I can't honestly say. Either way, I want this to happen. My curiosity is overflowing. The book made this sound incredibly sexy— so much so that when I finished reading about it, I had to use my fingers on myself to quell my arousal. That's not something I've done often, but the mental picture I had made it happen quite efficiently. It was fun, and I was happy to have a single room in case I need to take myself in hand more often. These men have created a monster in me, and I love it.

I'm lost in thought until I feel gentle hands stroking my bottom, and suddenly what I've asked for becomes quite real. Ollie speaks up and says, "On second thought, sweetheart, boost yourself up onto your knees so I can reach around and play with your clitoris while Troy and I loosen you up back here. The more relaxed you are, the better. And we both know it's a little strange at first to get used to this. Fun though." He kisses my back.

Now my butt is up in the air, and I feel like a wanton woman. This is not something I ever dreamed I'd be doing in my lifetime. Troy reminds me, "Spread your legs a little more, love."

A large, warm hand reaches around and slides into my folds, seeking my nerve bundle.

"Good lord, Troy. She's already soaked." Ollie kisses my back again, and Troy makes a happy growl.

Then I feel a large finger playing around with my backside. It's slippery as it circles round and round and then pushes in slightly. "That's it. Relax," Troy tells me.

Ollie's fingers have started a circular pattern on my sensitive bump, and it feels so good. *So* good. My breathing accelerates, and I can feel that wonderful sense of arousal growing deep within me. The finger at my backside pushes inside, and I cry out, "Oh!"

"Was that too fast? I don't want to hurt you," Troy says.

"Not too fast at all. I love it."

"Ollie's going to join me in here in a minute. We'll get you used to this first."

Ollie's manipulations increase in pressure and speed, and I feel myself nearly floating away. The sensations are almost more than I can handle. It's all so lovely.

Just as I'm on the very brink of an orgasm, a second finger slides into me. The pressure is nearly painful, but not really. It's so much, I detonate immediately and shake all over, moaning a sound that I've never made before. "Gahhohh!"

"Now, Ollie. Give her your finger too. She needs three now," Troy orders.

The third finger seems much larger, and it's a strain to stay relaxed enough to let him in, but I tell myself this is what we all want. And I'd do anything for my wonderful men. I take a deep breath and relax into the pressure. They begin to pump in and out of me, and I have never felt anything like this. My spasms are still making me shake and jolt, and the pressure in my bottom makes them stronger than ever.

The men thrust and thrust until Ollie says, "She's ready. Troy, lie down on the bed so I can help Rosalie onto your dick. I don't think I can take your combined weight on top of me just yet, so this will be the most comfortable for all of us."

Troy quickly takes his position, and his erection points at the ceiling, ready, red, and eager. Ollie helps me arrange myself over him and bends down to lick my clit. Carefully, slowly, I slide down onto Troy, facing away from him. He penetrates my backside with a groan. As we join together, it stings and stretches, but the pleasure is almost overwhelming.

"Oh my! That *is* a new sensation," I exclaim, shaking all over.

Crouching in front of me, Ollie's tongue licks all around my sensitive parts, and he makes a happy, satisfied sound. He reaches for a condom, slips it on, and says, "Here I come."

I must admit, it feels a little crowded at first as Ollie pushes himself into me. But then I feel them rubbing against one another *inside* me, and I'm positively transported with desire, especially when Ollie cries out, "Troy! I feel you. *This is fantastic.*"

Troy reaches around from behind me and begins to stroke me some more as Ollie starts to plunge his throbbing organ in and out of me. Troy groans, "Amazing!"

Another orgasm builds in me until I can't contain it any longer. Or maybe it's the same orgasm that never ended—but whatever it is, I feel like I might explode, so I let it sweep over me. My muscles contract, and I make a loud noise that makes Ollie smile. He increases the speed of his thrusts, and I swear Troy's growing larger and harder in my backside.

Suddenly, Troy grips my hips, and he makes a few strong thrusts upward into my body. He bellows out with a primal sound as my bottom fills with hot spurts of ejaculate. It's so dirty and exciting, I start to orgasm *again*. That triggers Ollie, who also makes a mammoth thrust into me and hollers, "Oh, my God!"

Needless to say, we are all enjoying ourselves tonight.

Ollie is the first to pull out. I am a little concerned when he moans, "Damn! Not again!"

I look down and see that once again the condom didn't hold. I can't really think about what this might mean, so I push it out of my mind.

My immediate need is to get into a taxi and get back before curfew because one glance at the clock lets me know I don't have a lot of time. It makes me sad to leave after such an intimate interlude. At least the guys have each other.

This sure was a lot of fun though, and it made a scary night much better.

When I get back to my own bed, it seems so lonely. I miss my men terribly, even though I just left them. Christmas Eve can't come soon enough, if you ask me. This place is great, and I've made some nice friends, but nothing can compare to Ollie and Troy.

I'M JUST FINISHING up breakfast the next morning when I sense the sudden excited energy wafting through the dining room. Women are giggling, whispering, nudging their friends, and looking toward the doorway behind me. Curious, I turn around and see Troy scanning the room, searching for me in the crowd. I stand up, and his nervous expression turns to joy as he sees me approach. Wordlessly, he takes me into his arms and bestows one of his blistering kisses on me.

"Good morning, darling," he growls into my ear.

I can hear more giggling and happy whispers behind me from the other women. But Troy's face is all business as he says quietly, "Can you come with me right now? Ray Falco called, and he's on his way to the house with some news for us. He wants to talk to all of us together."

I can't help but wonder what this is all about.

Chapter Thirty-Nine

OLLIE

I'M A NERVOUS WRECK. Troy went to get Rosalie, and I'm left here to wait for Ray to show up. Zelda isn't even here—not that she's all that much company. But it's her day to visit her friend, wherever that might be. I stay out of her business. I just know she usually comes home in a much better mood than when she left.

I'm also unhappy about what I heard from the car dealership. They have declared my poor car a total loss. They said it would cost more to fix it than makes sense, and I'd be better off getting a new one. Considering that it's already eight years old, it might be better to just take their advice, but I'm also aware they are in the business of selling cars. It wasn't built to last even that long anyway, so I have to decide what to do. It had about a six-year lifetime, and I took good care of it, making it last. I actually bought it used when we got to California so I could have something to drive to and from Santa Barbara, but otherwise, it hasn't had a lot of use. My thrifty nature says to fix it—even though that will cost quite a bit, but my more extravagant side says I can afford a much nicer new one. And they do have some great new models now—much more fun than what was available when I bought the one I wrecked.

I hear someone at the door, so I go to let Ray in. One of the guards he had us hire let him through the gate. That's been a nice plus of having them around, but I wish they weren't necessary.

Ray has an inscrutable expression on his face.

"Troy and Rosalie ought to be back any minute. Want some coffee? We also have cinnamon Danish."

"Sure. I wouldn't turn any of that down. Thanks." Ray has a large envelope in his hand, and my curiosity is piqued. I'll wait for the others before I pump him for information though, so I lead him into the kitchen and bustle around getting him coffee and a couple Danishes, setting it all out for him with cream and sugar. I just ate, so I pour myself more coffee.

He doesn't have much to say, and all I can think of that's had an impact around here is Troy's recent trip to the hospital, but that's Troy's business, so I keep my mouth shut. Ray knows about everything else. So we sit in awkward silence.

Thankfully, Troy and Rosalie show up after not too long.

After greeting one another, Ray begins by asking me,

"Mr. Shackleton, did you ever give a statement to the police about what happened the night you hit the tree?"

I think about it a moment and answer, "Not that I can remember. I know I was mostly out of it when they first got there, and I understand I said 'Call Ray' a few times, although I don't remember that. If I said anything to the cops, it probably wouldn't have made a lot of sense."

"Good, good. That's helpful. So they never came to you in the hospital later to take a statement?"

"No, I'm sure of that. Besides, Troy and Rosalie were there, so they'd have known about it if I did."

He nods. "So could it be possible that you were actually run off the road instead of dodging a raccoon or whatever?"

"Oh...well, it's possible, but not likely. I think I remember an animal."

"Forget the animal, okay? You were run off the road."

"Hmm." Troy and Rosalie look just as confused as I am.

"I located the driver of the car with the license plate G9 21 79, and it's the same person as the man who fell out of your tree and broke through the rotten wooden crate while attempting to take photos of all of you."

"He fell out of a tree?" Rosalie asks.

"Yep. I've spoken with him, and he confirmed he's the person Gloria Dumont hired. He has a painful sprained wrist, and that interferes with his picture-taking abilities, but I swear he's one of the dumbest people I've had the misfortune of talking to in a long while." Ray shakes his head. "And now he has an infected wound on his leg that he needs to take care of besides the sprained wrist. It wasn't too hard to get him to talk when I suggested he could be in a lot of trouble—or we could do him a favor."

"What kind of favor?" I ask and wonder to myself, *Do I even want to know?*

"I offered to buy any photos he's taken for double what Gloria Dumont offered him, and he was naïve enough to show me the negatives of what he'd taken. As I expected, the exposed film was nothing but a bunch of pitch-black frames and then a blurry mess of leaves and the top of your wall. He was already falling through the wooden crate when the camera went off the last time. I then pestered him into showing me what he'd taken from the tree the day he fell out of it, and there were a few shots from too far away of you, Mr. Shackleton, swimming and sitting on your patio at your typewriter. The only way I could tell it was you rather than Mr. Kingsley was because the hair looked blond rather than black. Your features were not recognizable because he shot the picture through a bunch of branches and leaves. And even if you could make out who the photo was of, you aren't doing anything the least bit interesting in any of them. You're just a guy enjoying his backyard on a nice day by your-self." He opens the envelope and pulls out prints of every-thing he just described. "I was almost considering paying him fifty bucks for this pile of nothing because I was honestly starting to feel sorry for the guy, and then I figured I could destroy the negatives, but as you can see, there's abso-lutely nothing here. I just laughed and told him they weren't worth a plugged nickel."

"How did you get them then?"

"I waited until the next day and checked his trash can. Sure enough, he'd dumped everything since he had decided they were worthless. I only grabbed them so I could show you what he'd done. I think he was hoping he could come back and try again, but he saw your guards and gave up. When I came through the gate, the guard said a car that matched the description of his has driven by here several times in the past few days, but when he saw the guards, he drove off."

"What about what he told Gloria that he saw?" Troy asks.

"He tried to make me believe he never said a word to her about you guys, but he started getting all shifty and wouldn't look at me. So he must have seen something and blabbed about it to her. Then he hoped he could try again and back up his claims with better pictures. What I wondered is how she might have suspected there was anything to talk about in the first place."

Troy speaks up and says, "She was probably hoping she could get a photo of Ollie having an affair with Rosalie, and that would ruin her reputation. It's also probably why Rosalie was followed; they were trying to catch her doing something wrong. I mentioned to Gloria one time that I had a majordomo who lives here, and she looked at me with her eyes all squinty. It takes someone who does vile things to think everyone else does them too, I think."

Ray nods. "Makes sense in a weirdly twisted way, I guess."

"So how are we supposed to deal with Gloria and her fat mouth?" I ask.

"I can have one of my buddies at the precinct take your statement now that your mind is clearer. You can tell him about the car that ran you off the road. You saw two people in it just like when Miss Channing saw the car with two in it, but you don't have to recount her story to the cops."

"You're recommending that I lie to the cops?"

Ray shrugs like it's nothing. "It happens all the time, and you're not going to be actually accusing anyone—just casting some possible blame. If you were planning to commit insurance fraud, I'd be a little more worried about this."

"I couldn't get anything for the car. I've already been told that. It's too old. Too many miles."

Satisfied, Ray continues, "A guy I've done some work for lives near here, and he often walks his dog at night. He can be persuaded to say he saw the car and remembered the license number, if it comes to that. The important thing is to convince Gloria that she may have been involved with something that could be serious."

"But we have no idea what she was doing that night."

Ray gets a sly grin on his face and answers, "As a matter of fact, I do know where she was. She was having an affair with a very famous and also married studio executive. If she needs an alibi, that guy would never, ever give her one."

"How do you know about that?" I ask

"Well, I can't reveal all of my secrets, but let's just say that I have eyes and ears in all of the major hotels around here, and for a small bit of persuasion, I'm privy to a lot of the hanky-panky that happens. Miss Dumont was involved that night in some very loud shenanigans that she doesn't want made public. Or rather, her partner would not want their goings-on to be common knowledge." He tips the last of his coffee into his mouth, and I pour him another. "Anyway, the idea is just to scare Gloria into believing you can blackmail her if she opens her mouth anymore about your relationship. You don't have to actually commit the blackmail; we just have to make her think you would. She has no proof since the pictures were worthless, and there's a good reason for her to shut up about this, so it ought to be enough."

Troy takes a deep breath and says, "I sure hope it is, but she's got a vendetta, and I don't trust her. I think she has a wide mean streak."

Rosalie speaks up then and says, "What if you do something she perceives as good for her instead, Troy? Like you get her a plum part in a great movie, or something like that? Wouldn't she be so grateful she'd stop trying to make life difficult for us?"

"That's possible, but I don't know what clout I'd have for that."

"I have an idea," she says. "Remember the book Ollie published a few years ago? The one about the woman who pretends to be nice, but she's really a serial killer?"

"*Goldilocks*?" I ask. It's a thriller that got rave reviews and still sells like crazy. Even though it wasn't my usual genre, I'm quite proud of its success. It actually helped us buy this house.

"That's the one. I've always thought it would make a spectacular movie. And Troy could also be in it but wouldn't have to kiss her." Rosalie smiles. "He'd be the lawyer trying to get her convicted. It's such a great plot, Ollie, it gave me the shivers. Anyway," she looks at Troy, "if you could present that story to the studio and they made a movie, Gloria might even win an Oscar. It's that exciting. You'd just have to work fast. When you think about it, Gloria is the best choice for the part, and it certainly ought to make her happy."

"Just don't blow my cover when you say it was written by Robert Oliver. I still prefer my anonymity."

"Even if it wins an Academy Award?" she asks me.

"Even then. That's a hard and fast rule."

"I'll get to work on that right away," Troy says with conviction. "First, I'll set up a meeting with John Packard and Harry Walken. I just have to be careful how I present it to them. I'll give them a call later today. You're a genius, darling! There is no guarantee that they'll do it, but if I sell it just right and let Gloria know I'll be pushing to get her hired for it, maybe this will turn her mouth off about us."

"I can't wait," Rosalie says with a laugh.

I grab her hand and say, "Brilliant. But is there anything else we can do about the photographer?"

She considers a moment and says, "Why don't we offer to pay for him to see a doctor about his infection and his wrist, with the signed promise that he'll stop talking about us. We'll threaten to sue him if he opens his mouth."

Ray speaks up, "That would be like suing a stray dog. He obviously has no money."

"Maybe, but you also said he's pretty dim-witted," she says. "He sounds like the kind of guy who'd be scared by the possibility of a lawsuit."

"True."

"Let's do it," I say. "Ray, can you contact him and let him know? We can have our lawyer write up a contract that you can give him on Monday."

And our plan is hatched. I feel better than I have in weeks now.

Chapter Forty

Rosalie

I'm pretty proud of my negotiation plan. So far, it's been working like a dream. The studio loved the idea of making a movie from Ollie's book, and Ollie is beyond excited about it. John Packard was already familiar with *Goldilocks*, and he saw the possibilities immediately.

Ollie's not a screenwriter, so the studio has gotten a couple of their writers to collaborate on the adaptation, but royalties will still go to Ollie. Ollie is happy with this arrangement because he doesn't want to be personally involved for privacy reasons. He understands alterations will be made to the story, and he's fine with it.

The word we hear about the shady photographer is that he's doing better. His wrist was actually broken, but it's healing well, and his leg wound isn't killing him anymore.

Ray recommended him to one of his former clients, so now the guy is gainfully employed as a theater usher. I doubt he can make too big a mess of that job. His camera was damaged in his fall from the wooden crate, so his photography days were over anyway since he couldn't afford to get it fixed.

In other good news, Gloria Dumont was ecstatic to be handed such a juicy role. Believe me, she won't be doing much acting. Her personality is perfect for the job—wicked to the core. And now she thinks Troy walks on water for recommending her for the part. She's done with the movie she made at Paramount, so she was more than ready to start something new.

I think Premier Works will start shooting *Goldilocks* now that since we're done with *Wild Horses*. Since Troy will play a leading role opposite Gloria, I'm not sure what the studio plans to do with me. Or maybe they'll have Troy take on another project with me before *Goldilocks* is ready to go. I'm not sure how long it takes to adapt a book.

We had the premiere for *Forever Yours*, and I was stunned and delighted when I saw the entire movie. It was beautiful, tremendously touching, and romantic. The reviews have been amazing, and now when Troy and I step out in public, people direct as many questions and requests for autographs to me as they do to Troy. My fame has skyrocketed like a Roman candle. It's strange how I've become a household name because of something I love to do. I'm so lucky, and I have Troy to thank for it. I feel like my life is from a storybook these days. Picking cherries hasn't crossed my mind in a long time now.

The wedding plans are taking shape well, and my gown is exquisite. The only unhappy news is that I wrote to my parents and told them about my upcoming plans to marry Troy, and I told them all about him and what a wonderful man he is. I offered to send them tickets if they'd like to fly or take the train out here for the wedding. They only responded by a postcard that said, "No thank you. Good for you." I guess I should be satisfied they bothered to respond at all. They still cash my checks, but that's the total extent of what I mean to them now. It breaks my heart to have them so uninvolved in my life, but I won't let myself dwell on it. Maybe the postcard was their way of congratulating me, but it certainly felt cold and disinterested.

Troy also heard from his family, and they were a lot nicer about their inability to come all the way from Ohio to the wedding. They can't leave the farm for as many days as the trip would take, so they wrote a lovely letter telling him how proud they were of him and wished him all the happiness in the world. They hope we can visit them sometime. They keep a huge scrapbook of articles and photos of him and mentioned in their letter how beautiful his bride is, and they love reading the stories about us. To me, that's much more like how a family ought to react. I hope I can meet them sometime.

The wedding is coming up in just a couple of days, and I can hardly grasp that I'll be married so soon. Between last-minute preparations and finishing up shooting *Wild Horses*, I'm exhausted.

It's been so bad the last few weeks that I haven't felt up for a trip out to Troy and Ollie's house. Instead, after work, I only have the energy to come back to the Studio Club, eat a quick dinner, and fall into bed. I haven't been feeling too well, either. I've had bouts of headaches and an upset stomach. I don't think I've been taking care of myself properly, and with all the stress, it's starting to take a toll.

So I've made the difficult decision to get as much sleep as I can during the week. I see Troy every day at the studio, but I've been missing out on seeing Ollie. I can't wait until I move in with both of my wonderful men.

Today, Sophie Packard is coming to the studio for our final fitting check for our gowns. She's going to look stunning in an elegantly draped chiffon dress that is the most gorgeous shade of scarlet. It's sophisticated and absolutely perfect for a Christmas wedding. She's been such a huge help with the plans, I don't know what I'd have done without her. She said she'd give me a lift back to the Studio Club after our appointment, so Troy is heading home. We've just finished with *Wild Horses*, but instead of jumping into a new project, the studio is closing from Christmas Eve to the day after New Years. Too many people needed to be with family, and several were traveling, so the studio was generous with the time off. It also conveniently (for them) coincided with our honeymoon. I wonder if that was the intent all along— making us think the Christmas Eve wedding was a spectacular idea. Well, I'm not upset. I'm delighted with how beautiful it will be.

The plan is to take off right after the wedding for our honeymoon. First, we'll fly to San Francisco and then board a Pan Am flight that will take nineteen hours to fly to Honolulu. I'm anxious to see the plane because it's supposed to be extremely luxurious, and it actually lands on the water. They call the Boeing 314 the "Yankee Clipper" because it's really a flying boat, and it's the largest aircraft in the world. They've booked us into a deluxe stateroom aboard it so we can relax in complete comfort. We'll have a few days at the Royal Hawaiian on Waikiki Beach to enjoy the sun and sightsee in Honolulu, and finally we'll board the Matson Lines cruise ship the SS Lurline to sail home. It all sounds wonderfully relaxing to me, and naturally the studio is making a big to-do about our travel plans. I guess it's another way of saying we're glamorous and famous, and everyone ought to take notice of us. I suspect Pan Am, the Royal Hawaiian, and Matson Lines have offered Premier Works big discounts for all the free advertising, but I'm not going to ask. I just plan to enjoy the time with Troy and the adventure of the trip.

I hope Ollie does alright while we're gone. He plans to head up to Santa Barbara to see his author friends for at least part of the time. I wish he could join us, but that's impossible.

Sophie arrives at my dressing room, and her knocking on my door wakes me up from a nap I hadn't even realized I was taking. She takes one look at me and narrows her eyes. She doesn't say anything, though, besides, "Ready to head over to the dressmaker?"

As we make our way to the design department, Sophie gives me a full account of all the deliveries and whatnot that have arrived at the Packards' house. She sounds as excited as I am for it all to come together. "The poinsettias all arrived today, and they're magnificent," she tells me proudly.

First, Sophie has a quick fitting, and all is determined to be perfect. She looks stunning, of course.

Then it's my turn, and I get a little dizzy in the dressing room. I shake my head to clear the cobwebs and step out. The designer, Irene, lends me a hand to step up on the fitting platform, and I feel so wobbly all of a sudden, I'm afraid I'm going to fall and ruin the dress. I grasp her arm and bend over, causing her to lose her balance momentarily. Sophie comes out of her dressing room to the sight of me hanging onto a stricken-looking Irene.

"What's the matter, ladies?"

Irene only says, "Umm—"

"I had a little dizzy spell. I'm fine now. It's passed." I look at Irene. "I'm sorry. I hope I didn't twist your arm off or anything. I promise, I'm fine now. I think I need some dinner since I missed lunch. Can we get on with this?" I shouldn't sound so cross. The poor woman was trying to help, and I'm acting like she was in the way.

"I'll get you some water," Sophie tells me.

Several minutes later, Irene is done, the dress is pronounced perfect, and I change back into my regular clothes. Sophie finally returns with a glass of cold water for me. It certainly took her a while to get it. We thank Irene and leave.

But on the way back to the Studio Club, I realize we're heading in the wrong direction. "What's going on, Sophie? Where are you taking me?"

"I made you an appointment, and he's fitting you in at the end of his workday, so we have to get there right away."

"An appointment?"

"With my doctor."

"Why? I'm fine. I just need to get something in my stomach, that's all."

"I'm sure you do. How long has this been going on, Rosalie?"

"Oh, uh...just a few days." I sure hope I'm not coming down with anything so close to the wedding. I try to give her a brave smile and add, "I'm sure it's nothing."

Sophie snorts. "It's probably something that will change your life, sweetie. My doctor will fix you all up depending on how you feel about it."

Change my life? A cold chill goes down my back, and I suddenly realize I haven't had my monthly visitor in a while. "You're kidding."

"I'm not kidding. There's nothing about this that's funny. But let's see what he says first."

"If you're insinuating that I'd even consider an...*abortion*, that's just...well, it's not happening." I can't even say the word out loud. It comes out in a whisper.

"We're almost there," she says matter-of-factly. She doesn't want to discuss it either.

AN HOUR LATER, we're on our way back to the Studio Club, and my head is spinning in a new way. I was asked to relieve myself in a cup, and the doctor told me he'd normally have the results in two days, but we'll have to wait extra long for these results because of Christmas. Just my luck. By the time the results are available, I'll be out of town.

I questioned him about how the pregnancy test worked, and I was appalled to hear that it involved injecting my urine into a vein in a rabbit's ear and then killing it to study the rabbit's ovaries. "Isn't there any other way?" I asked him.

His somewhat flippant reply was "You can always wait and see if your belly gets really big and a baby pops out, or you can use test mice. Both of those options take longer, though."

"Do the test mice also die?"

"They do, but that test takes four days to get an answer, so most women prefer the rabbit test for that reason."

"I want the mouse test. I can't be a part in killing a bunny to tell me what I already know, and I'll be in Hawaii anyway. You'll have to share what you find with Mrs. Packard, and she'll know where to reach me." I don't like killing anything, but mice are a pain in the neck, and it's not as if I'd get the results any faster if I did the unthinkable and had him kill a cute, fuzzy rabbit. It's decided.

"Are you going to tell Troy?" Sophie asks as she navigates the streets. I'm glad she didn't use the driver because it would be one more person who knew I'd seen a doctor.

"I guess I should probably wait until I have the answer for sure before I say anything."

"Don't wait too long."

"Sophie, I'm not going to do anything to end it if I'm pregnant."

"The studio might insist. It wouldn't be the first time."

I look at her, horrified. I know her husband works for the studio that employs me, but I absolutely cannot be a person who does that. It might be fine for some women, but it's just not for me. "They can't," I whisper.

"Look at your contract if you think they can't. It will depend on what they have planned for you in the next several months."

I vow to myself to make a call to Jack Cramer and ask him if the studio can enforce something that's illegal. For now, I'm putting any negative thoughts out of my mind. I'm getting married, and I'm a star in a major motion picture that's doing well. Life is good. It's all good. Even a baby would be good. Right?

I wonder how Troy is going to feel about it.

And Ollie too, since—

Stupid condoms. Can't they make them so they don't break, for heaven's sake?

Chapter Forty-One

OLLIE

ROSALIE MUST BE the most stunning bride anyone has ever seen. She's ethereally beautiful, and she has an inner glow I've never seen in her before. It's as if her love is gleaming out from her body in an aura of happiness. Her shimmery satin gown shines in the candlelight, and her face is lit up with joy. Her sparkling blue eyes draw me in like magnets.

I love this woman deeply.

The drawing room of the Packards' estate is exquisite. It's a chic Christmas delight for all the senses. The music is festive and charming, and the red and green seasonal decorations with all the gold highlights make the setting magical. The room smells of pine, cloves, and cinnamon, and the attendees are all dressed to the nines in formal attire. Hollywood's beautiful elite showed up with glittering jewels and designer elegance.

Troy looks good enough to eat in his tuxedo. He has eyes for no one but his bride.

John Packard said he'd be honored to escort Rosalie up the aisle for the ceremony, and his lovely wife Sophie makes a gorgeous matron of honor. There's nothing matronly about that woman in her flowing red gown. She's almost as captivating as Rosalie. I'm glad they've become such good friends. Rosalie needs a female friend who understands her and isn't jealous of her, but it must be challenging for Rosalie to keep the particulars of our relationship from Sophie. I guess it's possible she hasn't, now that I think about it, but that could be dangerous. If Sophie so much as whispered something to her husband...I can't think about that.

All of this goes through my mind as I stand proudly next to my best friend and lover. As the couple recite their vows, I remember that they both told me they would be saying them to me in their hearts every bit as much as they're saying them to each other. I take note when Rosalie's glance flicks to me and locks momentarily while she's speaking, and I feel her words in my very soul. That's some consolation, but I can't deny that my heart is breaking at the same time as it's soaring.

Why does it have to be like this? Can't the world accept a love that is not the norm? I know Troy and Rosalie love me equally, but I fear that at some point I may be their downfall, and that scares me to death. When the minister declares them man and wife, and the two of them kiss, it takes every shred of effort I can shore up to keep from crying like a baby. I want so badly to be a part of that kiss.

We've shared fantastic times in bed as three devoted lovers; although, in the most recent weeks, there was such a flurry of activity around them we didn't have a lot of time together. Their movie *Forever Yours* is a major box-office sensation, and the public's interest in them has been fueled successfully by innumerable photos and stories in newspapers and magazines. They've become the talk of the town—if not far wider circles as well. Our privacy is a challenge to maintain as the two of them are so scrutinized.

I despair about this loss of anonymity for Rosalie. It's new to her, whereas Troy has been able to adjust as his star rose steadily over several years in Hollywood. But for Rosalie? Well—there's no stopping the press and the way she feeds the public's fascination. Troy has seen even greater stardom as their couple-star rises. It's a lot to handle. I hope for their peace of mind that they'll be able to relax on their honeymoon.

The dinner service is superb, and we make it through the toasts and cutting the cake successfully. I barely remember what I said for my best man's speech, but I know people laughed and clapped. Honestly, a lot of it was lies because I left out everything pertinent to our real relationship. I couldn't say how Troy is the perfect man I've had the privilege to cherish for years now, and how he brought Rosalie into our circle of love so beautifully and with complete generosity. And I couldn't say that Rosalie is as precious to me as Troy is to both of us. I couldn't brag about how knowing I have their combined love is like oxygen to me.

I've heard the saying, "The truth will set you free," but in our case, the truth might send us to jail.

Although I've tried to be careful, perhaps I've had too much champagne because I'm feeling terribly maudlin. My favorite part of the evening is when I take Rosalie in my arms and waltz around the ballroom with her like we're Fred and Ginger. The swing orchestra is great, and Rosalie is light on her feet. Her dance lessons really paid off. She's a wonderful partner in so many ways. I'm crushed when the song ends and another eager gentleman claims her attention. Rosalie maintains a gracious smile as they foxtrot away from me. They spin around, and I catch a longing look in her eyes aimed right at me.

I peruse the dance floor and see that Troy is dancing with Packard's wife, but he keeps glancing over at Rosalie. Packard is dancing with Harry Walken's wife and looks a little bored. As best man, I should keep dancing with other ladies, but I'm losing my enthusiasm. This hideous pall of dread is seeping into my bones, and I have to hide it. I keep telling myself I am *not* losing them, but it's hard convincing myself. I know how badly things can go wrong if we're ever too obvious or have a slip of the tongue.

It's not terribly late when Rosalie tosses her bouquet to a bevy of laughing young ladies she's befriended at the Hollywood Studio Club, and all too soon it's time for her to leave with Troy. They change their clothes, and before they're whisked away by the Packards' chauffeur, I give them both ferocious hugs that I desperately wish could be more. They give me longing looks that I hope no one can read too much into and climb into the Packards' Rolls Royce to head to the airport. Once there, they will board a San Francisco-bound plane that will begin their honeymoon trip. I have to fight like the devil again to keep the tears at bay as I see the departing taillights leave me behind.

Most of the guests are still in the mood to party, and a few of those lovely single ladies have been flirting with me. But I find I have no more mood for socializing. I've tried to keep my drinking to a minimum, so I'm not afraid to drive my snazzy new Cadillac back to the house. I want a stiff drink when I get there and plan to leave for Santa Barbara sometime tomorrow. Zelda is going to take a week off to spend it with her friend. She seemed excited—for Zelda that's saying a lot—that they planned to spend a couple of days on Catalina Island. I haven't been myself, but I under-stand it's quite popular. She was looking forward to the casino, even though that seems out of character to me. Maybe I don't know her as well as I thought.

I've never felt so alone in my life.

Maybe I need to get a dog.

Merry Christmas to me.

Chapter Forty-Two

THE FLIGHT on the flying boat was an interesting experience. We were treated like royalty, I'll admit, but nineteen hours of being in an enclosed area was more than I needed, and it was by far the strangest Christmas Day of my life. We had fantastic meals, and the stateroom was comfortable, but I so wanted to get outside and breathe some fresh air and see the trees and the sun. Looking out the window wasn't anything to get excited about. Anyway, I was with Rosalie, and we had hours to ourselves like we'd never had since we met.

We made love I don't know how many times, but I know she was missing Ollie as strongly as I was. He's such a large presence, especially in bed, I wanted to reach out and touch him. I wanted to watch him make love to Rosalie and see her in a state of rapture from his touch. I wanted him inside me, and I wanted to be inside him while he made love to our wife. It's obvious that as much as we love each other, we both need our husband to make us whole.

Rosalie seemed a little preoccupied a few times, but I couldn't put my finger on why. I finally asked if everything was alright because she was in her own world. She curled up in my arms like a kitten, telling me, "Nothing is wrong, my dearest *husband*." Then she gave me her sweetest smile and said, "I love calling you my husband."

Now we're at the Royal Hawaiian, and it's much more to my liking than the flight was. The "Pink Palace of the Pacific" is as fancy as it gets in Hawaii, and we've enjoyed wandering through the lush gardens, lying on the beach in the sun, and taking dips in the ocean. Later today, we're going to take a private tour around the area. Mostly, though, people seem to come here to relax, and Rosalie and I certainly needed that.

Our suite is large and beautifully appointed. The bed is comfortable, and we've given it a good workout so far.

It's around noon of our third day here when there is a knock on the door. I open it to find a hotel worker holding a small envelope. "Telegram, sir, for your wife." I thank him, hand him a tip, and go find Rosalie. She was tired out after taking a long walk on the beach and is lying down.

"Darling? I'm sorry to bother you, but you have a telegram." I'm terribly worried this is bad news from her family or something. Who else would bother us on our honeymoon? I scowl inwardly at the thought of her family. I have little patience for those people and the way they treat Rosalie like their own personal piggybank. They made it clear, back when she was quite young, that a portion of what she earned would always belong to them. Rosalie confided that the only reason they didn't absolutely refuse to let her leave Idaho was because she promised to send them money regularly.

Rosalie sits up, and the lovely tan she's gotten seems to drain away to nothing on her face. I'm more worried than anything now, but I hand her the envelope.

She rips it open, and a curious mixture of emotions crosses her face in record time. "It's from Sophie," she says and hands it to me. I don't miss that her hand is shaking.

The telegram consists of one word, "Positive."

"What does this mean, dearest? What's positive?"

"It means...Sophie took me to see her doctor...she didn't want me to have to wait until we got home to find out the results of the pregnancy test I took—"

I hear the words "pregnancy test" and grab her, smothering her with kisses so she can't even finish her sentence. A baby!

"I know you said you wanted children, but are you really happy?" she asks in a timid voice.

"How can you even ask that? I'm thrilled! We're having a baby, Rosalie. A little girl or a little boy, and you're going to be the best mama ever. I can't wait. And I also can't wait to tell Ollie! This is the best news ever! I wish I knew how to contact him in Santa Barbara, but I'm not even sure they have a phone where he stays. They must, I guess, but I don't know how to find him. That's pretty dumb, now that I think about it. We'll have to tell him in person. He's going to be beside himself. Rosalie, we're having a baby!"

"You realize the chances are pretty good he's the father,

considering his luck with condoms," she points out with a happy grin.

"Yes, of course," I say with a gesture that indicates how little it bothers me. "That just means the kid will be tall, smart, and excessively good looking—a combination of you and Ollie. We'll all be this kid's parents though, and we'll do everything to make sure he or she has the best of everything."

She's full-on laughing at my exuberance now, and the relief on her face is adorable. How could she have been so worried? But then I think about what I've heard about studio contracts, and I immediately sober.

"Sweetheart, did you sign anything about not getting pregnant while you're under contract with Premier Works?"

In a small voice, she answers, "I don't honestly remember reading anything in the contract about that, but I was so shocked to be getting a major part in a movie as well as a husband, I was a little overloaded with information. It's possible it was there, and I missed it. I signed so many forms! But I'm going to check with Jack Cramer about it as soon as we get home. Sophie insinuated that the studios have forced some women to get abortions, but I can't believe that kind of thing is legal. They can't enforce a woman having an illegal procedure!"

"We'll have to check with Jack as soon as we get back," I say with lots more gravity in my voice. "You wouldn't actu- ally do it, would you? Even if they tried to force you?"

"Never. I don't care if it's the end of my career. I've made two movies now, and that's two more than I ever expected to make, so if that's it, then I'm satisfied. Being a mother is far more important to me. I just don't want to be sued over it."

"Yes, there's that. Let's go have a lovely celebratory lunch. We'll have fresh seafood and ripe fruit and fill ourselves to the gills with local goodies. And then we can buy you a bunch of those colorful loose dresses the locals call muumuus so you can wear them around the house when you get all big and round. Speaking of that, are your knockers bigger yet?" I reach for her blouse and push it up while she giggles at me. I nuzzle those sweet breasts and say, "We'll also have to buy Ollie and me some matching aloha shirts so we look as good as you do in your muumuu. I wonder if they have any in baby sizes."

We float around in a state of bliss for the rest of our stay, and I keep looking at Rosalie's flat belly, imagining what it will look like in a few months. Every time I do that, it makes me hard, so we've had to take care of my "problem" several times a day.

Ollie's going to be over the moon.

THE TRIP HOME is mostly fun. We have a nice, comfortable stateroom on the SS Lurline, and there is plenty of entertainment aboard the ship. During the day they have get-togethers, lectures, and games. People could play paddleball or swim, but it's actually too cold for that. Movies are a favorite pastime, and we sat down and watched a few, but not the one of mine they showed—that seemed way too egotistical, as if I were showing off. There are fancy dinners each night, and we can go dancing or listen to live music. It's basically a four-day party. Word travels quickly, however, that we're on board, and we draw a lot more attention than I'm thrilled with—especially after my movie is featured.

Most of the passengers are polite and just come up and tell us how much they enjoyed *Forever Yours* or they're looking forward to seeing it, but there are enough folks who think it's alright to flirt with someone on their honeymoon because we're public figures and therefore fair game. And there are others who shove things in our faces so we'll autograph them—and they don't care what we're doing when they make their demands. We've taken to looking for out-of-the-way, sheltered spots to relax in the sun, but that never lasts too long. We've had breakfast and lunch in our stateroom a few times because we're just tired of smiling at people and answering annoying questions. One thing I can say, however, is the food is magnificent.

And we have also met some nice passengers. We've been sitting with two couples for dinner, both a few years older than we are. One cheerful couple is from Chicago and came to Hawaii to get away from the cold winter for a while. The others are also newlyweds from Palo Alto. The husband is some kind of investor, and he hints at his interest in investing in a movie, but he only gives me his card and says we'll talk once we get back to California, "Because a honeymoon is not the time or place to do business," he adds.

I appreciate that tremendously and tell him so, but I also say that I know just the right people to introduce him to if he'd care to visit Hollywood. We shake hands at that and go back to talking about our favorite things we saw in Hawaii.

Rosalie and I have both caught ourselves a few times almost mentioning Ollie in a way that would make him sound like more than my best man or an employee. We need to be vigilant about how we talk about him in public, that's for sure. But it feels disingenuous to leave him out of conversation completely. What a dilemma. When you love someone, it's so hard to keep them a secret. I've had years of practice, but not as a threesome with him. Our relationship is magical, but it also has to be our dirty secret.

That's heartbreaking, but it's our life.

Chapter Forty-Three

OLLIE

MY DRIVE UP to Santa Barbara is more interesting this time. It's the first time I've had a radio in my car to listen to. This new car came with all the extras—unlike my old one. The sound gets a little distorted sometimes, but it's certainly better than endless engine noise as my only companion.

It's a beautiful trip, and I take it slowly so I can enjoy the view. It never fails to make me happy about moving out here with Troy—or I should say it's one *more* reason I'm happy about that. He's the main reason, of course, along with Rosalie. But the beauty of this state is inspiring, and I've used it as a colorful backdrop in several books now.

I'm feeling a little better about my life today, away from the pageantry of the wedding and worrying about exposing my true feelings in front of an audience. I awoke with a refreshed hope that everything would be alright for us. I'm also looking forward to spending time with my author friends at our retreat. I'm not sure who is going to show up since it's Christmas, but I'm not the only unmarried man who lives far from his family, so I have to hope a few more will be there.

It occurs to me now that I probably should have called more people than just my closest author friend, Ephraim. He promised he'd be there because he doesn't celebrate Christmas. I've missed seeing my writer friends because I skipped my last scheduled trip up here.

I can never get enough of smelling the salt air and watching the Pacific Ocean. Today the waves are huge, so I can't resist stopping at Three Mile Beach at Rincon Point. I love the name of the beach; it was called that because before the Pacific Coast Highway was built, the surfers had to hike for three miles to get out here to the good surfing. Imagine that—hiking three miles while lugging one of those huge boards. At least the surfboards are hollow now, so they're a lot lighter, but that's certainly devotion to a sport in any case. I park my car and head out to watch some surfers having a swell time out there. I laugh to myself that they are obviously skipping Christmas Day activities because the waves are so good. Their athleticism is impressive, but I keep thinking about how cold that water has to be. I'll stick to swimming laps at home. It was a big extravagance to have our pool heated, but well worth it considering how much it gets used.

As I relax and watch the surfers, it crosses my mind that perhaps Troy and Rosalie will soon be watching surfers at

Waikiki Beach, and that thought brings on a stab of pain right in my heart. I miss my lovers like a lost limb. And there goes my uplifted mood. Boom.

I get back into my car and raise the volume on the radio. Maybe I can cheer up before I see my buddies. There's a quiz show on, and it takes my mind off things for a while at least.

We always meet at a beach house that belongs to Stan—one of the authors—and as soon as I arrive, I see that Ephraim is already here. He tells me right away, "Stan took his family up to San Francisco for the holidays, so it turns out it will just be the two of us. I can stay until Friday, and then I'll have to head home for Shabbos." Ephraim is also from the Los Angeles area, but he lives in Boyle Heights, which is actually pretty far away or we'd probably do more together than just talk on the phone now and then. Stan, on the other hand, has his main residence in Fresno, but he keeps this beach house as a getaway, especially for the hot summer months. I'd sell the Fresno house and move to the beach if I were in his shoes, but it's his life.

During our getaways with one another, we all generally discuss the publishing issues and writing problems we encounter. It's always been helpful, and I've enjoyed the camaraderie immensely. There are nine of us in all, but the attendance varies from time to time.

I've never wanted to divulge much about my private life, but I've always sensed Ephraim could keep a secret, and I need someone to talk to. So after dinner, I pour us both a brandy and broach the topic that had been wearing on my mind. "Ephraim, if I told you something personal, would you be alright with keeping a secret? I don't want to put you in an uncomfortable position of knowing things you can't talk about to anyone, but I find my mind needs unburdening, and I'm tired of talking to myself about it." He looks taken aback, so I add, "I haven't done anything illegal if you're worried about that. Well...not anything violent or frightening anyway. The legality of it is debatable."

"I'm intrigued, mayn fraynd. If you trust me enough to confess, I'll keep your secrets. Don't worry; I'll take them to my grave."

I believe his sincerity, so I begin to tell him about Troy and how we happened to be living together in California. I don't name him—I only call him a "famous actor."

But when I get to the part that he's recently married a newly famous actress, Ephraim smiles and asks, "You've been living with Troy Kingsley? My wife has the biggest crush on him. Wonderful actor too, by the way. Is he as nice as he always seems in his interviews?"

"Even nicer," I reply. "He's been the love of my life for years. But the problem is, so is his new wife."

Ephraim wrinkles his brow in confusion. "You're worried that you want to split up their marriage? Pardon me, Ollie, but that doesn't sound like you."

"Thank you. No, nothing of the sort. I'm more worried about maintaining the relationship that all *three* of us have built over the past few months. Troy and I have been extremely careful to preserve our privacy so his career is protected and we aren't prosecuted for breaking any morals laws. It could get ugly if it were made common knowledge. And now they both have stellar careers to worry about. I don't believe my publisher would drop me the way the studio might do to them, so the liability is all theirs."

"I see. So, what is your biggest fear? Losing them or being exposed somehow?"

"That's the problem. I love them both with all my heart but feel like we're sitting on a powder keg that's about to detonate, and that scares me to death. See how easy it was for me to expose Troy and Rosalie to you by a slip of the tongue? I mentioned her as a newly famous actress, and you put two and two together immediately. I could do that and demolish our delicate house of cards by talking to the wrong person without even realizing I'm doing it. So I wonder if I should leave before we all get any more involved. I can see how wonderfully devoted they are to one another, and they profess to feel that way about me as well, but is it an impossible dream to think we could maintain our life together as a ménage à trois without that eventually becoming revealed?" I look into his eyes and say, "I'm so sorry, Ephraim, I don't want to embarrass you or tell you things that will make you not want to associate with me. Also, I must tell you that I've never been attracted to any other man in my whole life, so please don't think I'm shopping around for a replacement." I chuckle and relax a little when Ephraim does the same.

"I'm not worried. And even if you were, my devotion to my Esther is solid." He smiles kindly. "Ollie, I can't make up your mind for you, but I am aware of just how difficult the public can be with their opinions. We live in a difficult time with the continuation of the Great Depression having wreaked havoc on everyone for years now and the possibility of entering the war in Europe looming over our heads. It gives small people a warped sense of power if they can make themselves feel morally superior to someone else. People feel helpless because we might be dragged into a war that most Americans think is unnecessary. I do not personally agree, and I would gladly lay down my life if it would stop the Nazis, but I'm just one man in millions."

He takes a drink from his brandy and lets that sink in for me before he continues. "Your friends, however, provide a happy diversion from the problems we all face from day to day. They are beautiful people who are in love, and they make a trip to the movies something for people to look forward to and think about for days afterward. They offer us a wonderful escape from reality. People want to believe the love story. They need it. So doing anything to break that up would hurt not just them, but also many, many ordinary citizens around the country. Exposing Troy and his beautiful new wife and thereby changing public opinion of them would be a tragedy."

I have tears in my eyes as I listen to the sense he's making, and my gut churns with sadness and the cruelty of it all. But I know he's right. I will be jeopardizing something beautiful unless I remove myself from Troy and Rosalie's lives. Now I just have to figure out how to accomplish it cleanly and without too much heartbreak.

It just might kill me.

We don't talk about anything much other than writing after this conversation, but when Ephraim has to leave to get back to his family, he gives me a warm hug and says, "No matter what you decide, mayn fraynd, you will always have my friendship. I will pray for you, and I hope you achieve the happiness you deserve. Only you can decide what is best for you in this situation." He claps me on the back and says, "Best of luck with your next book! I enjoyed the parts you shared with me. Keep writing; you are a huge talent."

And off he goes to be with his family where *his* tremendous worry is for his relatives who still live in Europe. That puts things into perspective for me somewhat. There are problems that are far larger than mine in this world.

Chapter Forty-Four

Troy

It's midafternoon when the SS Lurline docks at berth 158 in the Port of Los Angeles. We're met by a cadre of photographers who want to record the momentous occasion of our return to California after our honeymoon. They're all hurling ridiculous questions at us that are barely discernible through the racket of everyone shouting at once. Honestly, I'm beginning to feel silly about all this attention, but Rosalie and I smile and wave like having our picture taken is the most fun we've had in ages. It's such a relief to climb into our waiting limo provided by the studio.

Quiet and privacy at last.

We're so anxious to see Ollie. We brought him a selection of truly garish aloha shirts and a beautifully crafted Hawaiian koa bowl he can either keep on his desk or his dresser, depending on where he'd like. But our biggest surprise is what we're dying to tell him. Rosalie's vibrating with excitement when we enter the house. But when we rush in and call out to him that we're back, we hear nothing in response.

Heading into the kitchen, I also look for Zelda. She's there cooking something that smells delicious, and she looks tan and quite pretty, but the expression on her face is worrisome. At least she tells us somewhat cheerfully, "Welcome home. It's good to see you. You both look wonderful."

"So do you, Zelda. Did you have a nice vacation?"

"I did."

"Have you seen Ollie?"

She takes a deep breath and says, "I expected him to be here, but I haven't heard a word from him yet. I hope he hasn't had car trouble or something."

"He hasn't called?"

"Nothing."

Rosalie's expression is worried and a little sad. She was so looking forward to giving him her happy news. I turn back to Zelda and ask, "Did he ever give you a contact name or a phone number for when he goes off for one of his writers' retreats?"

"Yeah, I have a phone number, but when he didn't come home all day, I called, and there was no answer. I don't know what to do." She hesitates for a moment and then our reliably stoic housekeeper admits, "I can't help but worry."

"Hmm. I don't really know what to do either. Ollie knew we'd all be home today."

Rosalie and I head up to unpack and find something

extremely distressing. We open the walk-in closet and realize that Ollie's clothes are gone. I guess Zelda didn't come looking for him in the closet.

"What the hell?"

Rosalie looks at me with tears sparkling in her eyes and asks, "What on earth do you think he's doing? He can't be leaving us, can he? He surely didn't take this much stuff for a few days in Santa Barbara."

I give Rosalie a hug and say, "I'm going to go make some calls. And if I can't find him, I'm calling Ray Falco. At least Ollie wouldn't pack up his stuff if he were in the hospital, so we can surmise that he's not sick or injured somewhere. He might have lost his mind for some reason, though."

I'm furious at Ollie for the first time ever. He's never done anything impulsive like...like *leaving* me.

I head down to Ollie's office and note that his typewriter is also gone. He may have taken that with him on his trip, but if he'd returned, he'd have placed it in its normal position on his desk. This bothers me even more than his missing clothes.

Over the next twenty minutes or so, I call every hotel I can think of and finally hit pay dirt when I call the Club Casa del Mar. I should have known Ollie would gravitate to a place on the water. I wait for the staff to locate him and discover he's in the hotel bar. They bring him a phone and before he answers, I think about what to say to him. It all goes out of my head when I hear his voice.

He sounds awful.

"Ollie, what on earth is going on? Why aren't you at home? We just got here, and we were all so anxious to see you, but what we found instead was the side of your closet empty!"

"I…I can't."

"You can't what? Are you drunk?"

"Maybe a little."

"Then I'm coming to get you. You need to hear something."

"Wait. I need to tell you something, Tr—" I hear a sob, and it breaks my heart. I still don't understand anything, though. "I have to leave. I can't ruin you and…her."

"What do you mean ruin? What are you talking about?"

In a rough whisper he says, "It's not private here, so I can't speak freely, but if I stay, I might ruin everything. I can't do that to you."

"Ollie, we love you. We need you. Don't say another damn word because I'm coming to get you. Go take a shower or something and sober up. Drink some water. I'll be there as soon as I can." I hang up before he can protest.

I take the stairs two at a time up to the bedroom and find Rosalie sad and confused sitting on the bed holding one of the shirts we bought him. "I found him," I tell her.

She looks up with hope in her eyes. "Where is he?"

"He's at a hotel in Santa Monica, and he's been drinking. He was spouting off some ridiculous garbage about possibly ruining us, so I'm heading over there right now to get him. We'll have to get his car later because he's not in any condition to be driving. Just sit tight and we'll sort things out when I get him back. I'm sure you're tired after our long trip, so why don't you lie down for a while?"

In a small voice, she says, "Yes, I think that sounds like a good idea. Bring him back, Troy. Convince him we need him, and we love him." She holds the garish shirt out to me. "Want to take this to him? It might make him smile at least."

Not wanting to disappoint her, I kiss her and take the shirt. I'm afraid it's going to take a lot more than a brilliantly colored shirt with hibiscus all over it to make Ollie feel better.

NATURALLY, traffic is awful on my way to the coast. What should take about twenty-five minutes is actually closer to forty-five. By the time I pull up to the hotel, my nerves are shot. I storm into the lobby and have to rein myself in because it won't do me any favors to snap someone's head off. I take a fast look into the bar and feel minute relief that Ollie isn't there. I head to the front desk and inquire politely about Ollie's room number. They must get plenty of celebrities here because the desk agent doesn't bat an eye when he answers, "He is in room 126, Mr. Kingsley. The elevators are just through there." He points to the left and pauses a second before adding, "Mr. Shackleton did not seem to be feeling well when I saw him head back upstairs about half an hour ago, so perhaps you'd like this. Congratulations on your recent marriage." He hands me a room key and goes back to whatever he was doing.

I take that to mean that Ollie was sloppy drunk, and this guy would like it if I took care of him. He obviously does not want anyone to make a spectacle of himself in his lobby.

It's a good thing I have a key because when I find him,

Ollie is flat on his face, fully clothed, shoes and all, diagonally across the bed. He stinks of booze.

I've never seen him like this, and it breaks my heart. I think about what to do and make a quick call to room service, asking for a plate of scrambled eggs, lots of bacon, and some buttered toast. I also order coffee and a glass of tomato juice. "Can you get that up to room 126 in about twenty-five minutes, please? We're not quite ready for it at this moment. Oh, and can you also send up some aspirin?"

"Yes, sir. Anything else?"

I'm also hungry, so I ask, "Actually yes, can you add a club sandwich to that and an iced tea?"

Once done with that, I turn on the shower and begin to remove Ollie's shoes. He stirs at that and gives me a silly grin. "Troy, you dog. Where'dja come from? Didja miss me?"

"Yes, now get the rest of your clothes off. You're taking a shower."

He tries to sit up and sways. "Not sure I can." He lets out a long burp, and phew—his breath smells like a brewery.

Sighing, I help him undress and begin to take my clothes off too. I can't have him falling and getting hurt. But when he sees what I'm doing, he grins at me and asks, "Kinda eager are ya?"

"I'm *not* here for sex."

He cranes his head around and asks, "Where's that pretty Rosa...Rosary...Rosie?"

His nonsense continues until I manage to get him into the hot water. It feels good to me, but it seems to be relaxing Ollie a bit too much. He's leaning heavily against me, and he weighs a ton, so I take a bracing breath and turn off the hot water tap. Icy spray peppers us, and he lets out a bellow. "Ack! Good God, man, are you tryna kill me?"

"No Ollie. Just sober you up. We need to get you in shape to come back and talk to Rosalie and me." When I start to shiver, I take pity on him and readjust the spray to a better temperature. At least he's standing up under his own steam now. I hand him the soap and shampoo his hair while he does the rest. He's looking and smelling lots better by the time I have him out and dried off.

We're dressed again by the time the food shows up. Ollie looks a little green, but I tell him, "Start with the aspirin and tomato juice and then the food." Fortunately, he pays attention and gives it a go. As he gradually begins to eat with more enthusiasm, I ask, "When was the last time you had anything to eat?"

"Dunno. Maybe in Santa Barbara." He looks away. "I had lunch with a realtor, and we looked at some houses, but after that I drove home, got my stuff, and checked into the hotel. I don't remember eating."

"Are you planning to invest in some property?"

He drops his head and answers, "Actually, I was thinking about moving up the coast. I like it in Santa Barbara. I like the beach."

"I see, so you were running away from home."

"Yeah, kinda." His eyes are bloodshot, and he appears to have the worries of the entire world bearing down on him.

"Ollie, look at me."

It takes some effort, but he does.

"I love you. Rosalie loves you. We missed you terribly while we were gone."

He nods sadly. "Yeah. Me too."

"Finish your toast and coffee, then brush your teeth, and we'll head back to the house."

"Troy..." Ollie starts. He looks up at me with a defeated expression. "I can't go back there. It was hard enough, leaving when you were away. Now...now I don't know if I'll have the strength to do it again. This is for the best, you'll see. The risk was just too great, for you and for Rosalie."

I swallow the protest that rises in my throat. I can tell he's not ready to hear it. Besides, the best argument for his return is waiting for us at home. I reach across and touch his cheek affectionately. "I know you're trying to do what you think is right," I say. "But you mean too much to us to just disappear like that. Rosalie needs to see you. She needs to hear what you're thinking and feeling. Come with me. If you still want to come back to this hotel after you see her, I promise, we'll put you in a taxi and send you back here tonight."

I've never seen Ollie so morose. It's breaking my heart, but I don't think pushing him is the way to make things better. At a red light on the drive home, I reach around behind the seat and grab the Hawaiian shirt I brought. "Here you go. Rosalie thought this would cheer you up. And in case this color isn't to your liking, we have more at home."

Ollie stares at it. "It's burning my eyes."

"It's the height of fashion in the Hawaiian Islands. Everybody wears them. Wait until you see what Rosalie has for herself to wear."

"Did you have fun?" he asks.

"Mostly, yes. There were some terribly pushy and nosy

people to deal with here and there, but other than that, we had a nice time. I'll be glad when the furor dies down from the wedding and the release of *Forever Yours*."

Ollie snorts. "Troy, come on. You're so beloved by everyone. You can't tell me you think interest in you and Rosalie will die down any time soon."

I sigh. "Maybe not, but it can't last forever."

"I read in the paper that the movie is doing great. Congratulations."

"Yes. Thanks."

In a sad voice, he says, "You know, while you were busy going to parties all the time, Zelda and I went to see *Forever Yours*. We loved it. The audience clapped when it was over."

I'm both touched that they went to see it and sad I couldn't have been with them. With a catch in my voice, I tell him, "Thanks, Ollie. That means a lot coming from you."

We drive the rest of the way in silence. I'm so anxious to get back to Rosalie and some semblance of normal, I can barely stand it.

This is not my Ollie at all. I hope he isn't about to break her heart. And mine.

Chapter Forty-Five

I FEEL a bit better after a nap and a quick shower, but I wish the guys would show up. Where are they? It's been over two hours. I thought Troy would just go get Ollie and bring him straight back. I try not to imagine the worst, but it's difficult, especially after Ollie's car accident before Christmas.

In addition to being worried, I'm getting terribly hungry. I'm always hungry these days, it seems. That was one great thing about traveling on the Lurline—there was always food around. Zelda is making something that smells delicious, but I don't want to eat without my men. Both of them.

Finally, I hear them coming in, and I rush downstairs to greet them.

The second I see Ollie, all memory of the last few hours flies out the window. "Ollie!" I wrap my arms around him and say, "We missed you so much!" I breathe in his scent and hold him close, even though his embrace is lackluster at best. He steps away from me after a moment, his eyes shifting away from mine. "How was Santa Barbara?" I ask.

"It was alright," he says, looking at the floor.

I shoot a worried glance at Troy, who gives me a grimace in response. "Would you like a cocktail before dinner?" I ask Ollie.

Troy answers quickly, "No, he would not."

I blink at his tone. Ah, that's right. Troy said Ollie had been drinking. I clear my throat and put on my best smile. "Well then, let's sit down and chat for a little while."

Troy marches into the living room and doesn't look back. Clearly, he expects us to follow. I take Ollie's arm, but he doesn't react other than to shuffle after Troy. I'm not even sure he's looked at me yet. I bite back the questions that threaten to spill off my tongue: *Is there someone else? Are you tired of us? Do you not love us anymore?* These horrible thoughts run unbidden through my mind and burn my insides.

As we enter the living room, Troy pats the seat next to him on the couch, and I curl up next to him with his protective arm around me, but Ollie selects an armchair across from us. He feels a hundred miles away.

"Alright, Ollie. Since you're the one who admits to running away from us and considering moving over two hours up the coast, I think you owe it to us to give us an explanation."

"Moving two hours away?" I repeat. "Ollie! How could

you? Why would you?" The words tumble out before I can stop them. "Did you...*do* something?"

He finally looks at me and catches onto what I'm implying, and his bloodshot eyes look even more remorseful suddenly. "No, I didn't *do* anything. I love you both with all my heart. It's just that while you were gone, I had a lot of time to reflect on how precarious our relationship is. I am scared to death that I'll do or say something that will jeopardize one or both of your careers. I thought it might be better to...remove myself...before we're even more involved."

"Ollie, how could you even think that?" I ask on a choking sob. "How could we be 'more involved' than we are already? We have professed our love and made promises. You've been in love with Troy for *years*, and you want to leave us?" I wipe my eyes with the back of my trembling hand. I am so hurt and upset. "You're making a unilateral decision about how we're all supposed to live?" I vow to myself then and there not to mention anything about being pregnant until he seems ready to hear about it. It would take all the joy out of the announcement to let him know while he's in this kind of mood, and I'm afraid he'd feel manipulated. Unfortunately, he looks so sad, I want to comfort him in the worst (or best) way. I don't know what to do or say to him at this point.

Troy looks shaken to the core when he says, "Ollie, you and I have successfully managed our relationship in private for a long time now. Why do you think we'll suddenly lose that ability? Do you want to be less private, and you're afraid of repercussions? I don't get it."

"No. You know I don't want public adoration for my

career or have a need for any of that. I enjoy my privacy. But I don't want to be the anchor that drags the two of you down and ruins your lives. I envision that happening all too easily if the public finds out we're doing something most people would call immoral."

"Then be careful," Troy says. "It won't be any harder than it's already been, and we've done fine. Are you sure there isn't something else bothering you? Are you jealous of my marriage to Rosalie? If so, you picked a terrible time to figure that out."

"I'm not jealous." He hangs his head and goes on, "I have an author friend named Ephraim. I'm sure I've mentioned him to you, Troy. I was worried and bothered by my thoughts and took him into confidence during our retreat together. It only took me about a minute to accidentally reveal enough that he figured out who the two of you are. He promises to keep silent, so don't worry about that, but he thinks that it would be a huge tragedy for all of your fans if the public perception of the two of you were to be tarnished in some way. He stressed how people *need* to believe in your love story with everything bad that's happening in the world. I can't blame my actions on Ephraim, but I'd feel terrible jeopardizing something that he also thinks is beautiful."

"So someone who doesn't even know us has it all figured out and has you worried about what the press might say if our relationship were uncovered?" Troy asks. "I don't give a damn about the press."

"But they could destroy you! I couldn't live with myself if

that happened. You've both worked so hard to establish your wonderful careers."

"No one is ruining anything if we're careful. Look, Ollie, I'm as crushed by your worries as Rosalie. I don't know why you're suddenly afraid to live your life the way you want and to hell with anyone who disapproves." Troy's face hardens and he asks, "You aren't ashamed of us, are you? Was the ménage à trois idea only alluring as a fantasy, but the reality of it actually feels wrong now that you've tried it? Is that it? If so, then maybe you ought to leave! We are who we are, Ollie. I thought your heart was bigger than that, and you could handle both of us the way Rosalie and I can handle you as a permanent part of our marriage. We *want* you to be a part of it." Then in a softer tone he adds, "We need you, Ollie."

Ollie gets up with tears pouring down his face and kneels in front of us. "I promise I'm not ashamed. I truly love both of you with my every fiber. I'm just so scared of the repercussions for both of you."

"Hang the repercussions," Troy says hoarsely. He clasps Ollie and brings him to his feet, cupping the nape of his neck and glaring at him fiercely. "Nothing matters more than this. Nothing matters more than our family." He leans forward and kisses Ollie deeply.

Ollie resists for a heartbeat, and then with a groan gives in, kissing Troy back with everything in his soul.

As they break apart, breathless, staring into each other's eyes, I get to my feet and approach, carefully. Ollie turns and wraps an arm around my shoulders, pulling me closer.

"I think we should go upstairs," I say softly. "Let us show you just how much we love you, Ollie."

Ollie looks shocked for a split second and then straightens up. When he stands, I see the evidence of his growing excitement in his pants. He dries his face and sighs, "Yes. Let's." Troy takes his hand and starts toward the stairs. Ollie looks back at me. "Rosalie? Are you coming?"

"You bet." I wink at him. "But you're going to have to excuse me for a moment first." I head for the kitchen to grab something to scarf down before I end up with a hunger headache. While there, I let Zelda know dinner will have to wait. She gives me a curt nod, but no complaints about the delay. I get the distinct impression she's relieved to see Ollie home.

I hear the guys trundling up the stairs, and after I slap together a cheese sandwich and eat it as quickly as possible, I rush up the stairs to meet them.

They are both naked and sitting on the edge of the bed when I walk in. They're kissing ferociously, roughly—unlike the way either of them has ever kissed me. I stand and stare at them, growing more excited by the sight. They have also taken hold of each other and are rubbing up and down on their erections. I'm suddenly craving touch and friction, so I rush in and brush my teeth (who wants cheesy kisses?) then tear my clothes off as quickly as I can. I'm not sure they were aware of my presence until I position myself in the middle of the bed behind them where I can touch both men at the same time. Now we're talking. I stroke their strong backs, and all is right with the world once more.

They turn to involve me in their kisses, each alternating taking my mouth and tasting my eager breasts. My nipples are hard and ultra-sensitive, and I squirm with their attention.

"You're both so gorgeous with your Hawaiian tans," Ollie says with reverence and looks at me. "You smell like gardenias and taste like sunshine."

"You smell and taste like Ollie, and that's perfect," I tell him. "Make love to me, Ollie. And let Troy make love to you, please?" I breathe out on a sigh. I lay back on the bed and spread my legs for him.

He smiles, and I tell myself it's not a little sad looking. "I don't want to turn that down." Ollie reaches between my legs and strokes my sensitive nub. "But if it's alright with you, can we both make love to you at the same time so I can feel Troy inside you? That feels like the closest we can be together. It's my favorite."

I'm already as wet as can be and begin to rub against him eagerly. "Oh, Ollie, whatever you want. Troy and I are here for you." I flip over and present my bottom to him, and I love the sound of his intake of breath.

"She's one in a million, Ollie," Troy tells him and hands him the tube of K-Y. "Have some fun."

I look back over my shoulder to see Troy kissing Ollie's neck and still stroking his erection. Ollie is squirting a dollop of jelly onto his finger and looks at me with wonder in his eyes. "Here we go, beautiful," he says and begins to prepare me.

It feels so good as his finger teases and strokes my bottom and gently prods its way inside. Troy's hand reaches around to dip inside me and draw moisture up and around my sensitive nub. Between the two men and their ministrations, I already feel the stirrings of an orgasm approaching. This was supposed to be all about Ollie, and I'm starting to feel selfish, but Ollie was the one who suggested this as his favorite.

Both men are now kissing me, and I'm squirming and shaking. Ollie shoves a second finger into my backside, and the sudden shock of it tips me over the edge. "Ohh!" I cry. "Yes! More!"

I can feel Ollie's grin against my neck, "More?" he asks.

"Always." I'm feeling greedy today. It feels so right to have him back. Our honeymoon lovemaking was wonderful, but just not as complete is this. We need to make sure he knows he's important to us and that we're not afraid of losing anything because of him. I squirm against his hand as he pushes a third finger into me. I can't deny it hurts, but I relish the stretch because I know how wonderful it's going to feel when they're both inside me.

"I love you both so much," I tell them.

"Look at her, Troy. She's perfect. She's taking almost my whole hand. Maybe we ought to both put our dicks in here together. She's so greedy."

I laugh. "No thanks, guys. One per orifice is plenty for now. Although, I remember reading about two men in one—just *not* the backside—and it sounds like an interesting idea. Maybe sometime we can try it. Ready, Ollie?"

He positions himself on the bed and smears K-Y all over his dick. I squat over him while Troy holds Ollie erect for me and helps lower me down on him. It's a tight fit, and even after three fingers, I feel the burn, and I love it. Ollie lets out a protracted sigh as I bottom out on him, and he grabs me by the hips.

Troy is watching all of this carefully with dilated eyes. Once I'm situated, he leans down and licks me from back to front, ending with sucking my clitoris deeply into his mouth and attacking it with his firm tongue. I cry out in surprise and delight.

It's too perfect. He sucks and sucks until I'm nearly screaming with an orgasm that wallops my senses like a magnificent cyclone—pulsating, beating me down, spinning me around until I'm nearly ready to pass out. But he's not done. He grabs his own erection and slams it into me, helped along by my juices and eagerness for him. In and out, in and out, he thrusts as Ollie and I moan our chorus of pleasure sounds.

How could this be anything but perfect? It's magical.

Behind me, Ollie is shaking with excitement. He cries out, "Yes! There you are, Troy. I feel you now inside her, and, ohh, it's so good." He starts making noises I've never heard from him. It's almost a sob, but at the same time a holy chant about his adoration of us.

In front of me, Troy has his eyes locked on mine, and he's grinning like the Cheshire cat. I think to myself, *Yes, Troy, we are all mad here. Madly in love.* We have all heard that Lewis Carroll was a bit eccentric in bed. I embrace *our* eccentricity—my Cheshire cat husband in front and my chanting, fevered husband behind. I love them more than I ever thought possible.

I feel so lucky with these two men. We're all shaking and sweating, making undecipherable noises of sheer bliss.

One after the other, my men pour the proof of their love into my body, shouting to the moon. It's sloppy and messy, and I adore every second of it. I squeeze my muscles and feel them both jolt. We stay fused together until they both finally slide out, completely spent.

How could I live without this?

After cleaning up, we all climb back into bed, a pile of tangled limbs, worn out physically and mentally. I wonder fleetingly if Ollie realized that Troy didn't use a condom, but he's so emotionally worn out—and possibly still a little tipsy—he probably missed it. We can discuss it in the morning. My last conscious thought before we fall into a deep sleep is that there is no way Ollie could doubt his need to be here with us after this.

Boy, am I wrong.

Chapter Forty-Six

Ollie

I wake up around four o'clock in the morning and begin to panic. My heart is pounding nearly out of my chest as I ask myself, *What am I doing in their bed?* I know we made promises to one another, but in the wee hours of the morning, I see things with a newfound clarity.

Am I a complete fool? Should I leave the best thing that's ever happened to me? Last night was incredible, but more than the sex, I saw just how deeply Troy and Rosalie are in love with me. I'm sure they were sincere—talented actors or not—but it's such a complicated situation. I could be responsible for so much heartache if we were found out.

And for what? I am superfluous to their relationship. On top of that, I believe they are naïve about the possible dangers here.

But I can't wake them up and tell them to their faces because I'm also a coward, and they need their sleep. They gave me their reasons last night anyway, so I'd just be hearing the same things all over again. There isn't anything else they can say that would make me stay and cause their downfall. I love them far too much to see it happen.

It would be easier to see them get angry with me than see them ruined. They'll get over it. Over me.

I decide to make my clean getaway and call them when I get somewhere that is not here. Not in their arms. Not in their bed.

With a generous amount of self-loathing, I slide out from under the sheets and gather my clothes. I sneak downstairs before dressing and call for a taxi. Then I slink out of the house like a cat burglar, leaving my shattered heart behind. I have no more use for it. They'll learn to thank me.

It's for the best.

Chapter Forty-Seven

TROY

I wake to the sound of a loud knock at the bedroom door. It's Zelda, calling out, "Hey, Troy! Get up. The studio wants you on the phone."

I take a look at the clock and realize it's nine already. The sun is out, so we must have slept in. I rub my eyes and tell Zelda, "Thanks, I'll be right there." I make a quick trip to the bathroom then grab a robe. Rosalie is just beginning to stir, but Ollie must have gotten up earlier. He's probably outside having his morning swim, or maybe he's having breakfast. I smile, thinking about how much he enjoys that heated pool during the colder months. It was expensive, but so worth it for him.

I rush downstairs and pick up the phone. It's Harry Walken's secretary who tells me in her clipped, businesslike tone, "Mr. Walken and Mr. Packard want to see you and Miss Channing at ten-thirty. Please see that you're on time."

I resist the temptation to correct her and say, "Mrs. Kingsley," but I'm in too good of a mood. "We'll be there. Thank you." I have to admit her summons has a bit of a threatening air about it, and that cools me down a little. Maybe it's just her way of talking. I hang up and head back upstairs to let Rosalie know.

"I'll be ready," she says. "Have you seen Ollie this morning? I woke up an hour or so ago and saw that he was out of bed, but I was still so tired, I went right back to sleep. This pregnancy stuff makes me want to sleep and eat, and nothing else, it seems. Well...I guess sex should also be on that list."

She winks at me, and I have to kiss her before answering, "I've only been downstairs to talk on the phone, but I didn't see him. I wonder if he's swimming. Anyway, we'll find him."

But after we're dressed and head down to breakfast, Ollie is nowhere to be found.

Zelda asks, "Isn't he still up in bed? I've been up since seven, and I haven't seen him."

"Oh no," I moan. "Excuse me, ladies, I'm going to go call the Club Casa del Mar." I head back to Ollie's office, place the call, and discover from the front desk that Ollie was there extremely early this morning. Then he checked out around six.

My head is spinning. That man is so stubborn. I don't know what to do now, but we have to get to the studio. I'm frustrated with him and madly in love with the man in equal measures. I dread telling Rosalie, but there's no getting around it.

"He *left*? Is he crazy?" she cries and tosses her toast onto her plate. "What's the matter with him, Troy?"

"Did you do something stupid, Troy?" Zelda asks, and I glare at her.

"No!" I am immediately sorry for yelling at her, but that was a pretty mean supposition on her part. "Look, Zelda, we have to get over to Premier Works, but if Ollie shows up again, please call Harry Walken's number and let me know, alright? We'll be in Harry's office. If you hear from Ollie, that also warrants a call. He's distraught, and he's not thinking particularly straight right now."

A few minutes later, we're on our way to the studio.

"Any idea what this meeting is about?" Rosalie asks.

"None, and I hate to speculate. Please don't get overly stressed, though. Whatever it is, we'll be fine." I have no idea why I think that. Maybe because I want it to be true so badly.

WHEN WE GET to Harry's office, he invites us to help ourselves to fresh coffee and pastries. I immediately take that as a good sign that we're not being fired, sued, sent to some hideous place for a location shoot, or anything else awful. I'm stuffed from breakfast, so I just help myself to coffee. Rosalie, however, selects a blueberry muffin. She's lost her taste for coffee lately, so she pours herself a water instead. She's also lost her taste for gin and tonic and prefers to drink nothing but water or lemonade these days.

Harry is all smiles, and as we're getting comfortable, John Packard bustles in looking overworked and completely satisfied with himself. He also grabs something to eat and pours himself a coffee.

"On behalf of all of us at Premier Works, welcome home. I trust your honeymoon was spectacular," Harry gloats. "Hawaii was my idea. Everyone thought the photos were terrific from yesterday when you disembarked."

"Thank you," I tell him. "We had a great time." I look at their smiling faces and ask, "So what did you want to see us about?"

"Oh, this and that. Do you have anything to report to us?"

I frown and look at Rosalie. She looks nervous, but she straightens in her chair and says, "Yes. I'm pregnant. And before you try to tell me to get rid of it, I want you to understand that I'll do everything in my power to ensure the safety of this child. If you want to fire me, so be it."

Well. *That's telling them, my dear mama bear.* I look at Harry and Packard, and I'm amazed to see them both grinning like fools.

Packard reaches out to grab my hand in a firm handshake and says, "Congratulations."

Harry chuckles happily and tells Rosalie, "That's wonderful. We're delighted for you. We actually heard the news while you were gone, and I couldn't wait to tell you how pleased we are." He gives me an inscrutable look and says, "Frankly, Troy, we weren't sure you had it in you. This is fantastic."

"What? Why did you think that?"

"Oh, come on, Troy. You came to town, bought a house and moved in with another man. You've never been seen around town with a woman on your arm until you showed such a strong interest in Miss Channing—"

"Mrs. Kingsley." I feel my insides knotting up.

"Right. You only supposedly had eyes for her. We know you made up some cock-and-bull story about Shackleton being your employee who manages your estate, but you don't have enough going on around there to warrant that. Managing a cook, a cleaning woman, and a gardener? Not exactly a full-time job. But you two kept to yourselves and didn't go out and party around with other guys who are...like you. I admire your discretion."

"Other guys like me?" I'm starting to see red.

"Yeah, I'm sure you know you have plenty of company with all the actors, entertainers, and various artistic types in this town."

"I see. And how did you come by this kind of information, may I ask?"

"Actors like you are a big investment, Troy. You're great looking and extremely talented. You make everyone love you —men and women—and we saw your potential immediately. It's why you get paid so handsomely. We've been in this business a long time, and we need to protect our investments. We generally hire someone to keep tabs on the new guys until we're satisfied you're not going to do something stupid or get yourself arrested for lewd behavior. You've been a real boy scout."

I put my hand over my eyes for a moment and try to calm down. They knew all along and didn't give a damn. All this worry for nothing. I'm feeling rather foolish for thinking we were covering our tracks so well. Obviously, we weren't.

"How did you know I'm expecting?" Rosalie asks with a tremor in her voice. "It wasn't Sophie, was it?" She looks imploringly at Packard.

"Absolutely not. Sophie doesn't even know I know. She would never rat out her friend, and I'm delighted she's taken to you the way she has. There is so much petty jealousy in Hollywood, I was thrilled for her when she met you and forged a tight bond. No, we got a call from her doctor as soon as the rabbit died."

"They killed a bunny? They were supposed to use mice!"

"Oh, sorry. It's just an expression women say when they get knocked up. If he was supposed to use that older test with mice, then he probably did. Don't be mad," Packard says.

"Hmm," she mutters. "He should be more careful about privacy."

"He answers to us regularly, actually." When Rosalie's eyes widen, he goes on to say, "You have to understand, it's important to know who's trying to conceal a pregnancy they ultimately don't want, but they're too afraid to talk about. If you wait too long, it's very...unhealthy. He's an excellent doctor, and he's taken care of a lot of our actresses over the past several years. Don't be too hard on him; just be happy he took you on as a patient."

Rosalie lets out a little snort of derision.

Packard adds, "You know, we aren't anywhere near as bad as some of the other studios. Some have actresses who get abortions as often as they go to the hairdresser because they'll get blackballed if they don't. Time is money, and if an actress can't work, they are considered expendable."

Rosalie crosses her arms and looks like she could spit nails.

Harry is still grinning when he says, "But you've solidified your husband's image, young lady. As we told Troy months ago, people start to wonder certain things about a guy who turns thirty and hasn't gotten married or even shown an interest in a particular lady. We were getting pretty worried about Troy as he approached thirty and thought it was high time to arrange a lavender marriage for him. I can't say we were too upset, though, when he took a pass on Gloria Dumont because she's...well...been around, shall we say? But when he made an enormous fuss about you, we thought it was just possible that he'd been looking for the right woman all along. This adds even more credibility to your great love story. And now that you're in the family way, we've written that into your next script. We have just the movie in mind for you, now that the shooting is over for *Wild Horses*. The movie Troy will make with Gloria will be shot after this one is done since we're still working on the screenplay adaptation for *Goldilocks*."

Packard looks seriously at Troy and asks, "We've tried several times to get in touch with him while you were gone, but there was no answer. Do you think Oliver Shackleton would like to work alongside our screenwriters? Sometimes authors like to have their own input."

I feel my face go white. "How on earth did you find out that Ollie is the author? That's a huge secret."

He laughs. "Ray Falco is the best there is."

"Falco works for you too?" I gape at him and then turn to Rosalie who is slack-jawed. Can this day get any stranger?

Packard looks taken aback. "Of course he works for us. He's the cagiest and best PI there is around here. How do you know about him?"

I shake my head. "Jack Cramer recommended him when I wanted to find out who was sneaking around and trying to take photos of us at home. It turned out there were no identifiable photos, but the guy got a bit of an eyeful once. The rest of the time he was just being a buffoon and almost got himself killed a couple of times by being careless."

"Great," Harry says. "Do we need to have words with the jerk?"

"You can if you want to, but he's happy now that he's working as a theater usher and out of the spy photographer business. He actually didn't know one end of a camera from the other. He was working for Gloria Dumont trying to get dirt on us, and it all failed."

"Wait...you knew Gloria was spying on you, and you came to us to strongly recommend her for a big part in a movie?" Harry blusters. "Are you nuts? Why are you being nice to that woman?"

"Just trying to keep my enemies close, that's all. She's so excited about the part, she'll never tell what she heard. Besides, she never actually had any proof of anything. It was all fabricated nonsense as far as she knows," I say. "And besides, who in Hollywood would make a better serial killer than Gloria Dumont? She has no morals that I can detect. Isn't it terrific type casting?" My question earns a big laugh.

"Alright. Let's not worry about Gloria for now. If she

starts to blab, we can keep her in line. And we can plant any story we want in the newspapers and magazines refuting gossip if she should try spreading any. Your image is safe in our hands, believe me. Just try to keep her happy while you're shooting. So, Troy...about Shackleton?" Harry asks. "The writers are working on the script now, but I think it could use some input from him because I'm afraid they're going off tangent a bit too much. Do you know how to find him?"

My heart drops, and I lose the smile on my face. "Ollie is having some trouble with personal issues, and I'm not sure how to reach him at the moment. It's possible he's heading up to Santa Barbara, or maybe he's even gone home to Ohio to see his parents. I'm not really sure." I look at Rosalie, who's struggling to keep the tears at bay. "We need to talk to him, but as of early this morning, we don't know how."

Harry reaches for his intercom and buzzes his secretary. "Eileen, get Ray Falco on the phone right away." He cuts her off before saying anything else and skewers me with a serious look. "Ray will find him."

Packard seems sympathetic as he says, "You two ought to go home and rest up. Take the afternoon off. Ray will undoubtedly have questions for you, so stay near a phone. He really can find anyone." He smiles at Rosalie. "Come back tomorrow, and I'll give you two the script for *Wedding Bells*. We thought it was a great follow-up to all the news about your wedding, and people will love a light, romantic film right now. In the movie, you'll get pregnant, so we'll have to pad your belly since I don't think you're far enough along to start showing for real yet. But audiences will eat it up." He's particularly smug when he adds, "We've never done anything as groundbreaking as showing a woman in the family way before. I can't wait to rattle the censors. If they don't allow the padded belly, we'll improvise." He laughs and adds, "I know for sure they'd swallow their tongues if we used the word 'pregnant,' so we'll need plenty of euphemisms."

"Could you both please not tell anyone about my pregnancy yet, though?" Rosalie asks. "I'd like some time to make sure everything is alright and let a few important people know before it becomes public knowledge."

"You got it, sweetheart," Harry assures us. "I'm sure your parents will be thrilled to find out they have a grandchild on the way."

Packard nods and shakes my hand once more. He looks at Rosalie with a huge smile and adds, "I'm proud to say you have something important in common with Sophie."

"Oh!" she gasps and then grins. "Wonderful news!"

Packard winks and strides out the door.

We start to leave too, but Harry says, "Wait a moment." His big smile disappears and he replaces it with a much more serious expression. "Look, you two. We're not stupid. Obviously, this pregnancy started before your honeymoon. If you'll remember, we said that whatever you two do or don't do in private is none of our business. But if word *ever* gets out that this isn't Troy's kid, I'll fire you both before you can say 'baby buggy.' We can deal with men of a *certain temperament*, but bastards are another story, and the stigma will follow the kid around forever. Consider that." He looks at me and then Rosalie and adds, "Now take off."

"Well, that was charming," Rosalie says under her breath as we make our way down the hall. Then she looks at me imploringly and asks, "Do you think Ray will be able to find Ollie?"

"I guess it depends on whether or not Ollie wants to be found."

Chapter Forty-Eight

Ollie

It's frigid and windy today, and the weather matches my lousy mood. I'm sitting on the cold sand as the waves tumble in. The ocean is choppy, and the surf is erratic. It's no wonder no one else is out here in this weather. I came to the beach to watch for the migrating gray whales on their way south to Mexico, but the visibility isn't very good. I think I saw one spout, but it could have been the turbulent water and my hopefulness fooling me. It's the prime season for whale watching, but a poor day for it. Normally, I love seeing their giant tails flip out of the water as they dive deep, but the best of all is when they jump straight up, breeching. No such luck today.

I'm feeling horribly low, even though it makes me feel guilty to admit it—even to myself. When I think of everyone who's in such dire financial straits with *real* troubles, I shouldn't be feeling so sorry for myself. I'm healthy, I have plenty of money, and I have...or *had*, I guess, two wonderful people who loved me. I know I'm doing the right thing by leaving them, though, and I promised myself I'd call them and let them know I'm alright. It's just too scary to think about hearing their voices. They might make me slip and want to go back to them. Or even worse, they might agree that I should stay out of their hair for good.

I've been up here in Santa Barbara for a few days, and already it feels as though it's been a month. I checked with him and found Stan's beach house was still vacant, so I decided to come enjoy the privacy. Hah. "Enjoy" is such a misnomer. I cry myself to sleep like a toddler who's lost their precious teddy bear, and the rest of the time I wander around like I'm in a trance.

I tried to get the realtor to find some more houses for me to look at, but nothing felt right. I could never express what was missing or objectionable about the houses he showed me—I just felt in my heart they were wrong for me. He finally got fed up with me. He told me he'd let me know if something new was listed, but I know when I'm getting the brush-off.

I need to pull myself out of this slump. As usual, I have a deadline looming, and I need to show some backbone and finish this damned book. Meanwhile, my typewriter gathers dust.

The phone has rung a couple of times, but I haven't answered. I know what I'm doing is self-destructive, and I need to have some healthy food and a normal conversation with someone, but I just can't do it yet. I've gone so far as to be tempted to start smoking again, but I don't have the gumption to go buy cigarettes. I've been living (barely) on bologna sandwiches and coffee.

My ass is starting to ache from the cold sand, my bare feet are freezing, and my eyes are watering from the wind (at least that's what I'm telling myself). I'm exhausted from my robust sitting around and doing nothing, so I resolve to go take a nap. At some point, I'll have to try to eat, but maybe not yet.

As I track sand into the house and head toward the bed I've claimed, my eye catches my cold, dusty typewriter glaring at me accusingly. "Shut up," I tell it and collapse onto the bed. One good thing about sleeping so poorly at night is that I've become great at it during the day. I'm asleep almost instantly.

I don't know how long I've been asleep, but I'm suddenly awakened by a gruff voice that grumbles at me, "Get up, Shackleton. People are looking for you. They need you, and you're being a jerk."

My eyes fly open to the sight of Ray Falco dripping water all over my gritty floor. Judging from the sound of rain pelting against the bedroom window, we're having quite the storm. He removes his raincoat, drapes it over the closest chair back, and scoops his wet hair out of his eyes. My first thought is that he looks tired and supremely cheesed off.

"How did you find me?" I ask stupidly.

"It's my job." He's always gotten right to the point.

"Did Troy send you?" I suppress any hope about how he'll answer.

"No, but he did provide some helpful information. The studio actually hired me to come get you and bring you back."

"What? Why?"

"As I understand, they're making a movie from your book, and they've decided they need you on the set, no matter what you call yourself."

"What? How do they know it's me, and how did you know to find me for them? This is an invasion of my privacy."

"Look, Ollie. It's not for me to tell, but they know who you are. You don't invest over a million dollars into a movie without knowing who you're dealing with. So clean yourself up and come back to Premier Works with me. And you might stop in and talk to Troy and Rosalie while you're there. They're pretty upset. I promised I'd get you back to them."

My heart warms knowing they still want to talk to me, but I'm also terrified at the idea of facing them.

"It's useless. They shouldn't want me."

"Well, I have it on good authority that they do, so let's either get moving or have some dinner and wait for this storm to blow over. Frankly, I'd prefer the latter because I'm cold, exhausted, and hungry. But I'm also going to call and let everyone know you're still alive like you should have done days ago." He glares at me. "They're good people, and they sure don't deserve this kind of treatment from you. And I warn you, you're not getting away with not talking to them and disappearing again."

"I...um...don't know what to say to them."

"Then why don't you start out by listening to what they have to say to you? And pay attention to them."

"Oh...uh..." I'm such a mess. I guess I owe them that much. "Look, Ray, if you're cold, why don't I light a fire, and I'll make us some sandwiches and hot coffee? That's all I have here. If you want something more substantial, we'll have to go out somewhere, although I'm not too crazy about seeing other people."

"How about we have a couple of your sandwiches tonight and then head back to LA first thing in the morning? I'm honestly sick to death of driving. I'll call Harry Walken while you're putting sandwiches together and let him know, and he can call Troy. That way you can think longer about what you want to say to everyone." He wanders away muttering something that sounds a lot like "chickenshit."

He's right, but I know I have to face the music sooner or later.

After having some really uninspired food, I have trouble sleeping again. I hope Ray got some sleep.

In the morning, I make us some toast and coffee and try to minimize the mess I've made of Stan's beach house. I change the sheets and run the vacuum, clean out the bathroom sink and shower, and decide that's about the best I can do. Ray is kind enough to clean up the kitchen. He isn't too talkative, but he does ask where he can buy some gas.

"I need it too before heading back, so you can follow me to the closest Texaco station," I tell him. I'm starting to feel nervous about seeing Troy and Rosalie, but I go throw my stuff into my suitcase and head out to the cars.

It's a much nicer day for a drive than the gloom of yesterday, but I still feel like I'm heading to the firing squad. After getting our cars filled up, tires and oil checked, and windows washed at the filling station, Ray stays close behind me for the hundred or so miles it takes us to get back to Troy's house. It's as if he's afraid to let me out of his sight for one minute, but I can hardly blame him. I have to remind myself that it's also *my* house we're heading to, but it feels strange to think of it that way right now. I'm so embarrassed for having run away from the two best people in the world. I still have to make them understand my position, though. I can't be the cause of their ruin. I just can't.

After a couple of hours and an uneventful trip, we're finally home. It occurs to me that Troy and Rosalie are probably not even around because they should be at work. I'll have to face Zelda's wrath, I suppose. After I pass through the gate, Ray blocks the driveway instead of taking off. Apparently, he doesn't trust me not to disappear now that I'm here, and he's standing guard. He only leaves after I park in the garage and head into the house.

Inside, I find Rosalie, Troy, and Zelda sitting in the kitchen having lunch. They even have a place set for me—unless they were expecting someone else.

"Oh...uh...hi." I choke out.

"Ollie!" Rosalie shouts. She jumps up and throws her arms around me, hugging me tight.

Troy also stands, and when Rosalie steps back, he gives me a silent hug.

Zelda glares at me, but she asks, "Want some lunch?"

"Um, sure, thanks, Zelda." I turn to Troy and ask, "Why are you here instead of at the studio?"

"Are you for real?" he asks, stupefied. "Harry told us to

take the day off so we could discuss with you why you ran off and left us."

"Harry? Why?" I'm starting to shiver. Maybe they've already been fired, and Troy doesn't want to unburden that little tidbit just yet.

"Sit down and eat. You look awful," Rosalie tells me.

So I sit. Zelda places a bowl of delicious-smelling soup in front of me with a big crusty roll. I take a spoonful and immediately feel minutely better. Everyone looks too calm for there to be terrible news, I realize.

"Ollie, it came as a big shock to us, but a few days ago we discovered from Harry and Packard that they have known about you and me since the day they hired me. They don't care!"

I set my roll down, and my eyes grow wide. "What do you mean they know about us and don't care? How can that be? We've been breaking the law, and it's alright with them?"

"Yep. They know, and they don't care. Apparently, it's a normal occurrence to have new men tailed when they show up in town, and—get this—they use Ray Falco to do it. So they know a lot about the actors they hire from the start. They found out right away that we bought a house together, and they didn't believe you were a majordomo for a minute. They say we're in good company with plenty of other actors in Hollywood, and they carefully manipulate the press images of their stars, so we're pretty much protected from any negative perception from the public. There's more to it than that, but it all boils down to this: we're all good. No one is getting canned or sued or ridiculed."

I don't even have words as I stare at him slack-jawed.

Zelda finally smiles and announces, "I need to go do some stuff in my quarters, so I'll leave the three of you to keep talking. And eating." She looks at me sternly. "But Ollie, I'm glad you're back, and I hope you're not going to be a horse's ass again and try to leave." She points a finger at me. "Listen to them," she gestures to Troy and Rosalie. "They have more things to tell you." And with that, she turns and marches out.

I'm already stunned. "More?" I ask.

Rosalie suddenly has tears in her eyes, and she blurts out, "We're having a baby!"

"A ba...what?"

"You heard her. Rosalie's in the family way, and the studio is thrilled because it solidifies my image as a stud or something." He laughs. "I'm thrilled because it's probably your kid! I mean it's gonna be mine too, but you were the one who kept ripping up condoms."

As Troy laughs, Rosalie wipes what appear to be happy tears from her eyes.

"Isn't it wonderful?" she asks. "You're a daddy, Ollie!"

I'm incapable of making words come out of my mouth, and the room starts to spin. Then next thing I know, I'm being propped up in Troy's strong arms. "Ohhh," I groan. "Tell me I didn't just pass out."

"Just for a little while," he says with a huge grin.

"What are you going to do about your job? Will they fire you?" I look closely at Rosalie, but her expression is all joyful and not the least bit worried.

"Nope. They're writing it into the script as far as the censors will allow. They're fine. I'll keep working until I don't feel as though I can. Are you happy too, Ollie?" Now she looks a little worried, and I feel like a complete heel if I caused that.

"Oh, sweetheart, I'm ecstatic. You know Troy and I have always wanted children." I reach for her hand. "When did you find out?"

"During our honeymoon. I got a telegram."

I jolt. "And you didn't tell me as soon as you got back? Why?"

"Why?" Troy asks a little too loudly. "We didn't feel like mentioning it because, except for while we were having sex, you were acting horrible and were probably too drunk to remember it the next day anyway. Rosalie was so excited to tell you until you pulled your disappearing act. We didn't know if we'd ever see you again or if you decided you couldn't handle our relationship. Give us a break, man. As much as we love you, you hurt us!"

I grit my teeth. I deserve that. "I understand completely what a jerk I've been, and I despise myself for it. But honestly, I thought I was protecting you. I just...you have both worked so hard to get what you have. If I were the reason you lost it..." I shake my head. "I'd never forgive myself."

"Ollie," Rosalie says softly, "you're more important than either of our careers. I was ready to give up my career if the studio had a problem with the pregnancy. Troy was ready to quit if they couldn't handle us as a threesome. That's how much we love you. You have to know this. Haven't we shown you enough how much we care for you? If we haven't, I'm so sorry."

"No, you're not to blame. It was all me and my crazy thinking." I look down at my bowl of soup, but it isn't giving me any great ideas of what to say, so I look at them pleadingly. "Can you both forgive me? I never doubted anyone's love, especially my own. It was killing me to be running away, but I really did think I needed to remove myself from the situation. I thought I'd find myself a house up in Santa Barbara, but each time I looked at one, it seemed like a prison rather than a home. It needed the people I love in it to make it right. I need you both, and I'm so thrilled there's going to be a baby, Rosalie. I can't even express how happy that makes me. Can you both please try to forget what an ass I've been? I love you both with my whole heart, and I'll never make anyone worry again...if I can manage that. I'm not perfect, but I'll do my best."

I kneel in front of Rosalie and lay my head against her belly. "I love you too, little one," I croon to our child. "Daddy's here to make a good life with your other daddy and mommy, and we promise to always do our best for you." I look up into Rosalie's shining eyes and say, "You're going to make the best mother." I hear sniffling beside me coming from Troy, and it makes me grin. Rosalie strokes her hand through my hair, and I almost purr at the tenderness of her touch. I rise and kiss her and then lean over to kiss Troy. "Let's finish lunch so we don't insult Zelda, and then can we all take a nap together? I haven't been sleeping much, and you both look a little tired."

So that's just what we do.

Chapter Forty-Nine

WE MAY HAVE all fallen into bed as if we hadn't slept in weeks, but we wake up a couple hours later in a very different frame of mind. Ollie is over his fears, and we all still have jobs. Tomorrow, we'll all go to Premier Works together so Ollie can confer with the screenwriters, and Troy and I will rehearse our new script. Now, however, we all have much more carnal ideas.

"Remember what you mentioned reading about last time?" Ollie asks me.

"I do. As I recall, there was a scene in the ménage book about a special kind of penetration involving my body. Do you think it's real, or was that made up for the book just to titillate readers?"

"I guess we'll never know unless we try," Troy says with a

hungry look that says he's all in. "And best of all, no more condoms."

"No?" Ollie asks.

Laughing, I answer, "I can't get any more pregnant than I already am."

We begin exploring each other's bodies like we've never seen them before. Every inch is fondled, kissed, and treasured. We're all positively vibrating with desire when Troy reaches for the drawer and pulls out the K-Y. "We need to start buying this by the case," he mutters with a gleam in his eye. Then he reaches for me and begins to probe me with his fingers as he licks my most sensitive part. He sucks me deeply into his mouth, and I jolt up off the bed; I'm feeling so sensitive. I see also that Ollie has captured Troy in his mouth and is sucking on him like a favorite lollipop. I can feel myself growing wetter, and I'm certain that's part of their plan.

Troy pulls back and says in a strained voice, "No more, Ollie. You're too good at that. I want to use it for Rosalie, so let's not go too far."

"Come here, Ollie," I order and begin sucking him the same way he was doing moments ago to Troy. I taste a salty flavor on his tip and know he's also nearly ready. But I have to let go of him soon for fear of biting him too hard when a climax rushes through me with an intensity I've never experienced. Both men look extremely satisfied.

Troy grabs Ollie and smears a good amount of jelly on his erection. Ollie closes his eyes, clearly enjoying Troy's attention. Then Troy does the same to himself and lies back on the bed. "Okay, darling, position yourself on top of me, but face

Ollie as you sink yourself down on me. I have the feeling this is going to be an extremely tight fit, having us both in the same place together, but we'll go slow. If it's too much, please say so, and we'll do this the way we've done it before with me in your bottom instead."

Just the thought of this process is making me aroused beyond belief, so I eagerly straddle Troy and slide easily down his shaft. He's large, but I'm wet and he's lubricated, so it's effortless. Once I bottom out with a satisfied shudder, Ollie leans in and sucks on my clitoris until I moan and shake. It's almost too much pleasure to handle, but more is coming, and I can't wait. Ollie slides his index finger inside me alongside Troy, and Troy starts to moan as loudly as I do.

"Oh, God, Ollie, this is incredible. I love how your finger is stroking me, and Rosalie is grasping me with her tight muscles at the same time. You've never felt anything like this! You won't believe it when you get inside next to me."

It's tight, but the feeling is incredible—Troy's right. But then Ollie inserts another finger, and...oh my. It's as if there is almost too much to feel. He's stroking Troy and stretching me while I can't help squeezing and releasing my muscles. I start to rise and fall over Troy's lovely erection. Oh, oh, *ohhh*. I gasp when Ollie forces a third digit inside me, and Troy grabs one of my breasts. His other hand seeks out my nub, where he and Ollie manipulate it together. It's the strangest, most delicious sensation. I feel swamped by affection, so I squeeze harder to let them know how much this excites me.

"Are you ready, sweetheart?" Ollie asks as he smears another dollop of jelly onto himself. He's red and hard, leaking everywhere, so I know he's beyond ready himself.

I'm a little scared about the pain I might feel but so excited, I lock the fear away.

"Now, Ollie, please!" I cry. "Troy and I need you."

His tip is warm and hard, but it's also smooth as he carefully lines himself up alongside Troy. He pushes and pushes, and I try to relax. It's not going in easily, but I'm determined for this to happen. So I squeeze my muscles really hard, and then instantly relax them and cry, "Push now, Ollie, push it in!"

He does, and I feel a sharp sting, but it all goes away as he shoves himself deeper and deeper inside. Troy's grip on my breast tightens almost painfully as he cries out, "Oh my God! This is incredible! I can feel every inch of you, Ollie. It's the best feeling ever with Rosalie squeezing us like this."

Ollie's eyes go huge as he looks at me and smiles. "We're in you together. Ohhh...this is...ohh my..." He pulls back slightly and pushes in again as Troy groans in supreme pleasure.

Over and over, Ollie pulls and pushes. It's a sensation that defies description. How do people enjoy just one lover at a time when this is a possibility? He alternates kissing me and then kissing Troy until the sensations almost become too much, and we're all panting.

Ollie shoves in and out, and I rhythmically squeeze and release my men. Ollie is using his hands now to balance, but Troy's fingers are still positioned over my clitoris where he's squashed against me by Ollie's body. The whole thing is messy and slightly uncoordinated, and...the most wonderful experience imaginable. Our moans and groans go on and on until I can't take it anymore and explode with pleasure so strong, it threatens to make me lose consciousness. I can't help shouting, "Yes, oh God, yes!" All of my muscles seize up and I jerk forward, shaking everywhere. Spasms of delight pulse through me over and over until I'm exhausted by them.

Troy lurches and lets out a sound that must have been dredged up from the underworld. It's a deep moan and a cry that ends with a laugh, and his arms tighten around me.

Ollie sucks in a huge breath and cries out, "This is the best moment of my entire life!" He shudders and collapses on top of us. We remain that way for a long time, our hearts pounding in sync. Gradually, they slow to a normal pace, and we still stay locked together in a heap. We're a beautiful mess.

Once we finally peel apart from each other and get cleaned up, I want to do it all over again. The men have cocky, satisfied grins, so I'm sure they feel the same.

Ollie is back for good. We're all going to be fine. Life is wonderful.

I just know it.

Epilogue

Troy

Although I felt she deserved it for her performance in *Forever Yours*, my wife lost the Academy Award for Best Actress to Vivien Leigh for *Gone with the Wind*. Still, it was fantastic that Rosalie was nominated, especially since it was her first movie ever. I can understand how *Gone with the Wind* won ten Oscars though, considering the scope and historical value of the film. Ours was much lighter fare. And half as long. Personally, I preferred *Forever Yours*, but that's just me.

I'm hoping Ollie will win Best Adapted Screenplay with the team of writers he's collaborated with on *Goldilocks*, though. We'll have to wait another year for that, but I know they'll be nominated. The film has received accolades from audiences and critics alike. Ollie loved writing with them, and the studio is considering another of his books for next year. We'll see if it might suit Rosalie and me acting together again. The public would certainly love that.

Incidentally, Ollie wrote with them as Oliver Shackleton, so Robert Oliver still maintains his privacy. His readers still think the author is a recluse.

Not to sound immodest, but Rosalie and I have definitely become the most beloved couple in Hollywood, especially after word got out that we were having a baby. This popularity of ours seems to have riled up Gloria Dumont something awful, though, because now she's spreading rumors that she turned down my proposal, and that was why I ended up with an "unknown" for a bride. We just laugh it off. There's no sense in making her feel important by giving her rumors any attention. She's finding it difficult to get good parts now, though. While she did quite well portraying a serial killer, that removed her from the running for romantic leads, and she's turned into a "character" actress when the studio can find something for her. It's too bad the Wicked Witch of the West was already done. She would have looked perfect with a green face and big hooked nose.

With the studio's consent, Rosalie stopped acting when she started showing too obviously, but she was still asked to give plenty of interviews about her latest movie. She looked so beautiful when she got really round. Despite her complaints about a sore back and tired feet, I know she loved it as much as Ollie and I did.

Our baby boy was born on August 29th, and he looks a lot like Rosalie. He's blond and has huge blue eyes. He's showing all the signs of being extra tall, and of course he's the most beautiful, beloved baby ever. He is the embodiment of the two finest people I've ever known, so how can he be any less than perfect? We named him Robert—Ollie's actual first name. His last name is Kingsley, however, as we didn't want to raise too much suspicion over that. Anyway, he looks like a Robbie to me, but Ollie prefers calling him Bert—so we do.

We arranged a contract adjustment with the studio for Rosalie. She can take more time off between movies to be home with Bert, and she's already talking about having more babies. The woman was born to be a mother. We hired a live-in nanny, however, so Rosalie could get back to work a couple of months after Bert was born. His nanny brings him for visits to the studio on days when he's not being fussy, and everyone loves that. Rosalie's lovely dressing room is now adorned with baby paraphernalia.

Rosalie has made it clear to the studio execs that she isn't a workhorse, and she will not work late into the night with a baby at home. Surprisingly, her demands have been accepted. I think some of this has to do with John Packard, who is besotted with his own brand-new baby girl, and he also wants to get home to her and Sophie at the end of the day. Funny how things get into proper perspective with the right encouragement.

Rosalie and Sophie are as thick as thieves, and they look forward to the day when Bert and little Clarissa fall in love and get married, solidifying our families as one. That might be quite a stretch, but stranger things have happened.

I've noticed a change in Ollie. Fatherhood and being a husband has relaxed him. He gets plenty of enjoyment working in collaboration with the studio writers and has befriended them the way he did with his author buddies in Santa Barbara. He routinely makes the effort to see his friend Ephraim here in Los Angeles and not just when all of them get together up north. Ollie and Ephraim are discussing collaborating on a political thriller novel, and it sounds as if they're both pretty excited about it. Ollie has certainly lost his need for privacy all the time, so I wonder how much of his previous life as a loner was self-imposed for fear of being exposed rather than comfort with isolation. He's also relaxed his schedule of churning out books at a rapid pace. He loves the camaraderie of working with others and feels more creative when he can stretch his mind in different directions. He seems to thrive on debating the finer points of a script, for instance, with the screenwriters. And he loves having time for his family.

He's anxious to teach Bert to swim, but that's going to wait a while. The little guy does love water, though.

And speaking of Ephraim, once Ollie explained how everything worked out to him, he was understanding and supportive of our relationship. That made Ollie extremely happy. It solidified their friendship even more. Ephraim has been a great source for parenting questions since he is the father of four. He's a great guy, and he's been over to the house now several times. It's good to have a friend you can trust.

Our only major worry happened in October when Ollie and I had to register for the draft. But we were relieved of that worry soon when the draft board discovered Ollie's atrocious eyesight and found out about my asthma. I was in such a panic when we went for our physical exams, I had a small asthma attack right in front of them, and that did it. The army didn't want to take chances with a soldier who had any trouble breathing and might not be able to get immediate medical attention.

So we remain in our glamorous, safe bubble of Hollywood. It seems like real-world issues barely touch us here. We feel for the rest of our hard-working citizens as well as the people in Europe, but we certainly cannot complain when we are so blessed.

Perhaps someday society will accept other kinds of relationships, and people who love each other the "wrong way" won't risk going to jail (and worse). If we don't live to see it, hopefully our children will. It would be so wonderful to be ourselves fully in the open, but, for now, that's not the world we live in.

The End

Acknowledgments

Inspiration is a strange and fickle thing. My apologies to anyone who has been waiting for the fourth installment in the "Honeybee Hollow" series. I was about a third of the way through writing it, enjoying the characters immensely, when I hit a brick wall. And just as suddenly, a kernel of an idea invited Troy, Ollie, and Rosalie into my head. They barged in and took over, and the rest is history—or rather historical romance. This is not the first time that's happened.

I've always explained to people who ask about my writing that I see my stories play out like movies in my head when most authors hear their characters talking. I've never had a single conversation with any of my people, but they do take over a lot of real estate in my brain with their shenanigans. I have to think that after studying art and being a professional artist for so long, that's just how my brain processes things. I also worked for several years as an animator and video editor, so that must have had an effect on my visual thinking.

You may have noticed that I've tried to position my historical romance stories *between* world-shattering events. I moved my San Francisco characters out of town before the devastating earthquake flattened the city and it burned to the ground. I also positioned my books as far away as possible from the Civil War. Likewise, in this book I wanted to acknowledge the Great Depression and the advancement of World War II, but I didn't wish to write about those terrible times directly. Plenty of people do a great job as historians, and they enjoy it, but I'd rather focus on the glitz and glamour of the strange phenomenon of Hollywood in 1939 and 1940.

Some of my original inspiration started with my beautiful, theatrical grandmother who became a Mack Sennett Bathing Beauty. However, there just wasn't enough material there for me to sink my teeth into. Her brief silver screen career predated the talkies. The Golden Age of Hollywood was another story completely. The anecdotes I found over and over were wonderful inspirations. So, thank you, Nonna, but your story might have to wait for another day and a different kind of book.

The other reason I have been drawn to writing these books is so that I could get a deeper understanding of my own family's history, and that's been a lot of fun. I have a few Easter eggs planted here and there, but you'd have to know me really, *really* well to find them.

Hollywood changed a lot in the years directly after this book ends, and that may be the subject for another book, but not necessarily as a sequel. The film noir mood became darker, and many patriotic movies were created during WWII. The country suffered shortages, and Hollywood was not exempt from those as well as lack of manpower. I still believe it was something of a safe bubble in many ways, however.

I have tried throughout this book to use verbiage that was correct for 1939 to 1940, so if your brain hiccupped over a few phrases, that's why. Sometimes old slang sounds utterly preposterous to us now, however, and I tried not to use too many of these little gems. It was pretty entertaining when I discovered them, though. For instance, I wasn't about to call a kiss a "honey cooler" or refer to an ambulance as a "meat wagon," and my characters definitely were not "pitching woo" or "making whoopie."

Writing a historical book is about 60 percent research and 40 percent writing. It just never ends. The tricky part for me was that this was the era when my parents were young. They would have been a few years behind my characters, but the way they talked is representative of many phrases I heard while growing up. Then I'd wonder whether the words I heard were newer adaptations as my parents evolved with the times, or if they were holdovers from the '30s and '40s. In any case, I had to research all of it to be correct.

It's always fun for me to revisit California by writing about it. I haven't lived there for many years, but I was born in Los Angeles and grew up in San Diego, so researching its history is a bit like going home for me. One of my special memories was being invited to Filoli for a party that was given by Lurline Matson Roth, who owned the Matson lines. She still lived there then, and it was not open to the public. I tried to model the Packards' ballroom after the one in that estate, but Filoli was *much* more incredible. I also used the château-like house that was featured on the *Beverly Hillbillies* as the inspiration for the Packards' home in Bel-Air, although I've never been to it.

An interesting fact about the SS Lurline for you history buffs out there is that when Pearl Harbor was attacked, the cruise ship was transporting over seven hundred passengers from Honolulu to San Fransico and had to go radio silent and blacked out at night to deliver people safely home. They took a circuitous route that finally got them back on December 10. Immediately after that, the ship was taken into service by the military and outfitted as a troopship. She was finally returned to Matson Lines after several years when the Lurline was extensively remodeled.

My family traveled to Hawaii on the Matson Line's SS Matsonia when I was eleven.

Santa Barbara was a place I loved to go to, and I owned a business for several years in Encinitas. So, there is a bit of me here and there in the book.

I have never aspired to having two husbands, however. ;)

I need to thank some people for their help and encouragement throughout the writing of this story. *Hollywood Glitz and Glamour* is probably my favorite project of all my books to date.

Thank you to Susan, my beta reader and bestie who lives too far away. She always provides wonderful input and support. I know she's busy with her life, but she makes time to check facts and ponder the mood of my writing, and I love her dearly for it.

A huge thank you has to go to Dar Albert of Wicked Smart Designs. She spent hours poring over old fashion magazines in a vintage clothing shop to get ideas for this gorgeous cover. I think she enjoyed creating it as much as I enjoy having it grace my book. It's so beautiful.

Amy Maranville, CEO & Founder of Kraken Communications, has been my editor now for several years, and it's always a wonderful experience working with her. So thank you to Amy for her flexibility and thoughtful ideas for how to make these books work.

Thanks also go to Mattie Davenport of Davenport Edits who is the final word on what works and what doesn't. She's supposedly my proofreader, but she's also a mentor, a friend, and just an all-around great person who is now so busy, it's fantastic.

Promotional assistance comes from Jen DeJong and Olivia Rose who do all the stuff I'm absolutely horrible at, and they do it extremely well. Also Anne Victory and Crystalle Berry are great at what they do in areas where I invariably mess up somehow. I couldn't do this without these ladies.

Thanks to my local author besties, Ava Cuvay and Sutton Bishop who are both terrific people and full of advice and ideas. It's lucky we ended up in the same small town. I love having friends who understand what it's like to be an author. This is also true for the ladies of the Kentuckiana Romance Writers group. Wonderful people.

As with all my books, my husband deserves a lot of gratitude. Dinners are late, I get a glassed-over look on my face sometimes when I'm not completely present in conversations because I'm working out a new scene in my head. And he listens to me, asks lots of questions, offers a man's point of view, and never reads a single word of my books. He helps tremendously, however, and he's never afraid to tell me when my idea is too over-the-top or just plain silly. That happens a lot, so he's a wonderful sounding board. I guess that kind of makes him the nonsense-booter-outer.

The biggest thank you of all goes to you, readers, for choosing my books for your entertainment. It means the world to me. I hope I've offered you an escape, maybe taught you something interesting, or just plain made you smile.

If you ever want to share an opinion about a book, I'd love to hear about it via a review. Amazon, BookBub, Goodreads, your own blog, TikTok, Facebook, Instagram, etc. are all welcome. Thank you to all of the advance readers who have already left reviews, and to everyone who does so in the future. Each review gives an author encouragement to keep up the good work.

www.ariellatalix.com

You can sign up for my newsletter here:

https://landing.mailerlite.com/webforms/landing/m6f3i7

Follow me at all the obvious places:

https://www.amazon.com/stores/Ariella-Talix/author/B07MKPB8TN

https://www.facebook.com/ariella.talix.1

https://www.bookbub.com/authors/ariella-talix

https://www.instagram.com/ariellatalix/

https://www.goodreads.com/author/show/18683284.Ariella_Talix

https://x.com/AriellaTalix

Books by Ariella Talix

Every book is a standalone story with no cliffhanger.

Each series is more fun when read in order, however. Often characters show up again because I can't help myself.

<u>Contemporary Romance</u>

The Drummonds:

Porter the Importer

Make Believe

The Artist

Lovers in Louisville (Spin-off from The Drummonds):

Save Her

Saving Him

Savor This

<u>Contemporary MMF Romance</u>

The Perfect Number (Spin-off from Savor This):

The Rule of 3

The Passion of 3

Living the Fantasy:

Just Curious

Compelling Urges

Standalone:

Group Hug

Honeybee Hollow Series:

Jack of Hearts MMF novella—a spin-off from Group Hug

Buddy System Small-town, MMF, Military romance

Everybody Knows Small-town MF Romance

Book #4 TBD

Historical MMF Romance

Hearts of Gold:

The Golden Rush

Fiddle and Fire

Casting Vows

Standalone:

Hollywood Glitz and Glamour

Anthologies and Box Sets

Double Down on Love (*Jack of Hearts*) with the Kentuckiana Romance Writers

The Drummonds

Lovers in Louisville

The Perfect Number

Living the Fantasy

Hearts of Gold

www.ingramcontent.com/pod-product-compliance
Lightning Source LLC
Chambersburg PA
CBHW051309300726

48976CB00002B/333